THE RAW LIGHT OF MORNING

THE RAW LIGHT OF MORNING

SHELLY KAWAJA

BREAKWATER
P.O. Box 2188, St. John's, NL, Canada, A1C 6E6
WWW.BREAKWATERBOOKS.COM

COPYRIGHT © 2022 Shelly Kawaja

ISBN 978-1-55081-946-5

A CIP catalogue record for this book is available from Library and Archives Canada.

ALL RIGHTS RESERVED. No part of this publication may be reproduced, stored in a retrieval system or transmitted, in any form or by any means, without the prior written consent of the publisher or a licence from The Canadian Copyright Licensing Agency (Access Copyright). For an Access Copyright licence, visit www.accesscopyright.ca or call toll free 1-800-893-5777.

We acknowledge the support of the Canada Council for the Arts. We acknowledge the financial support of the Government of Canada through the Department of Heritage and the Government of Newfoundland and Labrador through the Department of Tourism, Culture, Arts and Recreation for our publishing activities.

PRINTED AND BOUND IN CANADA.

 Canada Council Conseil des arts
for the Arts   du Canada
 Newfoundland Labrador

Breakwater Books is committed to choosing papers and materials for our books that help to protect our environment. To this end, this book is printed on recycled paper that is certified by the Forest Stewardship Council®.

to my mother

PART ONE

1993

ONE

DECEMBER

Wind howled across the narrow highway, cut through spruce and fir matted together in tangled stands, and shook Laurel's house at the end of Woods Road. Brass frames rattled on rose-coloured drywall. A lone lightbulb in the middle of the ceiling flickered, and the TV turned to black-and-white static. Laurel got off the couch and thumped the top of the set.

"Why does everyone pound on broken things?" Maxine blew into the room and dropped a laundry basket on the carpet. She squatted on the sofa chair. One of its legs had cracked once when Rick fell onto it drunk, and for a while Maxine had propped it up with a stack of books, but the books always shifted and eventually another leg snapped. Now the chair sat flat on the carpet and Laurel's mother's knees came up almost to her chin. She pulled a pair of Rick's Wranglers from the basket, folded them into a thick denim square and dropped them on the floor.

Laurel whacked the TV. Static sputtered and she turned it off.

"Can you watch Bud for me tonight?" Her mother folded two socks together.

Laurel paused in the middle of the room. Her mother's face, usually the colour of a low-hanging fog, had cheeks blushed pink and eyelashes bright with mascara. Even her lips looked polished.

"I'm going to run up to Una's." She paused, folding a T-shirt. "Just for a bit."

Rain slapped across the window. The light in the room turned grainy.

"In this?"

"Una's picking me up." Her mother folded the last of the clothes and put the neat stacks in the basket. She stood and flicked out her hair. Dark brown, almost black. She must have spent ages brushing it to get it that shiny. Her sweater was nice. Light green, cable knit. It stopped just above a snug pair of flared jeans. She yanked the curtains open. "The weather's easing off."

The window was a black square of wet rage. Headlights flashed across the pane. "What if the power goes out?"

"It won't." Her mother squeezed her cheeks and kissed her forehead. She went to a pile of coats and sweaters on the wall and rummaged around until she found her jacket. She pulled it out, slid her arms in and zipped it up. The black leather cinched her waist. Straightened her spine. She tugged her hair from the collar and fringes fell from her arms like angel wings. She looked through the shoes cluttered on the mat, crossed the entryway and disappeared down the hall. Skipped downstairs to the basement. Her room was down there, though really it was her and Rick's room now. Since he moved in last year, that room had become a space in the house off limits to Laurel.

Laurel stared at the empty TV screen.

Maxine came back with her knee-high tan boots. "These almost look real, right?" The boots tucked up under the flare of her jeans and zipped along her calves. "Back in a bit!" She spun around and her fringes fanned out, ready for takeoff. She flashed Laurel a smile, opened the door, and was swallowed up in a torrent.

The door slammed behind her. The coats on the wall rustled. A corner of the lace runner on the coffee table flipped up and settled back at a right-angled fold. Una's headlights flashed across the window and the glass returned to rain-streaked blackness.

On the kitchen wall, the apple clock ticked from seed to seed. Nine o'clock. Laurel took a bite of her toast, soggy with raspberry jam, and forced herself to chew at a normal pace. Her dad, Deon, had always sat there, in front of the apple clock. One knee up. His head in some Louis L'Amour western. Bud and her mother at opposite ends of the table. That's how it used to be every night. Bud snacked on blueberries picked from the field—fresh in summer, frozen in winter. Juice smeared over his face. Her mother read Anne Rice or V. C. Andrews, but eventually got up and banged around the kitchen. Took a moose roast out of the oven. Whipped up a pepper gravy. That was when Laurel wanted her father to stop reading too.

"Wanna know what we did in school?"

Her dad held the book open and ran his fingers through shaggy red hair. "What did you do?"

"It was sports day. I was the second fastest in all grade five. The second-fastest girl. We didn't race the boys, but I bet I was faster than all of them."

"Do you now? Boys are pretty fast."

"And I was the fastest on the monkey bars."

"That's not a surprise."

"There's no award for the monkey bars, but Horsey said I got the strongest arms."

"Show me." Instead of flexing to show off her plum-sized muscles, Laurel told him about the obstacle course, the long jump, the Frisbee toss, the beanbag throw, shot put and—

"Laurel." Her mother put a hand on her shoulder. "That's enough now, let Dad read his book."

"Javelin was the hardest." She vibrated in her seat. "You had to run as fast as you can. I'm really, really fast. And throw a spear. Far as you can."

"Did you throw it that far?" Her father flipped a page.

"So far. But Luke threw it farthest. He got gold. Daniel threw second farthest, but Bradley was almost just as far. In girls—"

"What's that sound?" Her mother paused her stirring.

Her father raised his brows. "I don't hear anything."

"A whoosh. Like a javelin flying through the kitchen."

"Or a Frisbee."

"It's gone now. It's quiet again." She spread her hands. "Perfect silence."

Bud grabbed a fistful of blueberries and shoved them in his face. He giggled.

"Perfect, perfect silence." Maxine opened the cupboard and pulled out a bag of flour.

"Mom." Laurel's mother could hear her, she was just trying to shush her up. "Mom?" She opened the bag and spooned flour into a Mason jar. "Dad?" Nothing. "It's not funny!"

"There it is again. A whoosh."

Her father turned another page.

"Bud, you hear me, right?"

Bud shook his head.

The phone rang. Maxine dropped the ladle in the gravy pan, wiped her hands down the sides of her pants and went to answer it. Deon closed his book.

"Hello? Yes, yes, he's here."

Blueberries fell from Bud's fingers and rolled under the table. Juicy blue streaks on the canvas floor.

Her father took the phone and her mother hovered with her ear tilted to the receiver, their voices wordless murmurs that crept up Laurel's spine.

When they hung up, her dad sat under the clock. Her mom

stood in the middle of the room. Bud paused mid-chew.

"What?" Laurel asked.

Tick-tick-tick.

"What?"

"We have to see the doctor in Stephenville tomorrow."

Her father rested his forehead on his palm. Knuckles heavy. Too big for his fingers. A question rose in her throat and stuck. Is the cancer back? Laurel coughed. She coughed and coughed until her mother pounded her on the back and she swallowed the question down.

A gust of wind rattled the fan in the range hood. Laurel crammed the last half-piece of raspberry toast into her mouth and got up. She flicked the light on over the stove. Turned the hall light on, and the light in her bedroom. The clock on her dresser read 9:14 p.m. She pushed the alarm button and the numbers changed to 6:30 a.m. When she let go, 9:14 p.m. returned. Laurel scanned the titles on the bookshelf. Every row. Left to right. Top to bottom. She could list the books from memory. The shelf used to be in the living room, but Rick hated clutter. Her mother had moved it into her room and Laurel fell asleep every night staring at the bowed shelves. Her parents' old novels. Her own collection of kids' books. The full set of the *Encyclopædia Britannica*. Her parents had purchased the set brand new, the only thing they had ever purchased brand new, and the rich burgundy-brown volumes looked warm and luxurious. She patted the spines until they lined up.

Laurel returned to the kitchen, cleared her plate and washed the dishes left on the counter. She stacked clean glasses in the drying rack, then wiped the counter and table down. When that was done, she swept the floor. There was a sticky spot where she'd dripped a bit of jam and she got down and scrubbed it with a dishcloth.

She went to the living room and stared out the window. Cupped her hands to the glass and willed Una's car to come up the driveway. Laurel turned the TV on and jumped at the roar of static. She lowered the volume, adjusted the antenna and fiddled with the wire at the back of the set until faint images and colour could be seen through the fuzz. A woman, a news anchor, sat at a desk and laughed at whatever the man next to her said.

Laurel tugged the blanket free from the back of the couch, wrapped it around herself and curled up in the corner. The man laughed silently at the woman. They both laughed, heads tilted together, mouths gaping holes of static and teeth.

TWO

A door slammed. Laurel jumped off the couch and ran to the living room window. No lights.

Nothing.

Heavy boots on the front steps.

The door banged open and Rick filled the doorway. Wind whistled around him.

Laurel's heels sank into the carpet.

"Where's your mother?" Rick slammed the door and pulled his boots off on the rubber mat. He stood and his head blocked the light in the ceiling. "Well?"

"Out."

"Out?" He drew his head back in disbelief.

"She's gone to Una's up the road."

"Una's-up-the-road?" He said this like Una's was made up. Something mythical.

"She just went for a bit. I thought . . . I thought—"

"You thought, you thought." His face twisted into a snarl. "No wonder you fuckin' knows it all."

"I don't . . ."

Rick stomped into the kitchen and Laurel caught the sour scent of booze.

"And what, you got every goddamn light on? You knows how to pay for that too do you?" Rick opened the cabinets above the stove and took out a bottle of Crown Royal.

Laurel snapped off the living room light, entryway light, and hallway light. She went into her room and the door closed with a quiet click. The lock could be picked with a butter knife or a hard fingernail, but she locked it, braced her feet on the carpet and shoved her dresser in front of the door. Her alarm clock slid across the dresser top.

11:35 p.m.

She sat on the bed and folded her hands. A cupboard door smacked closed. A glass banged down. The floor creaked as Rick paced the kitchen. She heard him fumble with the phone.

"Maxine there? Tell her to get her ass home. Now." The receiver banged down. It dinged in protest.

Laurel read the titles on the bookshelf out loud. Left to right. Top to bottom. Rick opened the fridge, and bottles clanked and rattled together so loud she thought something might break. She squeezed her eyes shut. Recited from memory. The oven door cracked open. There wasn't any supper. Nothing cooked. Rick cursed and swore and stomped around. The table shrieked across the floor and a chair hit her bedroom wall. Laurel jumped off the bed and stood in the middle of the room, clenching and unclenching her fists. Rick pushed the table back into place. He sat. A chair groaned as he settled into it.

She opened her curtains and looked out into the night. Woods Road stretched all way to Route 460, a slim, two-lane highway that joined Corner Brook and Stephenville. Both towns distant and far away, as mythical as Una's-up-the-road. Nothing but dark and wet and trees.

Laurel sat on the floor with her back to the wall and waited.

A car idled in the driveway. "Bye!" Maxine sang out. "Thank you! See you later!"

Laurel shoved her dresser out of the way and ran out of her room. "Mom! You're back."

"Hi, honey." Her mother bent to unzip her boots, hair like fresh air.

"You went out like that?" Rick barked from the table.

"Laurel, you should go to bed. It's late. I'll get you settled in."

Rick watched as Laurel was ushered to her room. Maxine locked the door, took off her jacket and dropped it on the bed. She pulled down the covers, her body shaking. "I'll lie down with you."

Laurel crawled in bed and her mother climbed in after her.

Rick pounded on the kitchen wall. "Get out here."

Laurel's breath caught. Her mother froze.

"Get out. Or I'm coming in."

"Shit," her mother hissed. "We should have gone to Bud's room." She flung the covers off. Laurel sat up. "You stay in bed." Her mother shushed her when she started to talk. "It'll be all right. I promise." She kissed Laurel's forehead, locked the door from the inside and shut it behind her.

Laurel lay stiff under the covers. Unmoving as she listened to her mother's quiet whispers in the kitchen. Her mother turned on the tap. Opened a cupboard. Shut the water off. Then she said something sharp and slammed a glass down on the counter.

A fist hit the table. Hit it again. A chair crashed to the floor. Laurel pulled the blankets over her head.

Rick shouted words Laurel would never repeat. Could never.

Her mother gasped. "Stop! You're hurting me!" A shuffling of feet. Hands slapping skin.

Laurel burrowed deep under the covers. A tight coil in the middle of her mattress. The last time Rick had drunk himself into a fit of rage, they'd locked themselves in Bud's room. Her brother asleep between them. Her dad's old hunting rifle propped against the dresser. His Winchester .30-30, what her mother had called "a precautionary measure."

Pots and dishes crashed to the kitchen floor. Glass shattered. Laurel pulled the blankets from her head and sat up. A body hit the ground. Her mother grunted. Heels drummed the floor. She was being dragged out of the kitchen.

The water in the bathroom came on. Full force. "Wash your face. There you go. Wash that off!"

Bang.

Laurel's eyes snapped open. The sound was hollow. Cavernous. Bone hitting porcelain.

Her mother's screams turned ragged. "Stop! Please stop. Please, please, please."

Again, the sound. *Bang.*

Laurel jumped out of bed. She undid her bedroom lock. Gripped the doorknob.

"Goddamn it! Look! You broke it!" Rick shouted. The water shut off. He dragged her mother out of the bathroom. Back to the kitchen.

"Up!" Rick boomed. "Up you go!"

"I'm sorry. I'm sorry." Her mother's voice was low, Laurel could hardly hear her.

She opened the door and ran to the kitchen. Rick pinned Maxine against the stove and wrapped his hands around her neck. Laurel stepped on broken glass. Slipped on wet tiles, but caught the counter before she fell. Her mother's eyes were wide and terrified. She scrambled at his hands. Laurel pried at his fingers, but they were slick, rubbery sausages that wouldn't budge from her mother's neck. She dug her nails into his knuckles. Into the sinew between thumb and forefinger. Rick laughed.

"Look at that! Look at your little *girl.*"

Laurel stopped scrambling at Rick's fingers. Her mother's eyes were bloodshot and swimming with wet. "Mom?"

Her mouth moved but no sound came out.

"Mom!" Laurel's voice shrilled. "Mom!" She stepped back. The knife her mother used to peel potatoes sat on the counter. Chunks of glass lay on the floor. Rick's hunched back was massive, and his neck was thick and corded. Her mother's eyes rolled closed.

Laurel spun and ran to Bud's room.

Her five-year-old brother was still asleep. His arm curled around Baker Dog. The bed gasped when she jumped onto it, but he didn't stir. She stood on the footboard and reached into his closet. Sweaters. Spare sheets. A knitted blanket. Her fingers brushed cold metal. She gripped the shelf and pulled herself to her toes. Something crashed in the kitchen. Laurel's fingers closed around the barrel. She tugged the gun from the closet and stumbled back against the wall. Bud rolled over, tucked Baker Dog under his face and snuggled into the fluff. Laurel held the rifle steady by the stock and checked the chamber for rounds. She laid the gun alongside her brother and stepped back on the footboard. Her hand slapped bare wood. Panic rose in her chest. She held her breath. Stretched and felt for the box of bullets. She jumped and batted at it. Swatted the box closer until it fell out of the closet. Bullets spilled on the floor and rolled under the bed. She jumped down, snatched up a single round and loaded the rifle. It had been years since her dad taught how to shoot, but she remembered his voice.

Cock the lever and lock it down.

Laurel cocked the lever. Locked it down and slipped out of the room with the loaded gun. She shut Bud's bedroom door and crept down the hall. Peered into the kitchen. Rick's back a wall of muscle between her and her mom.

She inched closer, bare feet landing flat and silent.

Ground yourself.

Laurel stopped and kneeled on one knee. Lifted the rifle and stared down the barrel. Muscles bunched in Rick's shoulders. Veins bulged in his neck.

Remove the safety.

She clicked the safety off. Rick's head snapped up.

Relax your shoulders. Line up your sights.

She adjusted the gun against her shoulder. Squinted. Lined up the sight posts. Aimed at the space between his shoulder blades. Finger tight on the trigger.

Breathe.

He spun around. Laurel let out her breath and squeezed.

The burnt metal smell of a pot boiled dry, scorched to the burner. A whiff of sour eggs. Blood roared in her ears. Laurel gasped for breath, but her chest was split in two. Air lodged in her breastbone. She patted her ribs. Pressed her fingers into her heart and tried to breathe. Her tongue worked to swallow, but her throat was parched, raw, burning. Laurel curled up and pushed on her ears until the painful ringing flatlined to a dull ache.

Maxine groaned.

Fog coalesced into two bodies. Rick, face down on the floor. Legs spread apart and twisted. His torso crossed atop her mother. Laurel scrambled into the blood that pooled around them. She tried to pull Rick off, but her hands slipped again and again. She screeched and pushed. Rick rolled and flopped. Laurel's arms were weak. Streaked now with blood. Her hands slick with it. They slapped the wet floor as she crawled closer to her mom. Her mother's face was ghastly pale. Neck mottled, swollen, and blue veins running over her jaw. "Mom!" Laurel patted her cheeks. "Mom-mom-mom-mom-mom . . ."

Laurel shook her, but her head only rolled from side to side. She pressed two fingers to the base of her mother's neck. The side of her throat, then the soft spot behind her jaw. She tapped at the skin. Pushed into soft tissue, searching for a pulse that she didn't know how to find. Laurel let go and scrambled for the phone.

"Laurel! Laurel!" Una shook her. Laurel lifted her head from Maxine's chest.

"I'm okay." Her mother's lips didn't move. She forced her words, thin and pasty, through clenched teeth. "ImokayImokayImokay."

Laurel's sob was big and soundless. It caught in her mouth. She couldn't breathe around it. She sagged forward. Pressed her forehead to her mom's.

Una tugged her shoulder. "Come on. Let's get her out of here."

Her mother's face was stained with blood. Laurel looked at her own hands and shook her head wildly. The room spun out of focus.

"Here!" Una caught her by the shoulders. "We have to get out of here. Okay?"

Laurel blinked at her.

"We have to go. Now." Una squeezed harder. "We need to take care of your mom. Think about everything else later." She leaned in close. "Okay?"

Horsey, Una's daughter, the only other girl Laurel's age on Woods Road, crouched next to her and slipped a hand under her armpit. "Okay. Here we go." Laurel stiffened, embarrassed for everything her friend was seeing.

"Is he . . . ?" Laurel looked to Una.

"I don't know," Una said. "But I'm not taking any chances."

Laurel found her balance as they guided her outside. The rain had stopped, but wind pulled at her hair. She sat down and pulled her knees to her chest. Horsey wrapped her arms around her shoulders.

"Horsey," Una said. "I need you."

Horsey nodded into Laurel's neck, then let go and followed Una back inside.

Laurel huddled on the steps. The night cold and round and moonless. She dug her nails into raw wood and gasped for air. Closed her eyes against the noises coming from inside. Una's orders. Horsey's responding movements as they scrabbled and banged around. And from the driveway, a faint *ding-ding-ding* came from Una's car where the driver's side door hung open. Damp air coursed down her throat, into her veins. She heard her mother groan and looked back as Una and Horsey shuffled outside with Maxine slumped between them. Laurel jumped up.

"Here." Una let Laurel take her place. "Can you get her in the car?" Una turned and went back in the house.

Maxine stumbled and the two girls helped her sit on the step. Laurel sat down and let her mother slump into her. She started to shake.

"Horsey?" Laurel said.

"Shh. I'm here." Horsey sat on the other side of Maxine and helped support the weight of her.

Una reappeared with Bud flopped over her shoulder and her arms crossed under his bum. "He's still asleep," she said, like it was the craziest thing she'd seen all night. "Come on. We need to get out of here."

Maxine nodded and closed her eyes.

"We got her," Horsey said.

"They need shoes." Una started down the steps. Bud's feet hung past her knees. Baker Dog dangled from her hand. Horsey got up and went inside.

Laurel shifted to handle her mother's full weight. "Should we call the police?"

"I already did." Una trotted across the driveway, Bud's arms and legs flapping. She managed to balance him against her shoulder and open the door. He groaned as she eased him into the backseat of the car.

Horsey returned with shoes and Laurel shoved her bloody feet into them. She shivered in her shorts and T-shirt.

Something crashed in the house.

"Come on!" Horsey bent to help Maxine into her shoes.

Another crash. Rick grunted and coughed.

Laurel slipped her arm around her mother. Horsey took the other side. They pulled her down the steps and stumbled to the car.

Una drove slow over the gravel driveway that travelled the length of Pateys' farm. Laurel rolled down her window to let the fresh air flush the smell of her blood-covered body from the cramped space. Wind clawed at her hair. Trees groaned as they bent at unnatural angles, offering a glimpse of the Pateys' farmhouse. Windows lit. Porch light on. Everything bright and yellow. Then dark again as the trees closed over it. Una sped up when they hit the pavement, her house just minutes away. Maxine huffed and clutched Laurel's shoulder. Laurel held her close and stared out into the night. Clouds shifted overhead and they raced down Woods Road under the narrow eye of the moon.

Horsey's driveway was as long and rough as Laurel's, but Una didn't slow again. She bumped and juddered over the gravel until she parked at her front door.

"Bud's still asleep." Una jumped out of the car, "I'll put him in my bed."

Laurel clung to that simple statement. Bud was still asleep. He'd missed all of it. She climbed out of the car and Horsey came around to help her with Maxine. Una disappeared inside the house with Bud.

Maxine's nose flared as she eased herself out of the backseat. Her fingers dug into Laurel's arm. Behind them, lights flashed down Woods Road. A car turned up the driveway. Another. Quiet flickers of red and blue over trees and across wet gravel.

Una returned and tried to take Laurel's place. "Go on now. Both of you. I got her."

Laurel held on. "I have to get her out of here."

"It's done." Una shoved her aside. "Go on. I'll talk to the cops."

Horsey grabbed Laurel's arm and pulled. Laurel followed, then turned to see her mother's knees buckle.

"Mom!"

Una caught her and Maxine collapsed against her side. The ambulance stopped in front of them.

Horsey yanked her arm. Laurel twisted and broke away, but Horsey caught her by the back of her T-shirt. The collar dug into her neck and snapped her back into a straightjacket hug. "She's all right. Come on."

Two people ran from the ambulance with a stretcher.

"Come on! Bud's in the house."

Laurel shoved, but Horsey was almost a year older, a foot taller and twice as strong. She stopped struggling.

"Okay?" Horsey relaxed her hold and they turned toward the house. Inside, Horsey shut the door, held Laurel's arm and led her through the kitchen to the bathroom.

"Get in the shower. I'll find you some clothes."

Laurel stared at herself in the mirror. A tangled mass of hair plastered to her forehead. Blood smeared across her face and down the sides of her neck. She touched her cheek and followed the path of a smear, down to her T-shirt. The fabric a patchwork of red, pink and raspberry all wet and run together. Her shorts were streaked with it. Her knees. Her legs. A clumpy bit of something stuck to her calf.

The room tilted. Laurel's stomach lurched. She bent over the toilet and heaved.

"Oh!" Horsey crouched next to her. She rubbed her back and pulled her hair back from her face. "It's okay. It's okay."

Horsey flushed the toilet and closed the lid. "Get in the shower and put these on when you get out." She set a pair of pyjamas on top of the toilet seat. "You'll feel better." Horsey hauled her up. "Think about it later, remember? Later. Right now, you gotta get cleaned up."

Laurel nodded as Horsey pulled her shirt over her head. She started to unbutton Laurel's shorts, but Laurel pushed her hands away and did it herself. Horsey turned on the water, gave Laurel's bare shoulders a squeeze and pushed her toward the shower. She shut the bathroom door and left.

Laurel got in and adjusted the tap until the shower was as hot as she could stand. She sat in the bottom of the tub with her arms around her knees, shivering despite the steam.

Goddamn it! Look! You broke it!

She covered her head and rocked back and forth, tried to push Rick's voice from her mind. A trickle of pink streaming toward the drain. The hot water ran out and cold pelted her skin until she was numb. Laurel stood and picked up the bar of soap and lathered her body. Her face. The soles of her feet. Her hair. She washed the froth away, but still, a steady drip of pink swirling down the drain.

Laurel picked the bar of soap up again.

Blood dripped. From *inside* her body. Drip, drip, drip, into the tub. Red dissolved to raspberry, dissolved to pink. Laurel returned the soap to the edge of the tub. She checked between her legs and her hand came away bloody. Horsey started her period long ago. This was bound to happen to her too, but the shock of it sank into her belly. Laurel trembled as she climbed out of the tub and rummaged under the sink. She knocked aside an empty bottle of shampoo, a bin of cleaning supplies, and rolls of toilet paper. She pulled a tube out of a box of Tampax, then held it up in front of her face. The paper wrapping crinkled as she turned it left and right. She shoved the tube back in the box, the box back in the cabinet and made do with a massive wad of toilet paper.

THREE

Water trickled down Laurel's back as she stood outside the bathroom door, bloody clothes in her hands. Two police officers filled Una's kitchen. One of them, a man, stood in the middle of the room with his fingers hooked in his belt. His head tilted to one side as if the ceiling was too low to stand to his full height. The other sat at the table with her hands folded. She gave Laurel a slow smile. Laurel balled her clothes up as small as she could.

The officer in the middle of the room stepped forward.

Una rushed past him. "Here. Let me take that."

He held out a Ziploc bag and Una dropped the clothes inside. She rubbed her hands on her pants and turned back to Laurel.

"Where's Mom?"

"She's gone to the hospital in Stephenville." Una pulled Laurel into a hug and squeezed her close. "We'll go see her first thing tomorrow. She's going to be okay."

"Can I call her?"

"First thing in the morning. I promise," Una whispered in her ear.

"Ma'am," the man said.

Una released Laurel, but kept both hands on her shoulders.

"Constable Hennessy," she said loudly, "wants to talk to you. Is that okay?"

"Am I going to jail?"

"No, my girl."

"You're not in trouble," the officer seated at the table said. "We just need to ask you a few questions."

Constable Hennessy cleared his throat. "Ma'am?" He took another step forward and Una's kitchen shrank around him.

"I'll stay right with you," Una said. "Just a quick chat. You tell the constable what happened, then we can all get some rest." Una nodded slowly. "Okay?"

Laurel mimicked the movement and nodded back.

"Okay." Una stretched her arm across Laurel's shoulders and steered her into the kitchen where she pulled out a chair. Laurel sat down and shifted to make sure the wad of tissue was still in place.

"I'm Constable Delphine." Delphine pushed another chair out from the table with her foot. "And this is Constable Hennessy."

Hennessy took the chair, but he sat away, as if the table was too small.

Constable Delphine leaned forward. "You can call me Delphine. I have a sister named Laurence. That sounds a lot like Laurel." She smiled as she spoke. "Maybe if she was born here, in Newfoundland, her name would be the same as you. But my sister was born in Quebec. So she is Laurence. And I am Delphine." She spread her hands as if these were just two of the many things in life she couldn't control. "I think you've had a very difficult night, Laurel. I just need you to tell me what happened. Can you do that?"

Flecks of nail polish were embedded in the woodgrain of the tabletop. An orangey pink, a violet purple. Red. Laurel dug the edge of a nail into the wood and scratched.

"Would you be more comfortable talking to me alone? We can

go to the detachment. Just me and you."

Horsey was in the living room. TV down low. A splinter caught under her fingernail.

"I can leave," Una said. "Would that be better? I can sit in there with Horsey and watch some TV. We won't even hear you. Do you want me to do that?"

Laurel shrugged, then shook her head. Una pulled out the last chair and sat down.

"This is my recorder." Delphine set it on the table. "So we can record our little talk, okay? Is that all right with you?"

"Sure," Laurel whispered. She cleared her throat. "Yes."

"Good. Can you begin by telling me your name?"

"Laurel Long."

"And how old are you, Laurel?"

"Fourteen."

"Can you tell me what happened tonight?"

Laurel nodded and sat back in her chair. She examined stains on the ceiling. Little green splatters, like someone had overcooked a pot of peas on the stove and it had exploded. A brown water-marked corner.

"You are not in any trouble. I just want to understand what happened."

The TV grew louder. Police sirens. Music. *Law and Order*.

Laurel cleared her throat again. "Is he . . . Is Rick . . . ?"

"Rick Warren is also in the hospital."

"I shot him. In the chest. I saw the blood fly out."

Delphine looked at Hennessy.

"Maybe we should—"

Delphine held up a hand and cut him off. She crossed her arms on the table. "Laurel, can you tell us what happened before that? Start from the beginning."

The beginning. It had started with her mother wearing makeup, and that jacket, and going out to Una's by herself in the middle of a rainstorm. But that wasn't the beginning. It started long before that. When Rick moved in about a year ago. At first, everything was fine. He ploughed the driveway with his truck. He bought a big TV and watched movies with Bud. He drank sometimes, but when he did, he just got loud. Then he sold his house and moved into their home. Their home was his home now. And he thought they were all his, too. He called everything clutter. Packed away her mom's stuff. And he had rules. No baths. Showers had to be kept short. Laurel tried to shower when he was out, but sometimes he came home early, pounded a fist on the bathroom door and barked, "That's enough water!" They had to wait for Rick to get home before they could eat supper. Even if it was late. Even if it was so late Bud nodded off at the supper table and Laurel had to poke him to keep him up. There were more rules for her mother. No makeup. No knee-high boots. No hippy leather jackets with fringes. No going out alone.

"He was choking her. He was choking her and her face was red. Her veins . . ." Laurel touched her neck. "I couldn't make him stop. I thought about kicking him, or hitting him, but that might have just made him worse. I got the gun from the closet."

"Was it loaded?" Hennessy asked.

"No. I couldn't reach the bullets, but then I did. I got one."

Delphine took the recorder from the table and clicked stop.

Laurel hugged herself. "Am I going to go to jail?"

"No," Delphine said. "Don't worry about that right now. Okay? There might be more questions for you later. Or maybe this is enough. I'm not sure. But it'll be okay. Okay?" Delphine reached into her front pocket, pulled out a card and handed it to Laurel. She indicated the phone number printed on the bottom. "You can call me anytime. Just ask for Delphine. Call me if you think of anything else you want to tell me. Or just want to talk. Okay?"

Laurel nodded.

She caught Laurel's hand. "I think you are a very brave girl.

Very strong." She made a fist over Laurel's for emphasis. "I think you saved your mother's life."

After the police left, Una turned her attention to Laurel. "Do you want anything? Are you hungry? Want me to fix you some tea?"

"No."

"You go on in your room," Una said to Horsey. "Laurel can sleep in my bed with Bud. I'll take the couch."

Una ushered Laurel to her bedroom, but Laurel went in ahead of her and shut the door before she could follow. She felt her way to the bed in the dark, climbed in and wound her arms around her little brother. The heat from his body helped ease the hollowness inside her. She curled tight around him, found Baker Dog, and squeezed the stuffed toy and her brother as tight as she dared. Bud's breathing hitched, then relaxed into deep, steady breaths.

Laurel squirmed and adjusted the tissue in her underwear. She matched her breathing to Bud's, buried her face in his neck and fell into darkness.

FOUR

Sunlight slanted through the window and across the bed. Horsey's parents' bed, but her dad was never home. He was always on the road, hauling another load of mill-paper across to the mainland. Laurel reached through the blankets for Bud but found only empty sheets. Her stomach cramped and she pulled down the sheets to check for bloodstains. Baker Dog flopped to the floor. She picked the stuffed toy up, tucked him under her cheek and covered herself again. She shut her eyes and saw her mother collapse in the flashing lights of the ambulance. Two people running with a stretcher like in a scene from *Law and Order*. Laurel sat up and pain shot from her shoulder across her back. She rolled her neck from side to side, but the stretch didn't help.

She had stared down the barrel of a rifle, at a man. Had lined up her sights on his back and breathed. Squeezed the trigger. She'd told the officers she had seen blood fly out of his chest but couldn't remember that now. There was only the crack of the bullet. The smell of burnt metal. Bad eggs. The shock, as the gun kicked back into her shoulder and knocked her to the ground. Maybe she hadn't hit Rick square in the chest like she thought. Maybe he was already up and prowling around the hospital corridors looking for her mom. Laurel bolted out of bed and flung the bedroom door open.

Three sets of eyes looked up at her from the living room carpet. Una, Horsey, and Bud sat around a Trouble game, Bud with his hand on the plastic bubble in the middle of the board.

"It's morning," Laurel said.

"I told Bud your mom wasn't feeling well and had to go to the hospital for a bit, but she's going to be okay," Una said.

Bud pushed the bubble and it made a clunky *pop-pop*.

"I told Bud we can go see her later, when she feels better."

"But—"

"And your mother already has some visitors this morning." Una widened her eyes at Laurel. "She'll feel better real soon."

The last thing Laurel wanted was to freak Bud out or see another police officer. She stood in the doorway until her heart calmed enough for her to limp across the living room and sit on the couch.

"You okay?" Horsey moved to make room.

"Get Laurel some breakfast, would you?"

"Me?"

"Yes you. I'm about to kick Bud's ass."

Bud giggled and clunked the bubble again. *Pop-pop*.

"I'm not hungry." Laurel rubbed her shoulder and shifted her position on the couch. Everything was brown in Horsey's house: the couch, the carpet, the panelled wallboard.

"Come on." Horsey got up from the floor. "We got toast, and we got toast. Welcome to the shack."

"Don't call your home a shack. Be grateful for the roof you got." Una clunked the bubble and rolled a six. "Ha! Bud, I told ya!" She picked up her game piece and clacked out six moves. "There's coffee on the counter."

The wooden slab that served as a counter ran the length of the kitchen wall. Laurel leaned against it as Horsey rummaged through open shelves underneath. She scavenged two slices of bread from a plastic bag and dropped them in the toaster.

"I'm not hungry."

Horsey banged around the wall cabinets, opening and closing the doors. "Mom! There's no dishes!"

"It was your turn to wash!" Una shouted back from the living room.

"Jesus." Horsey rolled her eyes and plucked the lone spoon from the drying rack next to the sink. She opened a jar of peanut butter and dipped it in. She offered it to Laurel, then stuck it in her own mouth. Horsey ran the water in the sink and squirted dish detergent into two dirty mugs. She washed them as she sucked on her spoon. The toast popped. "Butter or peanut butter?"

"No."

When the kettle shook and rattled, she whipped it off the stove and poured water in the wet mugs. She sucked the last of the peanut butter, gave the spoon a rinse, then used it to scoop coffee. Added tinned milk and sugar and handed a mug to Laurel. "It's good. I swear."

Laurel took the cup. Bubbles formed around the edge of the steaming brown liquid. It tasted as bitter as it smelled. Scalded her throat.

Horsey turned back to the toast. "Jam? We got jam. Raspberry I think."

The room shrank. She felt the way Constable Hennessy had looked the night before, crammed and suffocated. "I want to go outside."

"I'll come with you."

"No. I just . . . need some air. Do you have anything I can put on?"

"Help yourself."

Laurel went to Horsey's room and pulled on a pair of her jeans. She rolled the hems to her ankles, found a MuchMusic sweatshirt in a heap on the floor and tugged it over her head.

"Where you going?" Una asked.

"Nowhere." The shack was too hot, stuffy with smoke from the wood stove. She touched the wall for balance and looked through the clutter of shoes on the doormat. "I won't be long."

"Wear a pair of Horsey's."

Where were her own shoes? The ones she'd shoved her bloody feet into last night? The answer was in Una's pinched lips and furrowed brows. Laurel shoved her feet into Horsey's two-sizes-too-big black-and-white Champions and took off out the door.

Snow drifted in the air like Styrofoam. Laurel pulled the baggy collar of Horsey's sweatshirt up around her chin and started down the driveway. She wanted to curl up in her own bed, burrow under her covers like a baby rabbit until her mom came back, but as she walked Woods Road, she imagined her front door criss-crossed with yellow police tape and police officers stationed outside with buzzing walkie-talkies. Laurel slowed and listened for signs of life.

But the morning was still and quiet and open to echoes. Snow pattered in the trees. Gravel scraped underfoot. Laurel rounded the corner of her driveway and her house came into view. It looked the same as it always did. A perfect rectangle with a cement basement. Log siding to the top of the door, then clapboard that her mom had always wanted to paint cherry red but that had faded to driftwood grey. She climbed the plank steps. No police officers standing guard. No yellow tape. Laurel opened the door.

There was blood everywhere. It covered the floor. The walls. Kitchen table. Knocked-over chairs. Fridge. Cupboards. Counter. Stove. Laurel gasped for breath. Iron, and the tangy sweet smell of raspberries.

A broken Mason jar sat in a pool of jam. Her mother's jam was just boiled berries. No sugar. No pectin. Always tart and dripping with juice. Where Rick and her mother had fallen there was a thick pool of blood. The difference was obvious. Laurel stepped around broken glass and clumps of jam. She went to the bathroom.

The bathroom sink dangled from the wall like a twisted

creature. One of the two sticks that held it up had snapped. Laurel traced her fingers along the cool porcelain. *Goddammit! Look! You broke it!* She shut her eyes and tried to erase the image of her mother's head smacking the sink until the porcelain cracked. The bowl was smooth. Cool. Her mother hadn't broken the sink, only the stick that held it up.

Laurel lifted the sink and pushed it back against the wall, but the pipe was too bent. The sink slumped back down and hovered above the floor on its wasted neck. She opened the closet and found the box of pads her mom had kept there for her ever since she turned twelve. Two rows of little floral packets peeked up at her. She pulled down her pants, dropped the wad of bloody tissue in the toilet, flushed and replaced it with a pad. Laurel stuffed a handful of pads into her pocket, then hauled the thickest towel she could find out of the closet.

In the kitchen, she dropped the towel in a puddle of raspberry jam. The towel settled and soaked up juice. It dripped when she picked it up. Ripe red drops landed on Horsey's jeans. Juice had spattered the walls. Speckled the ceiling. And the blood. That thick, red pool that smelled of clotted rust. The heavy spray on the kitchen window. Laurel dropped the towel and ran.

She stumbled down the front steps. Horsey's sneakers squelched as she half-ran, half-slid across the wet grass around the back of the house to the tree line. Spruce boughs slapped her arms and legs as she crashed down the path to the river. She slowed only to hop or duck a fallen tree. Deep green moss gave way to roots, packed earth and rocks as she reached the shore, where river stones shifted and clacked under her feet and the roar of the current almost drowned her thoughts. Laurel stopped when the tips of her sneakers touched the water. She lifted her face to the sky and screamed.

Laurel lay flat on her back on the icy wet stones. A lone crow flew to the top of a skinny spruce. It landed on the tip and folded its wings. Crowed in a voice that sounded human.

She closed her eyes and pictured her mother cracking a dead tree branch over her knee. The fire they had built sat in a hole burned through the snow, a circle of ash around it. Maxine fed the branch to the flames, then looked up and watched a crow lift off, a crooked treetop swaying in its wake.

"Do you know your way home from here?"

Laurel had been only six years old. She looked at her mother, then back at the snowshoe tracks twisting into the trees behind them and pointed in their direction.

Her mother adjusted her woods coat and tucked it tight inside the bib of her snow pants. She took off her mitts and squatted down to fill a pot with snow. "That's just the way we walked. What about the river? Think."

Black spruce and balsam fir crowded close, their branches frosted with snow. Every direction the same. In the summer, they went to the swimming hole and the sun was always in her eyes on the way there. She pointed in the direction of the sun.

"That's right." Her mother pulled her coat sleeves over her hands and lifted the pot on the fire. "Once you reach the river, you can follow it to the swimming hole. You know your way home from there. If you overshoot the swimming hole, you'll reach the farm. The important thing is to walk in a straight line. Keep the sun in your eyes or at your back, so you don't go in circles."

Her mother stood and shoved her hands in her pockets, her face a silhouette as Laurel squinted at her.

"What do I do when there isn't any sun?"

"Oh, that part's trickier." Her mother bounced her knees against the cold. Rubbed her hands together. Shivered and looked up. "Just think."

"Laurel!"

The light snow turned to hail. She sat up to see Jimmy emerge, tall and lanky, from the path, shielding his eyes from the onslaught.

"Laurel, what are you doing?"

She pushed herself up from the ground. Laurel, Jimmy and Horsey spent forty minutes together twice a day, squished together in the back of the school bus. "What are you doing here?" Her voice lost to ringing hail and roaring water.

"Come on!" Jimmy grabbed her hand and tugged her upriver. His whole body bent against the hail.

She yanked free but followed him along the riverbank.

"Horsey called," Jimmy shouted.

"What'd she say?"

"Nothing. She was looking for you." He veered back into the woods on another path, one that led to Pateys' farm. The trees trembled in the ice storm but sheltered them from the worst of it. Jimmy led her out of the woods and into a pasture where wind whipped across an open expanse of field. Laurel put her head down and trudged behind him. Every few steps she squinted into the mess to make sure he was still in front of her. She walked into him when he stopped.

Jimmy hauled the door of the old hay barn open.

The wind was instantly muffled inside. Air warm with the deep-earth smell of stacked hay. Jimmy stomped his feet and pulled the door closed. He brushed past her, wiped caked ice from his coat, jumped on a bale, then climbed up another. At the top, he turned and reached down a hand. Laurel wedged a foot into one of the divots and pushed herself up. She worked her way to a space between hay bales that offered enough room for her to stand. Jimmy had to duck his head, but he sat down and drew his knees into his chest. Laurel sat opposite him and wedged her hands between the damp denim of her thighs.

"What'd you say?"

"What?" She looked at her hands. Her wet jeans. Hay. Anything but Jimmy.

"Outside?"

"Why was Horsey looking for me?"

"'Cause you disappeared in an ice storm. When you weren't at your house, I figured you were out in the woods."

"You went to my house?" Laurel's gaze fastened onto Jimmy. "Did you go in?"

"No. I . . . I just knocked." Jimmy turned ash-pale.

"Did you go in my house?" Laurel's voice pitched an octave higher.

"I didn't." He raised his hands.

Had she even shut the door? If Jimmy had gone inside, he probably wouldn't be here right now. Laurel let her head fall back on the wall of hay behind her.

"What were you doing out there?"

"Nothing."

"It looked like you were about to crawl into a river."

"No it didn't."

"That's how I saw it."

"Whatever, I get it. You saved me."

"Well, no, I—never mind." Jimmy manoeuvred himself around the nook until he sat next to her. He stretched out his legs, leaned his head back and let out a long, dramatic Jimmy sigh. "You gave me a fright. That's all."

"I'm fine. It was nothing." She stretched her legs alongside his and rested her hands by her sides.

Her eyes were closed when Jimmy put his hand on top of hers. She held still in case he had done it by accident. The barn was warm. Like they had burrowed deep, deep, deep into the ground, but the warmth didn't reach her bones. Laurel shivered and pulled her hand free, careful to make it seem like she hadn't noticed his at all.

"I should go. I'm soaked." Horsey's sweatshirt hung limp from her shoulders as she stood.

"I'll walk you back to Horsey's."

"How'd you know I was going to Horsey's?"
"I just assumed."
"Why would you assume that?"
"I don't know. She—"
"I'm not fucking homeless."
"What?"
"I can walk fine on my own." Laurel jumped from the hay bale. The hail had turned to rain and her entire body stung with cold when she burst out of the barn. She sprinted across the pasture, sweatshirt plastered across her chest. Lungs burning as she wailed.

FIVE

The wood stove roared in the shack, but Laurel spent the rest of the day shivering in bed, buried under covers, teeth chattering.

Una laid a hand on her forehead.

"You're burning up. Horsey!" Una shouted. "Where's the thermometer?"

"How the hell should I know?" Horsey shouted back. A moment later she appeared in the doorway with a small glass thermometer. She passed it to her mom, then hovered by the bed as Una put it under Laurel's tongue. Laurel tried not to smash it with her teeth.

Una inspected the line on the glass. "You got a fever."

"I'm freezing." Laurel gritted her teeth.

"That's how it works sometimes. Horsey, go see if we got any Tylenol." She pulled the blankets off and left Laurel with only a bedsheet. Laurel groaned and wrapped the thin cotton around her body.

"You'll warm up when your fever comes down."

Laurel was too busy shivering to argue.

"This is all I could find." Horsey came in with a bottle of Children's Tylenol and a spoon. Bud lingered behind her.

"There's nothing for adults?"

"This is it. Or Dad's shine."

Una shook the bottle and handed it to Laurel. "Drink whatever's in there."

Laurel eased herself up, pulling the sheet with her like a second skin. She tipped the bottle and drank. The cherry flavour tasted like sore throats on summer days. Stolen horse rides on Jimmy's farm and rope dives into the swimming hole. The sweet syrup coated the back of her tongue.

"Will I catch it?" Bud climbed on the bed and crawled under the sheet.

"I don't know." Una screwed the cover back on the empty bottle. "Probably."

Bud wiggled closer to Laurel and stretched his little arm across her waist.

"I'll be all right, buddy."

Laurel didn't notice Horsey had left the room until she reappeared.

"Want some orange juice? I mixed it up in the blender so it's nice and frothy."

Laurel reached for the glass.

"Right? There you go."

She drank as much as she could and handed the glass back to Horsey.

"Let her rest now," Una said. "Come on, Bud."

"He's okay." Laurel turned away from Bud so she wouldn't breathe her germs directly in his face.

Horsey left the juice on the bedside table and they both faded from the room. Laurel shifted until her back pressed against Bud's belly and chattered herself into oblivion.

Asleep, she dreamed of the woods behind her house. A bruised and swollen sky. Snow drifting in a clearing and catching in her mother's hair as she fed branches to flames. Wood popped. Sparks sprayed and settled in an ashy ring. Her mother turned away. Snow crunched as she marched into the trees and the red and black of her coat disappeared.

Wait! Laurel got up to follow, but her boots sank in fresh powder. She stretched her stride and gripped branches to pull herself from one of her mother's snowshoe prints to the next. Mucus ran down the back of her throat. *Wait!*

Her mother came into view. A rigid figure between the trees. Rifle tight to her shoulder. Head cocked as she stared down the barrel.

Laurel scanned the trees, but there was nothing there. She scrambled forward. Her legs a whoosh of nylon snow pants as she panted and reached for the next footprint and the next.

The crack of the rifle echoed. Laurel fell back and patted her chest, her stomach, her legs. Blood seeped into the snow around her. That's when she saw it. The black carcass of a bear, only a few feet away. The length of a kitchen. *Mom!* Laurel turned in every direction. Trees and shadows packed tight together. The rifle, in her arms now, heavy and leaden. Her finger locked around the trigger.

"Laurel."

Laurel tried to open her eyes but only managed to groan.

"Shh." Una.

A cold cloth on her forehead.

"Shh. Your fever broke. You're going to be okay."

Laurel reached through the sheets, but Bud was gone. Sunlight beamed in through Una's bedroom window. She tried to sit, but Una guided her back to the pillow.

"Shh-shh-shh." Una ran the cold cloth over Laurel's face and neck.

"Mom?"

"I talked to her," Una said softly. The facecloth rested on Laurel's forehead, then her left temple. Her mother was still in the hospital, but she was doing well. She had three broken ribs. A fractured jaw. A torn larynx. A lot of bruising. She needed time and rest, but she was healing.

She was also three months pregnant.

Laurel coughed, but her throat was sawdust.

"She's going to be fine. And the baby's going to be fine." Una gave her leg a pat under the blanket. "You will be, too." Laurel nodded into her pillow. Una gently stroked her hair and shushed, *shh-shh-shh*, as she rocked on the bed.

"Rick?" His name caught in her mouth like a woodchip.

Una bent over her, shook her face against Laurel's hair. "He's no longer with us." She squeezed tight. "Sometimes, the strongest, most extraordinary things grow in the hardest places." Una rubbed her shoulder, quick and firm like she was trying to erase something, as if something could ever be erased. "You hold on to that. Hold on to that as tight as you can."

PART TWO

1993

SIX

FEBRUARY

The ten-plex took up one whole side of Royal Avenue, a lane tucked behind Main Street with as many potholes as Woods Road. There were no trees or fences behind the building, only a frozen stretch of field and more pavement hard-packed with snow. Their new home was exposed to every pedestrian, car, truck, and snowmobile that whined past, clunking over potholes. Everyone in Stephenville knew the ten-plex as the Crown. Everyone also knew that living in the Crown meant being on welfare. They had ushered in a new year huddled at the back end of Woods Road while their driveway filled with snow. School abandoned. A Christmas that never happened. Meals and grocery shopping forced on them by Una. Their only other visitor was Tina, the social worker, who came more often than anyone liked. She managed to get them into a unit in just two months. What Tina called a miracle. Laurel pulled the screen door shut and walked back through the empty apartment. A place to live where she hadn't shot anyone. A kitchen where her mother hadn't been choked almost to death. Square ceramic tiles that Rick hadn't bled all over. White walls that smelled of fresh paint.

Laurel stepped outside. "Not bad."

Her mother sheathed the shovel in the snowbank. "Yeah. There's light fixtures." She rested her hands on her hips and relaxed into a sigh. The flaps of her winter coat hung open on either side of her belly, too big now for the zipper to close over it. "And you can see the ocean."

In the distance, over the tops of houses and a row of industrial buildings, a sliver of grey Atlantic gazed back at her.

Laurel grabbed the shovel. Her mother stepped back and nodded her relief as Laurel flung snow at the snowbank between apartments four and five. Snug in his snowsuit, Bud dodged her shovelfuls until she caught him and knocked him off an ice boulder.

"Hey!"

"Come help!"

"There's only one shovel."

"Use that one." Laurel gestured at a scoop propped against the far side of the front step they shared with apartment six. The driveway was shared, too. And the side in front of number six was clear. It would be much easier to grab that scoop and push the snow over there, but Laurel resisted the urge to dump snow in someone else's driveway. She heaved another shovelful at the bank and got Bud in the face.

"Mom!"

The screen door of apartment six snapped open and a guy in a Polaris Ski-doo jacket strutted onto the step. Laurel pushed her shovel deep in the snow. She had never talked to Brax Randall in her life, but she knew—just like every kid at Stephenville Integrated knew—he was expelled, repeatedly, for selling vials of hash oil and spit-licky joints on school grounds.

"Need some help?" he said.

"My God, yes." Her mother leaned against the truck and massaged her belly.

"New neighbours, is it?" Brax plucked out the scoop and pushed it back and forth across the driveway. He made quick work of the snow and grinned at Laurel when he shoved the final scoopful into the bank directly under Bud, who made for higher ground.

"I'll back up the truck," her mother said.

Brax looked at the furniture piled in the pan of the pickup. "I don't think I'm off the hook just yet."

"If you wouldn't mind?"

He stuck the scoop in the snow, rested his arms on the handle. "I can never say no to the ladies. The cute ones anyway."

Her mother raised her eyebrows, cracked open the driver's side door and climbed in. "Well, they don't make 'em like you anymore."

Brax smiled at Laurel.

Laurel kicked a bit of the snow off the step.

Her mother eased the truck into the freshly cleared driveway. Brax dropped the tailgate before she had the engine turned off and wiggled the coffee table until the legs came free from a mess of garbage bags filled with blankets, pillows, dishrags and towels. Laurel caught a bag before it fell and lugged it into the house. Brax carried the coffee table in behind her. He dropped it in the living room and held the door on the way out. "After you."

Her mother came up the steps with a bag hugged to her chest. "Think you guys can handle the dresser?"

"Depends how tough she is." Brax nodded at Laurel.

Laurel paused on the driveway. "*She* is Laurel."

Her mother's gaze ran over her. "She's pretty tough," she said, then disappeared inside.

Brax's eyebrows came together. "I know. Grade nine, right?"

Laurel climbed into the back of the truck, squeezed around her mom's heavy oak dresser and shoved it, bit by bit, over the tailgate.

Brax caught the edge and hauled it forward. "Now you climb out."

She scrambled down and they hefted the dresser off the truck.

"You take the front. I'll take the weight at the back."

As much as she wanted to say it didn't matter, her fingers were already strained. There wasn't much to grip and the bulk of the weight rested across her knuckles.

Laurel backed into the house and up the stairs. She reminded herself to breathe and not drop the dresser on her feet. Her fingers throbbed. They were halfway up when Brax asked if she needed a break. She spread her feet and let go. The dresser banged down on the step.

Brax squared his shoulders and braced himself but continued to hold the bottom end while she flexed and squeezed her fingers. "You know my name?"

"No."

"Braxton."

She worked her neck from side to side. "Let's finish this." Laurel lifted the dresser and took another backward step, practically bent double.

They reached the landing and she straightened her spine as best she could. Puffed air through her nose like she was pumping a tire with her nostrils and eased the dresser around the corner to her mother's room. A metal strip on the floor separating the carpet in the hallway from the carpet in the bedroom curled up and Laurel stepped on the sharp edge. She paused, puffed and carried on.

"Where to?" Brax wasn't even out of breath.

Laurel dropped her end on the thin, industrial berber. "Here's good."

Brax lowered his side and shoved the dresser into place against the wall. Laurel wrung her hands. The window in her mother's room faced the backyard, the road behind it, and the rear of a Tim Hortons drive-through.

"So. What brings you to the Crown?"

He could have said, what are you in for? And she could have said, murder. But Laurel shrugged and started back downstairs.

"I don't know. I guess Mom likes this place."

Brax laughed like it was the funniest thing he'd ever heard.

The couch groaned under the weight of the social worker whenever she moved. Tina wore a black wool coat that ended at the tops of her knees. Beige pants poked out from under it and hung down over socks that looked much too white, much too clean, even for their new apartment that smelled of paint and Lysol. She balanced a notebook on her lap and looked around the room. "This is good. Better."

Laurel sat on a box. The cardboard crumpled underneath her and she slid gracefully to the floor, where she sat crossed-legged next to Bud, who sprawled on the carpet with his head on her mother's foot. They had left the sofa chair with no legs behind on Woods Road, so her mother sat on a kitchen chair in the corner. She rested her elbows on her knees, her forehead on a fist.

"Yeah." Her mother ran her hands through her hair, sat up, then leaned back and looked to the ceiling. "Better."

"You couldn't stay there on your own with no support. Thirty minutes out of town. And that driveway." The couch creaked.

The first winter after her father had died, her mother had pulled them to the bus stop in a sled. She'd made a game of it, bumping over drifts and making sharp turns in the powder. That was before Rick showed up with his truck and the plough attached to the front like a claw. He cleared their driveway every morning before the bus came.

"And that wood stove."

Her mother had managed just fine with the wood.

"You have easy access to clinics here in Stephenville. The hospital. Support groups. And soon there'll be a baby to consider." Tina's voice bounced off the bare living room walls. "How's our young man? All ready to get back to kindergarten?"

Bud nodded. He grinned and exposed the gap between his front teeth.

"Laurel." Tina's voice as grave as a headstone. "How do you feel about school?"

Laurel chewed the corner of her thumbnail. "Fine."

Local man dies at Sir Thomas Roddick Hospital of fatal gunshot wound. That had been the headline in the *Western Star*. The details were sparse. It provided his name, where he was from, and the date of his death. At the end of the short article, it said, "Foul play is not suspected." Her mother had gone to court, but Laurel's initial statement was the only one she ever had to make, and as a minor, she was protected under the Youth Criminal Justice Act. The few people who knew what really happened—police officers, social workers, doctors—were prohibited from releasing that information. Whenever anyone asked, her mother said it was a hunting accident and that she didn't want to talk about it.

A hunting accident. Laurel repeated it over and over in her head until she almost believed it. As long as nobody knew the truth, as long as nobody knew what she did, things could go back to normal. All they had to do was take that entire section of their lives, from the moment Rick walked in their front door to the night he was shot, ball it up, toss it in a Ziploc bag, and forget.

"It's been over two months now."

Laurel nodded again and chewed the other side of her thumb. They saw Tina regularly and Laurel had already muttered every sentence she could think of that meant she was fine. I'm good. I'm ready to move on. Promise.

"She needs a few things for school. They both do. And now, with rent." Her mother's nostrils flared.

"Rent is subsidized." Tina smiled. "You have a full basement and a backyard. When are you due?"

"June." She folded her arms.

"And you have someone to watch Laurel and Bud when you go

to the hospital?"

"I know how to have a baby." Her mother rubbed the back of Bud's head with her big toe. "I'll talk to Una. She can come . . . She can stay with them for a couple days."

"Do that sooner rather than later. These things don't happen on a schedule."

They had free cable, left over from the previous tenants. After pre-cooked chicken tenders and fries—a late supper their mother picked up from Foodland—Laurel and Bud clicked through thirteen channels of sports, news, and French programming.

"Oh, I've seen that." Her mother paused in the middle of pulling pillows from a garbage bag. "*Batteries Not Included.*"

"Is it good?" Laurel stopped turning the dial. She increased the volume to a level Rick never would have allowed.

"I liked it." Her mother threw pillows on top of Bud and hauled out a blanket.

"Will I like it?" Bud said, under the pile.

"Maybe. There's aliens."

"Is it scary?"

"They're nice aliens, little flying robots." Her mother thought the movie was only about a quarter of the way through, so they tore open a bag of ketchup chips, turned off the light, and sat in a nest of pillows and blankets. Bud, in the middle, was asleep after a handful of chips. Her mother's head tilted back, and her eyes closed.

"Mom?"

She snorted and looked back at the TV. Then her head nodded again and she was out.

Laurel ate chips in the glow of the screen until her tongue hurt. She watched the movie to the end and didn't get off the couch until Frank and Faye Riley said goodbye to the little mechanical aliens who had made them finally feel whole, if only for a brief time. Laurel dragged a blanket and a pillow up to her new room and curled up on her old mattress.

On the other side of her bedroom wall, in apartment six, an exchange of male voices rose and fell. Laurel got up and went in search of another blanket. She ripped open a bag in her mom's room and pulled out an oversized comforter. It was big enough that she spread it across her mattress and pulled it over her body like a sleeping bag. A door slammed, followed by a sharp outburst. A hand smacked a wall—she knew the sound. Feet pounded upstairs. Another door—slam!

Laurel blinked into the wan street light from her window and waited for more shouts. More feet pounding stairs. More slams.

Outside, a car revved its engine and squealed down Main Street.

SEVEN

"Time to get up. Get ready for school." Maxine sat on the edge of Laurel's bed.

She sounded normal, like any mom on the first day of school. Laurel blinked to adjust the lens on her new reality. The reality where her mother played the part of Any Mom, and she, Any Daughter. Simple, like putting on new school clothes. If she had new school clothes. "I can't."

"Yes, you can." Her mother tugged the blankets down. "One day at a time." She tapped Laurel's shoulder as if releasing a spring and got off the bed. Laurel pulled the blankets back up and closed her eyes.

Breakfast was peanut butter toast and orange juice. Coffee landed in front of her, heaped full of milk and sugar.

"Here," her mother said. "Try this."

Laurel chugged it.

Her mother leaned against the counter with both hands on her belly. She ran them up under her chest and pressed them into her ribs, arched her spine and breathed deep.

Laurel put the mug down.

"It's just the baby." Her mother dropped her hands. "Time to go." She ushered them out of the kitchen. Instructed Bud into his winter clothes and pulled on her own. They left the apartment together but went separate ways at the end of Royal Avenue. Bud's elementary school was over a kilometre away now, but Laurel could walk to high school in ten minutes. She had almost reached school grounds when she paused to watch her mom and Bud cross a bridge in the distance. Her mother walked with a stoop, but maybe that was just the baby.

Stephenville Integrated High, a stout brick building, sat behind a circular driveway where buses rolled up. Laurel joined the stream of students with her shoulders tight and avoided eye contact as she made her way down the corridor to her locker. She stuffed her coat inside and went to homeroom.

The voices and movement in Mrs. Harding's grade nine class almost knocked her back. Conversations snagged in her hair and caught in her clothes. "Good morning, Laurel," Mrs. Harding said. "Welcome back."

Laurel ducked into her seat at the back of the classroom as the PA clicked on and Bev, the school secretary, started the morning announcements. She unzipped her backpack, pulled out a textbook and let it fall open to a random page. The page swam with math equations in italicized examples, $x+y$ $/z=whatever$. In the seam of the book, wedged deep between the pages, a tiny dead body winked at her. Laurel picked it out with a fingernail.

The infestation began right after Rick had moved in. They never figured out where the fleas came from, but living in the woods, there were all sorts of bugs. Her mom bought powders that she sprinkled over the carpet. They washed their bedsheets and clothes in hot water, but the fleas burrowed deep in the carpet fibres and hung on for most of the year. Laurel ended up with tiny red bites all over her arms and legs. They left scars.

She flicked the remains to the classroom floor.

"Laurel?" Mrs. Harding looked down at her. The classroom was empty. "Are you okay?"

Laurel slapped her book shut. "I thought I had math now."

"You have French, with Mr. Mercer. Listen." Mrs. Harding rested a hand on Laurel's chair, blocking her escape route. "You've had a hard year, a hard . . . few years. First your dad. Now your mom's boyfriend."

Laurel felt tiny insects crawl up her shoulders. Up her neck. Into her hair. She held her hands together on top of her desk.

"If you ever want to talk. To me, or the guidance counsellor . . . ?"

"I talk to Tina."

"Who?"

"My social worker?" A flea bit her scalp. Another. One of their hard bodies ticked down her forehead and landed in her eyebrow. Laurel twitched and squeezed her knuckles together.

"Okay, I just wanted to make sure you're talking to somebody. You've always done well in school, Laurel. How's Bud?"

"Fine."

"All right." The teacher stepped back. Her arm dropped like a starting gate and Laurel jumped up. "Well, if you ever want to talk."

"I know. You're here." She bolted.

Laurel moved through the corridors in a fog. Lockers slammed. Kids shouted. She kept watch for Horsey, but Horsey was in grade ten. Grades ten to twelve were upstairs and the stairwell divided the school like an electric fence. At lunchtime, she queued up for the cafeteria and her gaze shifted from the brick walls to the wide tiled floor to the back of the kid's head in front of her. Back to the brick walls. An eighth-grader pushed ahead of her. Alayna, or Allayne, A-something-with-a-y. "Excuse me?"

Alayna turned to face her. She leaned a shoulder against the bricks and blinked clumpy blue mascara. "My dad listens to the police scanner. He heard all about your house."

Laurel reached for the wall. Her fingernails scraped across the bricks until they snagged a jagged edge and held on.

The grade eight stood on her tiptoes. Chin jutted forward. Crooked bangs. Greasy lip-gloss. Laurel made a fist against the wall. Her scalp itched. Alayna's shiny mouth moved, but all Laurel heard was "bloodbath."

"What?"

"Raspberry jam. That's why it looked like a massacre. There was jam everywhere." Alayna looked proud of knowing this.

The muscles in her legs cramped.

"There was real blood, too. Lots of it, but the jam made it look way worse. Was that your mom's boyfriend? They said he beat her up real bad and she shot 'im."

Laurel leaned in close. "Your dad's a drug dealer?"

"What? No."

"Is he a cop?"

"No."

"Besides cops, only drug dealers have police scanners." Laurel shoved past and Alayna stumbled into the brick wall. Laurel strolled up to the cafeteria doors, looked through the windows as if to investigate the holdup, then flipped her hair over her shoulder and continued down the corridor.

When she was out of sight, she ran. She pounded down the empty hall to the library and slammed through the door. The librarian's desk at the front of the room was vacant and she ran past it, into the rows of bookshelves to the back of the stacks. Laurel cupped her hands over her mouth and breathed hard into her palms. She dug raw, chewed fingertips into the corners of her eyes. Scraped the rough edge of a nail across her eyelid. A fluorescent light flickered overhead. Grey carpet blinked in and out of focus.

She sat under the faulty light, hidden by books and shadows, until first bell. The signal that lunch was over. Laurel got up, bent upside down and shook out her hair. She ran her nails over her scalp, rubbed her eyebrows, her temples, her arms. Second bell. There were no bites. No fleas. That was a thing of the past, and that's where it had to stay, zipped up in a baggie with her bloody clothes. She would survive this place the same way she had survived Rick: head down. One day at a time. Laurel gave her arms one last shake and left the library.

Laurel walked out of the building at ten minutes after three. Brax was already up on the smoke hill with a cluster of students. She slung her bookbag over her shoulder and moved fast.

"Laurel!"

Brax broke away from the group and bounded over the bank. He skidded down the slick ice, arms swinging for balance, and fell in step next to her. "Let me walk you home. I'm headed in the same direction."

"Sure."

Brax walked with his hands stuffed in his pockets, elbows out and bouncing with every step. He talked the whole way. He told her that he missed school sometimes. Not classes or teachers, he hated those, but there were other things, you know? The stage in the gymnasium had this room under it where you could take girls and no one ever checked in on you. Brax smirked at her.

She stared straight ahead at the street sign for Royal Avenue. If she said anything, he would probably plunge into details. What girls. How many. What they did. Eagerness flew from his elbows like spores. He walked her to the front door.

Laurel hauled the screen open, but Brax caught it, pushed inside and shouted into the apartment, "Hallooo, Maxeeene!"

Her mother came down the hall with her hands in a dishtowel. "Oh, Brax! Come on in. I wanted to thank you. Why don't you stay for supper?"

The racket of the range hood fan increased whenever the wind gusted and sucked air through the building's vents. Her mother left it on even after she finished cooking. She placed a large pot of spaghetti on the supper table, directly in front of Brax. He grinned and rubbed his hands together. Laurel sighed and got up to turn off the fan.

Her mother sat across from him with a smile plastered on her face and kept up a steady conversation. Where's your Mom? Oh she's in Alberta. With your sister? I didn't know you had a sister. Older or younger? Older, okay. It's nice to have an older sister, like Bud. How long have they been gone? A year. That's a long time. That must be hard. Oh, yes, I hope that works out. It'd be great if she got you a job. Lots of work in Alberta. Do you have a girlfriend?

"For godsakes, Mom!"

"What?"

"Nothing." Laurel picked up her glass and gulped her water. It went down the wrong way. She gasped and banged her glass down. It almost tipped over, but Bud caught it before the water spilled.

Brax reached out. "You all right?"

Laurel pushed out from the table. Tears rolled down her face. Brax rubbed her back as she coughed. Her mother laughed. Laurel flinched and twisted away from Brax.

"It just went down the wrong hole," her mother said with a wave.

Laurel's breathing eased. Her face was hot, but she sat back down and cleared her throat. "I'm okay." She forced out a laugh to demonstrate. "I'm fine."

Brax clapped her on the shoulder and sat, too. Bud twisted spaghetti around his fork and stuck it in his mouth.

"How was school?" her mother asked.

"Fine." Laurel coughed.

"Bud?"

"Okay," Bud said around a mouthful of noodles.

"Careful," Brax said. "You might choke."

Maxine laughed along with Brax, her new best friend. Bud rolled his eyes. Laurel dropped her fork on her plate, sat back and folded her arms.

Usually, her mother let the dishes fester for a few hours, or days, before she bothered to wash them, but after Brax left, she cleared the table. She turned on the tap, squirted dish soap into running water and nodded toward the towel hanging on the oven. "You can dry."

Laurel grabbed the towel.

"Could you hear that racket last night?" Her mother slid a stack of plates into the sink.

"What racket?"

"Next door. Brax's dad. He sounds like a real . . . " She scrubbed a plate so roughly it slipped from her grip back into the water. She fished it out again.

"I thought you were asleep on the couch."

"It woke me up. He sounds like a real . . . asshole." Her mother said *asshole* under her breath.

"Yeah, I heard."

"You know what I think? The world is full of assholes." She whispered *asshole* again. "Full of them. We should invite him back over."

Laurel took the plate and dried it. "Who?"

"Brax! He could probably use the break from his dad."

"Mom, no. Once was enough. My God, Mom."

"He's just a kid."

"He's older than me."

"He's sixteen, still just a kid. I'd like to think someone would do the same for you if you needed it."

Laurel picked up another plate. She didn't tell her mother that Brax sold drugs at school or mention the room under the stage in the gym. "I think he's a bit of an *asshole*."

"Nah. He's just a kid." Her mother finished washing the last of the dishes and pulled the plug from the bottom of the sink. Water drained in noisy slurps. "Tea?"

"No."

Her mother filled the kettle, put it on and hit the switch in the range hood. The fan rattled back to life.

EIGHT

Laurel slipped a coat on a hanger, hung it in the closet, then pulled her mom's fringed leather jacket from the bottom of a box. She shook it until the fringes untangled, flipped it around and noticed a dark spot in the leather. She touched it to see if it was wet. Someone knocked on the screen door. Laurel dropped the coat back in the box.

Aunt Cora's blond hair bobbed as she waved on the other side of the glass, then she hauled the screen door open herself. "We saw the truck, but we weren't sure if it was this apartment or number six."

"Mom!"

Aunt Cora, Uncle Rol, and Laurel's cousin Denise clambered into their front porch. Laurel couldn't remember when she had last seen them. They used to come by Woods Road all the time for backyard bonfires and snowshoe trips. After her dad died, Uncle Rol checked in regularly for a while, but his visits grew infrequent, then when Rick moved in, they stopped.

"Well, this is unexpected." Her mother came up behind her. "We were just clearing away supper."

Rol started to speak, but Cora cut him off. "We were out

shopping. Thought we'd pop by." She handed Laurel a container of cinnamon rolls.

"We're still getting settled," Maxine said. "But . . . come in! Want tea?"

"Oh, don't go to any trouble." Cora popped off her furry ankle boots. "We stopped by Timmies already. Maxine, you look ready to bust!"

She rubbed her belly. "I got a ways to go yet."

Bud poked his head into the hall and Cora spotted him.

"Bud! Aren't you big?" Cora backhanded Rol in the chest. "He's all grown up." Bud licked a milk moustache. Cora pushed past Maxine to get to him. "He looks just like his father. Doesn't he Rol?"

Laurel waited for her cousin while Rol and her mom followed Cora into the kitchen. "Um, you went shopping?"

Denise was four years older and in her first year at College of the North Atlantic. "Yeah, just a few things. Nice pyjamas."

Laurel adjusted the waistband of her ratty red-on-white polka-dot pyjama pants, which had twisted to the side. She laughed and offered her cousin a cinnamon roll. Denise smiled, then struggled to open the plastic container while Laurel held it. They each took a roll, then Laurel carried the rest to the kitchen.

Maxine put the kettle on. Cora leaned against the counter and Rol peeked inside the flaps of a cardboard box. Laurel sat at the table. Bud immediately opened the container and chose the biggest roll that was left. He topped up his glass and spilled milk over the sides; a thin stream ran across the table and dripped on the floor. Denise stood behind an empty chair.

"I remember this thing." Rol pulled the apple clock out of the box. "Used to be Mom's."

"Want it back?" Maxine hauled three mugs down from the cupboard.

He chuckled. "Looks like you brought Woods Road with you."

"It's nice here." Cora looked around at the white walls, the white cabinets, the countertop mactacked to look like marble.

Rol went into the back porch and opened the door. "Nice yard." He pulled the door closed, then knocked on the door to the basement. "What's it like down there?"

"It's nice." Her mother dropped a tea bag in each mug.

"Is it finished?" Cora asked.

"I guess. It's a basement. There's a washer. A dryer." She rested her tailbone against the stove. The kettle ticked as it heated up.

"You know what you need now?" Cora said. "A job. Your very own job."

"Hmm-hmm."

Laurel reached for Bud's milk, but he moved the glass out of her range. She leaned back and chewed, determined to enjoy the cinnamon flavour even as the dry bun sucked saliva from her mouth. Denise's roll was still untouched in her hand.

"I heard Foodland is hiring. They provide benefits, I think."

Aunt Cora was older than her mom, but she didn't look it. She looked younger, softer, like a well-watered plant. A plump aloe in a Wind River sweatshirt. The last time Laurel had seen her had been at Foodland. Laurel had been embarrassed of her mother that day, so ashamed she'd moved around opposing sections of the store, dairy, produce, meats. When she saw her mother come down one aisle, she'd turned and gone up another. They could have bumped into anyone at the grocery store. A student from her class. A teacher. Someone's parent.

Her mother had been in the checkout line, and Laurel had watched from a magazine rack as Aunt Cora walked into the store, cheeks flushed with cold. She almost walked right by her mother, but her mother leaned over and got her attention. Cora stopped. She smiled and gave her a careful hug, as if the bruise on her cheek might be contagious.

Laurel had gone over and stood between her mom and her aunt. They were talking about Denise. She had joined figure skating. Could you believe that Stephenville had figure skating now? Her mother couldn't. Laurel looked back and forth as they talked, and each time she looked at the bruise it grew bigger, like a moon in eclipse. The whole world could see it.

"It's been way too long. You should come by my place for a visit sometime. You know, when you come out to Stephenville on grocery day or what have you." Cora had left then, with a happy smile and a little wave.

The kettle screeched to a boil. Maxine snatched it off the stove. She poured three cups full of hot water. "Laurel." She put the kettle back down, crossed the kitchen, and grabbed her winter coat from the back of a chair. "Before I have my tea, I'm going out for a smoke."

"What?" Laurel hissed.

"Just a quick puff." Her mother pulled out a pack of Players Light, her little red Bic; she shuffled past Rol, who raised his eyebrows at Cora. She shoved on her boots in the back porch and scuffed out to the yard.

Denise slumped down on the chair.

Rol rose up on his toes and the bones in his feet made tiny popping sounds. Laurel swallowed a lump of bun. "Did you want tea?"

"No, no. Thank you Laurel." Cora checked her watch. "Oh!" She hopped a little. "I have something for you. Rol, go get that bag from the car."

"Wha—"

Cora shook her hands. "You know, the one we were going to drop at Goodwill. Denise's old clothes might fit Laurel. I bet they will."

Rol came down flat on his feet and went to do as he was told. He returned a minute later with an overstuffed garbage bag. He lugged it into the middle of the kitchen and let it flop on the floor. The bag tipped to one side, rolled into the puddle of milk and smooshed to a stop against Bud's chair.

Music came on next door. AC/DC pumped through the kitchen wall. Cora looked around trying to find the source of the noise, but the opening riff of "Hells Bells" ricocheted off every surface.

"Oh!" she said, hands raised. "Well. Lots to try on."

I'm gonna get ya! Satan get ya!

"Mom?" Denise still hadn't had a bite of her cinnamon roll.

"Okay, yes. Maybe it's time to go."

Hells Bells!

Cora wrung her hands and looked at Rol. "Should we say goodbye to Maxine?"

Rol stepped into the porch and opened the door. The music grew louder, as if the open door was an invitation for it to expand and flow through the apartment. "We're going now, nice to see ya!"

"Yes!" Cora shouted. "It was good to see you!" She smiled at Laurel, squeezed the back of Bud's shoulders, then Aunt Cora, Uncle Rol and Denise banged out of the apartment as quickly as they banged in. Denise's cinnamon roll left behind on the table.

"I thought you quit," Laurel said when her mom came back.

Her mother shrugged out of her coat. "It's only one."

"You just left me here!"

"I know. I'm sorry. I really, really needed some air." Her mother returned to her tea, pressed the bag against the edge of the mug with her spoon, and took it out. The music paused for a moment, then a new track pumped through the walls.

"Mom," Laurel started again. "What did you expect them to do the past year, invite us over for supper, with Rick?"

Her mother sat down and picked a cinnamon roll from the tray. She bit into the pastry and spoke around the bread. "That. Exactly that."

Music continued late into the evening. Laurel's bedroom wall throbbed. Each song heavier than the one before. In her pyjamas, with her face washed and teeth brushed, Laurel unpacked the rest of her clothes and organized everything in her dresser and closet. Her walls were still bare. It would be nice to have a framed picture of her family, but her dad had always had a thing about photographs. Stills of people kind of freaked him out and her mother respected that even now. Laurel adjusted the Polaroid stuck in the frame of her full-length mirror. A picture of her dad sitting on the front step of their house holding a baby—Laurel stuffed in a hand-me-down snowsuit two sizes too big. He grinned straight at the camera, revealing the wide gap between his front teeth. Laurel touched her finger to his mouth. Bud's grin.

A shout next door. Heavy metal hitched up another notch.

Laurel switched off the light and climbed into bed, but cymbals crashed. Guitars shrieked. She shifted deep under the blankets. Pressed her head into her pillow. Bass drums dug into her spine. Hollow and cavernous, like a skull hitting a porcelain amphitheatre. Laurel sat up and pounded her fist on the bedroom wall.

The music stopped. She sat frozen. Listening. After a few minutes, she lay back down and pulled the blankets up to her chin. She was almost asleep when she heard a tap. Gentle. Quiet. *Tap-tap-tap.* Like an apology.

NINE

February slipped into March, but winter held fast. Laurel zipped her coat to her chin and pulled her sleeves down over her hands. Bud sped up when he saw her waiting under the street sign for Royal Avenue. His bookbag bounced about his shoulders until it dropped and hung from his elbows. His winter boots flapped against his shins. "Hey Bud," she said when he caught up. "How was your day?"

"All right."

Laurel helped him out of his bookbag and slung it across her shoulder on top of her own as they turned down the street. "That's it? A whole day and nothing interesting?"

"Logan got sent to the principal's office."

"Who's Logan?"

"He's in my class."

"What'd he do?"

Bud grinned up at her. Gap-toothed. "He threw ham at the wall."

"Like, from his sandwich?"

"Yeah. He was the helper today." Bud's school calendar, taped to the fridge, named a class helper for each day of the week. He counted down the days, every day, for his turn to pass out worksheets and stand at the head of the class lineups.

"Well, he did a crap job."

"The ham stuck to the wall. He had to peel it off in pieces."

"Gross. You're a way better helper than that." Laurel opened the door to apartment five.

Bud clambered in ahead of her, braced his arm against the wall and kicked his boots off with a flick-flick of each foot. "Then. He ate it!"

"Nice work, Logan."

The apartment was hot and humid and smelled of paint. Wet, straight-from-the-can latex. "Mom?" Laurel followed the *swoosh, swoosh, swoosh* of a paint roller to the kitchen, where her mom stood on top of a chair in her bathing suit and a pair of cut-offs. Her arms pumped up and down as she worked. Over half the room already transformed.

The paint tray sat on a plastic bag on the counter. Her mother dropped the roller in the tray and climbed down from the chair. The spandex of her swimsuit stretched from black to almost-transparent grey over her belly. She'd left the button of her jean shorts undone and a hair elastic held the waistband together. "All that white was depressing. We needed some colour. And look!" She adjusted the straps behind her neck and indicated several cans of paint in front of the basement door. "They had all this marked fifty per cent off. I just picked the best of the lot. Green for the kitchen. Mauve for the living room—"

"Are the fumes okay for the baby?"

"It's just latex. I got grey-blue for Bud's room."

"Mauve?"

"Mauve. Two cans. It should be enough to do the living room. And the hall. Or your room?"

"Not my room."

"Well, I don't have a man around to tell me not to paint a room mauve, so it's all going mauve." She swiped her hands downward as if flinging dirt from her fingers.

Laurel looked away. The last man they'd had around bled out on the kitchen floor. She cleared her throat. "Our old kitchen was green."

"This is brighter. They said people return paint all the time and they have to sell it half off. I'll drop back later in the week and see what else they got. You should come pick something out for your room." Her mother flapped her arms to air out her pits. "I'm roasting!"

Laurel checked the thermostat on the far wall. "It's twenty-four degrees in here!"

"It was freezing cold all morning."

Laurel managed to reduce her eye roll to a slow blink. She clamped her lips together and set the thermostat on nineteen, then adjusted it to eighteen and a half.

"Grab a brush. You can do the trim." Her mother climbed back on the chair and picked up her roller. "Let's make a fresh go of it."

"I'll just get changed first."

In the living room, Bud sat on the couch with a box of saltines he must have found lying around somewhere. He kicked his legs and nibbled bleached wheat as he watched TV.

"Mom's painting. Want to help?" Laurel asked through the archway.

He shoved the cracker in his mouth. "I don't have a bathing suit."

"That's fair."

They worked until it was dark outside. Laurel painted the edges of the wall and held a plastic placemat against the ceiling so she wouldn't get green splotches over it. Her mother rolled paint full force until she complained her shoulders were sore, then she held the roller straight out in front of her and bent at the knees. Her whole body bobbed as she painted the wall. Paint ran down the roller handle and dripped on the floor. "Bud!" her mother yelled. She took a break as Bud jumped off the couch and ran, heavy-footed, from the living room to the kitchen. With an exaggerated pant, he grabbed the rag from the sink and scrubbed the floor until it was clean. "You're an awesome helper, Bud."

Once the kitchen was as bright as a Granny Smith, her mother mounted the apple clock above the table and fixed the time. It was 5:45. "It's chilly in here again now." She rubbed her bare arms.

Bud opened and closed the fridge, then poked around the kitchen cupboards. "What's for supper?"

Laurel washed her paintbrush in the sink. Hot water steamed. She pushed the bristles against the drain and let the force of the water remove the last of the green paint from the base.

Her mother pried open another can. "I just want to see how it looks." She stirred the gallon with a paint stick, then poured the tray full of frothy purple paint. The handle of her roller was caked green, as were her hands, but she slipped a fluffy new cover onto the frame and rolled it into the paint, back and forth, until the fluff was uniformly mauve. She rolled a streak up the edge of the wall, where green kitchen would meet mauve hallway. "Look at that," she breathed.

"It's pink," Bud said.

"No." She rolled another streak.

"That's definitely pink."

Laurel set the paintbrush on the plastic bag to dry. "What's wrong with pink?" She turned off the water and stood next to Bud. "I think my room used to be that colour."

Her mother stopped rolling and stepped back. She looked at the paint from different angles, then let the roller drop to her side. "Shit. That's *pink*."

"Pinkish-purple?" Laurel offered.

Her mother looked from the wall to the half-filled paint tray, to the open can of mauve, to the unopened can of mauve next to it. "Is there much green left?" She dropped the roller in the tray and lifted the can of green. "I could probably mix it?"

"I don't know." Laurel folded her arms.

"Can we get supper now?" Bud slouched against a chair.

"I'll just . . ." She set the can down and picked the roller back up. "I'll finish this bit, then run out and grab something." She quickly turned the pink streaks on the wall into a four-foot-wide block of colour as Laurel and Bud watched.

"Nice, Mom."

"It'll be nice when I'm done. Promise." She huffed into her bangs and wiped her forehead. "I'm roasting again now."

Laurel sighed and took the tray from her mom. "You get supper. I'll clean this up."

"You sure?"

"Go."

Her mother released her grip. "I should probably get dressed first. How's Chester Chicken sound?"

"Sounds *awesome*." Bud collapsed into his chair.

By the time her mother changed out of her swimsuit, rummaged through the apartment for her bank card, repeated the search for her truck keys, and headed out, it was well past seven o'clock. Laurel tied the wet roller and paint tray inside a plastic bag and put it in the fridge for her mother to deal with later. Bud sat with his head on the table, kicking his legs.

It was past eight when her mother came back, arms heavy with two paper bags. "Let's eat in here." She carried the bags to the living room. Chicken, taters, tub of gravy, and a two-litre of Pepsi. "We earned ourselves a treat."

Bud turned on the TV and clicked through ten channels of snow. "The cable's gone! We got NTV, CBC, and *French*." His mouth hung open as he turned the dial back and forth.

Laurel unstoppered the Pepsi.

"*The Nature of Things*," her mother said. "My favourite show." She heaped taters onto a plate. "I know it's late. I just wanted to get this done before the baby comes. Oh! You guys want coleslaw?"

After supper, Bud and Laurel went to bed, but their mother stayed up to have another look at the paint. Their house on Woods Road had never been finished. The back side was tarpaper. Front steps rough-sawed lumber. For years, the only rooms that were livable were Laurel's and Bud's. Her parents slept in the basement by the wood stove and worked on the house late into the evenings. They hung drywall and plastered. Rolled out long spools of canvas flooring. Cut and hammered up trim. She had played in the open frames of walls, then inside the rooms her parents built while they covered outlets with plastic wall plates. Painted the kitchen green. Laurel listened in bed as her mother popped open paint cans and moved about downstairs by herself. Eventually, she drifted off to the steady *swoosh, swoosh, swoosh* of the roller.

TEN

Stephenville felt a bit like an American frontier town that had gotten lost at sea and come ashore in western Newfoundland. Main Street looked like the main drag in a western movie, only with pavement and dollar stores. Most of the establishments were small wooden structures with flat roofs and large painted sign-boards that indicated ownership. Debbie's Video, Byrne's Shoes, Danny's Bakery, Lee's Takeout. The place had grown from a small village to a town when the Americans set up an army training base there in the 1940s. After the war ended and the Americans left to go home, it's said they sold the base to the town for a dollar. The residents embraced the American influence that was left behind, and the value of a dollar. Laurel and Bud followed their mother down an alley between the Dollar Store and a laundromat. They cut across the back parking lot to Birch Lane, a narrow road lined with bungalows and skeletal birch trees with hard little buds that waited for spring to be warm enough to bloom.

Laurel knew almost nothing about her mom's parents. All Maxine had ever told her was that she had never met her dad and her mom had run off when she was little. She'd been raised by her grandmother on Birch Lane, just a short walk from Royal Avenue. They'd been living in the ten-plex for three months, when Maxine got up on a Sunday morning in May and said, "I s'pose we should visit Gran Keane."

They stopped in front of a faded burgundy bungalow with a black Honda Accord in the driveway. "New car." Maxine peered in through the windows. "She probably never drives it."

Laurel stood on the pavement while her mother walked up to the front door and knocked. When there was no answer, she hammered it with a closed fist. Another moment and she tried the doorknob. She looked back at them, opened the door and went inside.

"Come on." Laurel sighed and pushed Bud toward the house.

The sounds of *Jeopardy!* mingled with the smell of lemon cleaner and mothballs. Her mother went in with her shoes on, but Laurel paused on the mat and took hers off. She gestured for Bud to do the same.

The toes of her mother's sneakers touched the ivory living room carpet. She braced the archway above her head and leaned into the room. "Hi, Gran." Her voice rose above the TV.

Gran sat in the middle of a velvet floral couch. Her attention fixed on the screen. A loose sweatshirt sagged in her lap. "Thought that was you."

"I moved back to Stephenville. We're just over there, on Royal Avenue."

"The Crown?" Gran turned a rheumy gaze on Maxine, down to her sneakers then back up to her head. She snorted and looked back at the TV. "Suits you."

"The kids." She ushered Laurel forward. "You haven't seen Laurel since she was just a baby." Laurel took a step closer. Gran frowned at her. Her scalp was visible through the wisps of her hair. Skin hung from her jaws in angry folds. Laurel pushed back against her mother. "And this is Bud. Your great-grandkids. And there's another." She put a hand to her stomach. "Another one on the way."

Caribbean banana, a dessert flambeed with this liquor, may be topped with vanilla ice cream.

"Rum!" Gran shouted and thumped a foot on the floor.

Laurel flinched. Her mother's sneakers sank into the carpet and she sat on the only chair in the room, a velvet floral piece. Bud sat on the arm of the chair and Laurel squeezed onto it next to him as best she could.

Gran shouted answers after every question. Most of them were wrong. "Fucked if I knows," she said when the show paused for a commercial break. She looked at Laurel. Laurel stiffened and held her breath until Gran's gaze slid to Bud. Back to Maxine. "Always in heat," she said. "Just like your mother."

Maxine ducked her head. She slid her arm around Laurel and squeezed her a little closer. Laurel's left butt cheek slipped off the chair. She scrambled back on and leaned into her mom to keep from falling off again. "Have you ever . . ."

Gran turned back to watch the commercials.

"Have you ever heard from her? Mom?"

Gran grunted. Saliva hocked in the back of her throat and her voice was thick when she said, "No. Nothing."

Laurel shifted. Stood up. Sat back down. Bud shoved her and she shoved him back.

"Shh!" Their mother glared at them.

"They always like that?"

"What?" Maxine snapped. Laurel froze. Bud fell off the chair and windmilled to the floor.

Gran sawed her lips together from side to side, sucked spit from her glands. "You're not still sending her birthday cards, are you?" Furrows bunched and knotted between her brows. A smile twitched at the corners of her mouth. "On your own birthdays?" Her chuckle was an awful, raspy sound that reminded Laurel of a wasp. "Your birthday and you sends that woman a card."

"It was that one time. I was five!"

"You did it more than once."

"You probably didn't even send it."

"I didn't know where that hot ass had run off to. She was always chasing stray dogs." Laurel's thigh cramped. She kicked her leg back and forth. The smell of cleaner was overwhelming. Gran's gaze landed on her again. "That one be knocked up next," Gran inhaled hard through her nose and chewed the inside of her cheek. "Then you be a grandma."

Laurel's leg froze. Her mother slapped the arms of the chair and sprung up so fast she and Bud tumbled to the floor in a tangle.

"Well," her mother said. "Thought you might need some help around the house, but it all looks—"

"I don't need no help."

"Maybe we'll pop by sometime. Just to look in."

"Don't need no lookin' in on."

"Just so we're clear then." Her mother extended her arm and guided them away from the only blood relative of hers they had ever met.

On the walk home, Laurel held Bud's hand. Her mother followed behind with her head down, one arm wrapped around her ribcage as her belly led the way forward. Laurel tugged Bud to a stop and they waited until she caught up. Maxine tilted her head to one side as if to ask why they were just standing there, waiting. The grass on the side of the road was green, dandelion buds looked ready to bust open, but fat snowflakes drifted down with barely a breath of wind. Bud lifted his face to the sky and stuck out his tongue. Laurel closed her eyes and stuck hers out, too. A truck drove past and blew its horn. A quick double-beep that made Laurel laugh while her tongue still jutted from her mouth. She took her mom's hand. Bud hopped around the sidewalk and took her hand on the other side. He swung his arms back and forth and sang, "It's snowing. It's snowing." The three of them laughed and headed back to the Crown.

ELEVEN

Maxine shook Laurel awake. "Get up. You need to call Una. The baby's coming."

The phone rang and rang. Laurel was about to hang up and try again when Una finally answered. "Mom's having the baby."

"That's—" On the other end of the line, Una cleared the sleep from her voice. "That's wonderful."

"She told me . . ." Laurel paused. Her mother hadn't made any arrangements with Una at all. "She told me to call you."

"Are you at the hospital?" Una was on Woods Road, about thirty minutes away and it took longer to drive in the dark.

"Should I call a taxi? What should I do?"

"No. I'm on my way."

Laurel found her mom upstairs making her bed. "Una's coming. I thought you were in labour?"

She smoothed out the bedspread, then plonked down on the quilted top "It takes time."

"Then why didn't you call Una?"

"I was having a contraction." She gestured at the other side of the room. "Can you get me a bag?"

Laurel rummaged through her mom's closet until she pulled

out her old duffle bag, the black one with a fluorescent yellow CAT logo. "Now what?"

"Nothing. I'll pack it. Put it here." Her mother patted the bed next to her and eased out a breath. "Sit."

Laurel placed the bag next to her mom and sat on the other side of it. Her mother's breathing grew heavy. One of her legs shook and she leaned forward, brow wrinkled in concentration. She moaned. A deep guttural sound that reminded Laurel of an animal. She'd seen a goat on Jimmy's farm give birth once. The thing had shaken and bleated, but it had been over when Jimmy's dad hauled the baby out by the back legs.

Laurel moved the duffle bag onto her lap and held it.

Her mother sat up again. She leaned and stretched her spine. Took the bag from Laurel's lap and put it back in the designated bag spot. "Here." She got up, went to her dresser and started to pack.

Laurel hadn't actually seen the baby goat come out. She had looked at every other thing in the barn: barn board, hay, and more hay. And Jimmy. He'd stood back out of the way and all his dad had to do was wave or gesture and Jimmy knew what he wanted. When the baby landed on all fours, shaky and bloody, Jimmy had grinned at her. A grin that erupted into a laugh. And for the first time since her dad died, Laurel had laughed, too.

Her mother opened the bottom drawer and reached around her belly for a change of pants.

"You okay?"

She nodded.

"Should I do that for you?"

"You're fine there."

Laurel opened the bag wider whenever she shoved something into it. Pyjamas. Socks. Underwear. Until her mother slapped her hands out of the way; then Laurel sat there and did nothing as her mother shuffled around the room with a full-grown baby inside her. A baby that was about to be hauled, or pushed, or whatever, into this family, with no say in the matter at all. With no knowledge of past events. For this baby, Woods Road didn't exist, or at least maybe it didn't have to. Fleas. The chair with no legs. The bathroom sink hanging off the wall. Laurel down on one knee with a rifle pressed to her shoulder. This new baby in this new apartment could be the beginning of something. Her mother zipped the duffle bag closed.

"I'm going to wake Bud up." Laurel jumped off the bed.

"Why?"

"Because we're going with you."

The hospital was on base, at the top of Minnesota Drive, a blocky, over-large structure left behind by the Americans. The nurse tended to Laurel's mother in a room that had three unoccupied beds. Dusty pink curtains hung open on metal tracks between them. The nurse put a fetal monitor on her mother's belly, stuck tabs on her chest, and brought ice chips for her to snack on. Laurel watched the quick rhythm of the baby's heartbeat on the screen and let her mom squeeze her hand with every contraction. Bud focused on the monitor and ate his mother's ice chips. Una and Horsey lingered just inside the doorway, but when the contractions were only three minutes apart, the nurse suggested they all wait outside. Laurel held her mother's hand, but Maxine pulled free and waved them off. Said not to worry. She'd be fine.

In the waiting room, Bud led the way to a row of chairs directly in front of the TV. A muted Bob Barker introduced the great spinning wheel of the Showcase Showdown. Una sat next to Bud, took off her coat and draped it over his lap. He leaned into her, exhausted. Laurel and Horsey wandered off and rattled around the hospital hallways.

"How's life next door to Brax Randall?" Horsey balanced along a line of blue tape, one foot in front of the other, like on a balance beam.

Laurel followed a red line and focused on her steps without answering.

"Do you hear him in his room, like, you know, with girls?"

"No! I mean, do you think . . . ?"

Horsey nodded and her eyes bugged.

"He plays music a lot. Like AC/DC? It's brutal. Sometimes I can't take it and I pound on the wall."

"Does it work?"

"Yeah. Sometimes, he knocks back." Laurel tapped the air.

"That's an invitation."

"For what?"

Horsey's eyes were about to pop from their sockets. "Laurel!"

"I don't think it's like that. I think it's an apology for the loud music. Like, it's really loud sometimes."

"It's exactly like that." Horsey stopped at a vending machine and checked the coin slot for change.

"Mom thinks he's nice."

"Ha! Maxine would." A bag of ketchup chips dangled from its metal coil. Horsey rocked the machine back and forth, but the bag held on. She crouched down and reached up inside the dispenser. "Shit." She half-grinned as she tried to pull it back out again.

A nurse came down the hallway in a hush of white sneakers. She slowed as she reached them. "What are you doing?"

"Nothing." Horsey tugged her arm free and winced.

The nurse raised her eyebrows but continued along the hall.

"Fuck." Horsey rubbed her elbow. "You got seventy-five cents?"

"No."

They turned back toward the waiting room, in the opposite direction from the nurse. Once they rounded a corner, Horsey relaxed and walked next to her with her hands in her pockets. "It's going to be weird," she said. "Having a baby around."

"I guess."

"Your mom's got you to help out, anyway."

"It'll be fine."

"Mom thinks it'll be hard. For you."

"Babies are cute."

"I didn't say they weren't cute."

They turned into the waiting room. Bud was sprawled across the row of chairs with his head on Una's lap, asleep. The *Late Night News* was on NTV. Una looked back at them when they sat behind her. "No word yet."

The nurse who had caught Horsey with her arm in the vending machine walked in. Horsey stiffened, but the nurse smiled and said, "Mother and baby are doing just fine."

"Oh, my goodness." Una put a hand on her heart. "Is it a boy or girl?"

"Come see for yourself. She's asking for you."

Laurel left the waiting area and crept into her mother's hospital room with Una at her shoulder and a sleepy Bud clinging to her hand. In the far corner, her mother sat propped against a pillow with a baby hidden in folds of cotton. A floppy wool hat on its head. The window a phosphorescent glow behind them.

"I didn't know if you were all still here." Her mother's cheeks were flushed, hair plastered to her forehead. "Come meet her."

"It's a girl?" Laurel asked.

"Your sister. Want to hold her?"

Laurel took the little bundle. Her sister's face a squishy, squirmy peach. Had she ever seen anything so small? Bud must have been just as tiny when he was born, but she couldn't remember.

"Careful, her head," Una said, hovering at Laurel's elbow just in case she dropped the baby on the floor.

"I have a name," Maxine said. "Braya. Like the flower."

"Braya." Una's smile twitched. "What flower?"

"There's a flower that grows up the coast. In Flower's Cove, or Savage Cove. I can't remember now, but Rick brought us there once in the camper. Remember, Laurel? We parked by the ocean, then had to move because the wind was so fierce, but there were these tiny little flowers that grew right up out of the rocks, sheltered in the cracks. Rick found them. You don't remember that? We were so amazed that anything could grow there on the barrens. Rick said it was the most incredible thing he'd ever seen. I remember that, plain as day. 'Incredible,' he said. You picked one and then on the drive home we saw a sign on the side of the highway, "Home of the rare Long's Braya flower." We figured they were rare, but apparently, they're impossibly rare. They don't grow anywhere else in the world, only there in those rocks. And I let you pick one! I told you not to show anyone and you hid it in one of your books." There was urgency behind her smile, as if Laurel had to remember that moment. As if everything depended on it.

Laurel looked at her baby sister and tried to remember. She and Bud had sat in the camper as the truck whizzed along the highway. The Strait of Belle Isle a glitter of grey, and on the other side of it, the cliffs of Labrador. Bud had bounced up and down on the bench that could turn into a bed while Laurel wrote a note and held it up to the window for her mom to read: *Bud has to pea!!!* Her mother had laughed at her spelling, silent on the other side of the glass, and they pulled off to the side of the road. "I don't . . ."

"Memories are tricky things." Una reached for the baby, but Laurel held her sister to her chest and tried harder. She had run along the white limestone slabs of the coastal barrens, as close to the waves as she dared. Her mother had shouted for her to be careful. Rick loped from one slab to the next, short and stocky, holding her mother's hand, pulling her along.

"I can't . . ." Laurel felt dizzy. Rick wasn't much taller than her mother, but his back was twice as broad. Bunched and muscular. His neck thick. Veins bulged. He had her pinned against the stove. The kitchen counter. A jar of jam at his elbow. Fleas crawled out from the crevices of the chair with no legs and into the carpet. Laurel squeezed her sister to her chest as they scuttled onto the canvas floor, *tick-tick-tick*.

"Here." Una pulled Braya from Laurel's arms. "You need to sit down." She guided Laurel to a chair. Laurel tried to laugh. It was silly to stand there not-remembering, but it hiccupped into a sob.

"Oh, honey."

Dawn crept over the Crown as Una, Horsey and Bud slept in apartment five while her mother spent the night at the hospital with the baby. Laurel stared into the dark, wide awake. She couldn't remember anything about that day on the beach except snippets of waves. Shattered limestone. Had they had a day like that? A day on the beach with Rick, picking flowers out of rocks. A day when she hadn't spent every minute afraid. Light began to slant through her bedroom window, across the floor and up the length of her mirror. Laurel got out of bed in her nightdress and plucked the Polaroid from the frame. She stared into her dad's goofy grin one last time. Then, without looking at the title, she pulled a book from her shelf and tucked the picture deep into the pages.

PART THREE

1995

TWELVE

MAY

Two-year-old Braya toddled around the coffee table. Her chubby fingers clamping the edge as she moved in an oval. She could walk on her own, but she built up so much momentum on the curves that when she let go and dashed across the room, her body moved too fast for her feet and she fell face-first on the floor. Footsteps quickened down the stairs, but Laurel was already there. She scooped Braya up.

"She okay?"

Laurel nodded at Maxine. Braya popped a finger into her mouth and her wailing turned into sniffs and sucking sounds. She curled a tiny finger into Laurel's hair.

"That was quite a thunk."

"She's okay."

Braya hadn't started out with tentative baby steps, she just walked one day at about fourteen months old. Her face a gummy smile and her hair a cloud that bobbed on top of her head. She would mad-dash from her mother to Bud to Laurel to the couch to the coffee table, but whenever she paused, even for a second, she fell over. The way she used to drop, stiff and straight, reminded Laurel of a cut tree. Timber! And her massive baby head would hit the floor with a bang that rivaled the heavy metal in the next-door apartment. Laurel inspected the newest bump.

Her mother leaned close as she shoved her arms into her jacket. "She's tough." She zipped up her coat. "Okay. You got to get to school. Bud!"

Laurel let go as her mother pulled Braya from her arms. Bud bounded down the stairs and came around the turn with his coat on, bookbag bouncing.

"Hand me that?" Her mother pointed to the duffle on the floor, but before Laurel could lift it, she crouched down and shuffled through the contents. "Diapers, wipes, Cheerios, instant formula. Am I missing anything?"

"Her blanky?"

"Shit, can you run up and get it?"

Laurel ran upstairs and grabbed the knitted square Una had made. It was about the size of a cup towel, but her baby sister couldn't sleep without it. On her way back down, Bud barged in from outside.

"It's raining! Can we take the truck?"

"I wish." Maxine tugged Bud's hood up over his head. "Go on, you'll be okay."

Laurel stuffed the blanket into the duffle as it swung from her mom's shoulder, then held the door. "How're you getting to work?"

"I got two feet and a heartbeat, same as you." Her mother led Braya outside into the drizzle. Laurel ducked her face against it as she pulled the door closed. Braya whimpered. A bubbly sound that meant she was about to lose her shit. Her mother hefted her up. "Lynne can watch her until three-thirty. You won't be late?"

"Why would I be late?" Lynne lived in apartment one at the end of the ten-plex.

"Get her right after school. Come back here with her and Bud.

I'll be home by five."

"From Queen Street Extension?" Laurel's jacket didn't have a hood. Water trickled down the back of her neck.

"I'll take a cab. Five-thirty, latest."

"That's kind of a lot, Mom."

"It gets us off welfare." Her mother hurried down the driveway, Braya and the duffle bumping out of sync.

The spring melt had exposed the truck's two flat tires, sagging off the rims in a sorry heap on the pavement. Rust ran along the bottom of both doors and ate through to the other side. It needed a new transmission. New starter. New tires. And probably a new battery. But her mom had a new job as a home care worker. They should have it back on the road again soon. Laurel whacked the hood with her already-damp mitt and trotted after Bud, who was halfway down the road.

In the library, the faulty fluorescent tube had long ago given out and no one had bothered to replace it. Laurel was grateful for the atmosphere the broken light created at her booth in the back corner. Light enough to read, but dark enough to feel hidden away. It wasn't just the lighting that brought on this sense of peace—the heft of the wooden chair as she pulled it into the desk, the hush of carpet, the smell of books, all made her comfortably sleepy. Not that she slept—instead she ate her lunch and read. In the past two years, she'd made her way through the library's motley collection of fantasy novels: Anne Rice, J. R. R. Tolkien, Madeleine L'Engle, Octavia E. Butler. She'd read every science-fiction book. Every western. There weren't many of either, not a single Louis L'Amour, but she'd read so much that characters and worlds started to blur together. She was partway through *The Summer Tree* by Guy Gavriel Kay when she realized she'd read it before. Laurel closed the book. It was time for another genre.

The bookshelves weren't much taller than she was, but the aisles between them were narrow. In Historical Fiction, Laurel ran her finger along spines, waiting for something to catch her interest. Her finger paused on *The Thorn Birds*, and she was about to haul it out to inspect the back cover when the door at the front of the library opened.

Footsteps across the floor. A hand brushed along the top of the librarian's desk.

Laurel crouched low and moved deeper into the stacks. Her lunch bag sat on top of her booth. A half-eaten sandwich on top of it. Ham and mayo. If she crawled under her booth, they would see her lunch on top, and her squatting behind the chair legs. The bookshelf ended at her booth. There was nowhere else to go. Laurel pulled out her chair, sat down and picked up her sandwich. She took a bite.

"Hello?" A female voice. "Students aren't allowed in here lunchtime."

Laurel turned. It was a high school student one year ahead of her, in grade twelve. She recognized the girl as a hall prefect but couldn't remember her name.

"And you can't eat in here. Ever."

Laurel forced herself to swallow, then stuffed the rest of her sandwich in her lunch bag.

"You don't need to get all contrary about it."

Laurel shook her head as she shoved her lunch in her book-bag.

"I'm just doing my job. Don't shoot the prefect, you know?" She raised her hands and took a step back. A purple T-shirt with ROXY stretched across her boobs.

"It's all good." Laurel got up, brushed past the prefect and slammed out through the doors. She walked through the cafeteria staring straight ahead. Imagined every head turning, every mouth moving. *Killer. Psycho. Murderer.* Horsey was probably there, sitting with her grade twelves. And Jimmy must be somewhere there, too. But she couldn't sit with them. It was fine if Horsey came by her locker when she wanted to come over after school, but that was different. That wasn't the cafeteria, where every movement was under scrutiny. Who sat where, with who, and why: all predetermined by some unwritten hierarchy. She was at the bottom of that hierarchy, deep in a rabbit hole. Laurel strode past tables to the far end of the cafeteria and out through the double doors, keeping up the same clipped pace, coatless in the cold drizzle. Bookbag over one shoulder like she didn't give a fuck about any of it. She didn't stop until she was back in her room in apartment number five, where she crawled in bed and read *The Summer Tree* until it was time to get Braya.

For the rest of the week Laurel walked home for lunch. The fifty-minute period gave her enough time to get home, shove food in her mouth and rush back to school. She was late most days, and on Friday, she skipped her second afternoon of the week. The following Monday, Mrs. Harding, her old grade nine teacher, stopped her after homeroom.

"Do you have a minute?"

Laurel paused with her math book pressed to her chest. The teacher gestured for Laurel to follow. She was the only teacher in school who wore heels and she clacked down the corridor to the library. The door swung closed behind them and Mrs. Harding's shoes dimpled the carpet as she made for the librarian's desk.

"Our librarian, Mrs. Mercer, is out for the rest of the year."

"Oh, ah, I hope she's okay?"

"I hope she is, too. Until the end of term, I'll be holding down the fort, as much as I can anyway." Mrs. Harding pulled a desk drawer open and rummaged through papers. "I could use some help." She found a clipboard and flipped through sheets shackled by a metal clip. "We used to have a library prefect, years ago." The teacher unclipped the pages, threw the top half into the garbage and thrust the clipboard at Laurel. "There's quite a bit of work I'm afraid. It'll take up your lunch period."

Laurel adjusted the clipboard on top of her math book and skimmed the checklist: turn on lights, look for trash, change stamp for the day, check books out and in, put items on cart in alphanumeric order, straighten books and magazines, vacuum if necessary—

"Of course, some of that will already be done in the morning when I come in, and nobody checks books out at lunchtime, but you could deliver the holds to the classrooms. That is, if you're interested?"

Laurel gave a slow nod.

"Great!" Mrs. Harding clapped the top of the desk. Laurel blinked to keep from jumping. "You can start today. Lunchtime."

"Can I—"

"Bring your lunch. It's you that gets to clean up now anyway, isn't it?" Mrs. Harding sashayed across the room toward the door. "I'll leave a prefect pin on the desk here for you later. Check for it at lunchtime." The door closed just as first bell rang. Laurel finished reading the checklist, then looked around the empty library. The room suddenly looked different, like she was seeing it for the first time. Book stacks. Book cart. The desk in the middle of the room. The smell of old carpet. The books. She was responsible for all of it, during lunchtimes anyway, but that was a start. The start of what she wasn't exactly sure, but Laurel turned on her heel and headed for class. She'd make homeroom before second bell.

Each day with her mother working felt endless. Laurel walked home from school, dropped off her bookbag, then picked Braya and her immense diaper bag up at apartment one. Whatever Lynne fed her baby sister wasn't enough, because both Braya and Bud were starved and begging for food by four o'clock. Laurel had to fend them off while she put something together. Chicken nuggets and fries. Chicken burgers and fries. Breaded chicken in any form went great with fries, but her specialty was goulash. A chef's kiss of macaroni, stewed tomatoes, and hamburger meat that lasted for days. When her mother got home, usually after six, everyone was fed and sitting in front of the TV. Maxine ate whatever was left over or wolfed down four slices of peanut butter toast. She had been mildly impressed with Laurel's new role as prefect, but she was probably too exhausted to be excited. When Laurel asked how her job was going, she shook her head and made a pinched expression. "That man," she said. "That man is disgusting." Laurel didn't ask again.

Horsey came over regularly after school. Maybe she was bored, maybe Una had asked her to help out. Either way, Laurel was happy about it. Horsey seemed less happy. She was the only kid Laurel knew who wasn't financially better off than herself, yet somehow Una always managed to have the shack stocked with food.

Horsey banged around the kitchen, opening and closing cupboard doors. "There's nothing to eat. Nothing. Like, your cupboards are actually empty." She picked a plate off the top of a stack of dirty dishes on the counter and it came away with a sticky rip.

"Mom gets paid today. She'll get groceries tomorrow. Maybe we should wash these." Every dish in the house was piled on the counter. Glasses stacked inside glasses, mugs on top of mugs, pots and pans overfilled the sink.

Horsey eyed the mess. "I'm cooking."

"You're boiling noodles."

"Yeah, well, it's not easy to make spaghetti when there's no sauce." No sauce, no stewed tomatoes, no fresh tomatoes. There were a few things in the cupboard, but nothing that went together. Macaroni but no cheese, a packet of taco mix but no tacos, a bottle of maraschino cherries.

Horsey opened the box of spaghetti. "There's not much in

there." She tipped a thin stream of noodles into the boiling water.

Laurel left the kitchen and went downstairs to check the freezer in the basement. Since they'd moved in, the basement had remained untouched. Stacked boxes, unpacked and forgotten, obstructed the far wall. A washer and dryer sat against the back wall and under a small window squatted the freezer. She yanked the door open and found it half-full of frozen moose. Laurel pushed packages out of the way until she found a small roast that looked manageable.

She lifted it out and brought it upstairs. "Look what I found."

"Ugh."

Laurel had seen her mom cook a roast plenty of times, but she'd never paid much attention to the process. It couldn't be that hard. She cleared the dirty pans from the sink and dropped the moose in hot water to defrost while the oven preheated to 350 degrees. Then increased the temperature to 450 degrees just to be sure. The roast fit squarely in the roasting pan. Laurel gave it a generous sprinkle of salt and pepper, covered it with the lid and slid it in the oven.

Heat stung her eyes when she opened the oven an hour later. She turned her head and pulled out the roaster with dish towels wrapped around her hands. The roast was dark, almost black, and covered with tiny cracks like fissures in chapped lips. It sat stiff in the bottom of the pan, a ring of burnt juice smoking around it. Bud lifted up on his toes for a closer look. Braya slapped her high-chair tray with two chubby palms and ate chopped-up pieces of maraschino cherry. The roast looked overcooked to Laurel, but when she cut into it, the meat was raw.

"Gross." Horsey leaned in.

Bud tugged a jagged bit of burnt meat and tore it away.

Braya slapped her tray harder. Cherry juice splashed across her face and she started to cry.

"Let's just fry it." Laurel found the bread knife poking up out of a water jug. She scrubbed it under hot water as Braya wailed and Bud tore a piece from his strip of burnt meat and offered it to her. Laurel hacked into the roast. She sawed off skinny slivers as best she could. Horsey unloaded dirty forks and knives from the frying pan, then washed the pan and set it on the stove. "Got any oil?"

"Butter works."

Horsey dropped a cold chunk of butter on the pan and waited for it to sizzle.

Covered in butter, more salt and more pepper, the crispy slivers of meat weren't so bad. Laurel cut tiny bits for Braya. Bud gnawed a strip like jerky. Horsey doused hers with soya sauce.

"Hmm, it's like Lee's Takeout, with no rice."

"Or chicken balls."

"Or egg rolls."

"Or cherry sauce."

Horsey raised her eyebrows and ran a strip of meat across Braya's juicy tray. "Not bad," she said, "not bad at all."

THIRTEEN

Brax and his dad were quiet now, but Laurel strained to catch a familiar bang or slap or grumble that could escalate into another shouting match. The noises next door sounded like furniture being knocked around, smacks to tabletops and walls. Laurel didn't think they hit each other, but she couldn't be sure. She imagined their hands wrapped around each other's throats. Two purple faces. Swollen necks. Bulged eye-to-eye stares. Who would let go first?

She reached out and knocked on the wall.

Nothing.

She knocked again, louder.

When there was still no response, she kicked off her covers and got up. She stood for a moment with her eyes closed. Deep breaths. In and out. That's what Tina had told her to do when her heart raced like that and she couldn't control the images in her head. Her mom's swollen face. Her eyes red and pleading. "Stop."

Deep breath in. Deep breath out. It didn't work. It never worked, not like she told Tina it did. Neither did counting down backwards from a hundred.

Something crashed inside her apartment. Laurel's eyes snapped open. "Mom?"

Laurel rushed out of her room and into the hall. She opened her mother's bedroom door and switched on the light.

Maxine sat on the foot of her bed. "Laurel! Jesus, you gave me a fright. What are you doing?" She shielded her eyes. Her other hand hung out the open window. "Turn the light back off! You're going to wake Braya."

"What was that?"

"Nothing." Her mother waved. "Something just fell."

Laurel caught a whiff of smoke. It wasn't a cigarette. She had smelled that dank, boggy smell before. Once, when she and Horsey had hung out behind Danny's Bakery. Horsey had followed Andrew around Main Street all night while he tracked down a bit of hash oil. Andrew was Jimmy's cousin. He lived in Stephenville, but he'd spent summers at Jimmy's house on Woods Road ever since Jimmy had moved there from Ontario. Laurel had never tried hash. Horsey either. But they had huddled together in the cold as Andrew and his friends passed a joint around in a slow circle.

Braya was asleep in her crib, curled up under a blanket.

"I can't sleep."

Her mother's eyes were bloodshot. "Me either. Turn the light off, please."

Laurel folded her arms. The room was cold with the window open like that. Her mother extended her arm farther outside. "Fine," Laurel said. "Good night."

"Night, sweet heart. Get some sleep."

Laurel turned off the light and closed the door.

Back in bed, she listened to the quiet apartment. If she went to sleep now, she would get exactly four hours and . . . twenty-three minutes of sleep. The tiny red dots on her alarm clock reformed from a seven to an eight. Four hours and twenty-two minutes. If she kept staring at the numbers, she would have to fall asleep eventually. Watching a clock would put anyone to sleep. Why didn't Tina recommend that? Laurel became aware of each blink. She counted the seconds between them until the space between blinks grew longer and her eyes started to water. One minute passed. Laurel rolled over, touched her fingers to the wall. She'd knocked on the wall whenever she heard Brax and his dad fight. He always knocked back. It was their code. *Are you okay?* And the reply, *I'm fine.* She tapped.

Nothing.

A few moments later she heard movement next door. She tossed onto her back and listened with both ears. Footsteps—someone going downstairs. The front door opened and closed. Then, on her own front door, very lightly, he tapped.

Laurel's heart raced as she got out of bed. She crept past her mom's room and down the stairs. She paused halfway down, then pounded down the rest of the steps, turned the deadbolt and opened the door to see Brax in his sock feet. Hands stuffed in his jeans pockets. He hunched forward into them.

"Hey."

Laurel's jogging pants were old and saggy. Her T-shirt too small to wear out of the house anymore. The cold pricked her bare arms as she opened the door wider and stepped back.

"Thanks." He shuffled past her. "Seriously. You have no idea." Brax sat on the couch in the living room, shook his head, and let out a slow, agitated breath. He balled his hands into fists on top of his knees and looked at the ceiling.

Laurel perched on the arm of the chair. "You okay?"

His hair bounced when he jabbed an elbow into the couch. *Jab-jab-jab.* "Sorry. Shit." He ran his hands through his hair. Rested his elbows on his knees. "I'm okay," he said in a rush of breath. "I'm okay now. It's my dad. He's just—" Brax leaned back, patted the cushion next to him, and smiled. All of his aggression spent on three sharp jabs to the couch.

Laurel slid from the arm to the cushion. He jerked his head for her to come closer still. When she didn't, he shifted down until their thighs touched and rested his head on her shoulder. They never talked about their code. Their knocks back and forth on the bedroom wall. In real life, they acted as if nothing ever happened. But it happened all the time. "What about your mom?"

"What about her?"

"Do you talk much?"

"She's saving up for a plane ticket to get me to Fort Mac. There's a ton of jobs up there. She'll hook me up. I just got to get there first." He burrowed his head deeper into her neck. "But she's not like Maxine or anything."

"Mom? Mom's a mess."

"She loves you to pieces. What more do you want?"

Brax's hair made her face itch and she rolled her head away. "I don't know. It'd be nice if she paid attention sometimes."

"Well." He wrapped an arm around her waist and raised his mouth to her ear. "If it's attention you want."

She laughed to hide the shiver that ran up the back of her neck. "I don't think so."

"Okay, okay." Brax raised his hands in a gesture of peace. "Here." He lifted his legs and stretched them out behind her. "We can just lie down. I swear."

Laurel let him pull her down next to him. The couch groaned and squeaked as they found comfortable positions around each other's bodies. She settled with her back against his chest. His arms around her. Laurel remembered waking up sometimes to find her parents asleep like this. It was weird to make the same shape with Brax, like she was trying too hard to be a grown-up, or maybe she was too grown up to be sixteen. Brax squeezed her close and his breath hit the soft hollow behind her ear. Laurel's body went rigid. He loosened his grip on her.

Laurel took slow, shallow breaths as a cramp formed in her left hip. She flexed her ass cheek, but it only made the cramp worse. She clenched her teeth and pushed her heel toward her toes.

Cold ribboned down her leg and into her foot. Her arch clenched. Brax squeezed her closer to his chest, ran a hand over her stomach, down to her throbbing hip and back up to her rib cage. There he paused and traced the line of her breast back and forth with his thumb. Laurel's breath caught. Pain shot up her spine to the back of her skull. Brax pushed the front of his pants up against her backside, where her joggers did nothing to hide the bump she knew was an actual penis.

"Don't."

"Sorry." He drew back.

Laurel could have sat up in the same moment. She could have uncoiled her knees and let the blood rush gleefully back to her feet. Instead, she shifted, just a bit, and extended her legs farther down the couch.

Brax brushed her hair aside. "You're nice."

"Hmm hm." She meant that to sound like *You're nice too, but not that nice* and emphasized her meaning with a deep I'm-almost-asleep-now sigh. He put his arm back over her. Slid his hand down her belly.

Laurel shifted away.

"Fine." He sighed and rolled over to face the back of the couch. Eventually, Brax Randall's breathing grew slow and steady. And his breaths deepened. Laurel got up and went back to her room.

When her alarm went off the next morning she wasn't sure if it woke her up or if she'd been awake all night. In the bathroom, Laurel splashed water on her face to clear the fog from her head and soften the lines printed into the curve of her cheek. Braya babbled in her mom's room. Laurel dried her face and ran downstairs. Brax was already gone.

FOURTEEN

Maxine had carted a load of groceries home in a cab less than a week ago and already they were back down to spaghetti noodles and butter. Laurel smacked the cold block down on the counter and hacked off a chunk as Horsey stirred the noodles in the pot.

"Nu-nu," Braya babbled from the floor.

Horsey picked a few dry noodles out of the box and handed them down to her. "What the hell was that?"

"What?" Laurel spun around. She'd heard something too, an animal scampering across the floor.

"A cat! It just ran down the hall."

Bud came into the kitchen and they stared at him. He looked himself over. "What?"

"Did you let a cat in the house?"

"Oh," he said. "That's Furry Lewis."

He picked up the box of spaghetti and poured some into his hand. Braya reached for more.

"What the hell, Bud?" Laurel found the cat in the living room sniffing around an empty bowl tucked between the couch and the wall. An orange ring stained the bottom. "You've been feeding this thing? It probably has fleas!"

"It don't have fleas."

"There's a collar you can get. To make sure it doesn't get fleas." Horsey squatted down to pet the cat. The animal snaked around her arm and purred when she scratched its head. Horsey laughed.

Laurel huffed, picked up the bowl and brought it out to the kitchen, where she added it to the stack of dirty dishes. "What have you been feeding it?"

"I don't know." Bud followed behind her. "She likes everything."

"She? Furry Lewis is a *she*?" Bud got in her way as she carried the pot to the sink to drain the spaghetti. "This is scalding hot for God's sakes. Watch out!" Laurel held the lid against the flow of water so the noodles wouldn't end up in the sink. Steam whacked her in the face. She squinted as she poured. "There's no way that cat is getting any noodles."

"She loves buttered noodles."

"Not. Happening."

"Fine!" Bud opened the fridge and closed it again. He climbed up on the counter and rummaged into the back of the cupboards.

"There's nothing else here." The cat circled Horsey's feet and rubbed the length of its speckled grey and brown body against her ankles as she stood in the middle of the kitchen. Laurel made a show of moving around them and set the pot back on the stove. She dropped the hacked-off chunks of butter into it.

Braya reached after the cat. "Fur!"

Horsey crouched next to her. "Did you hear that? She just said Furry! Didn't you? Yes, you did! You're so smart! Did you hear that, Laurel?"

Laurel crossed back to the sink and washed just enough dishes for the four of them to eat supper. Her. Braya. Horsey. Bud.

"Okay." Horsey stood back up with her hands on her hips. "Furry Lewis needs cat food. I'm sick of noodles . . ."

Bud raised his hand. "I'm sick of noodles."

"I'm going shopping."

"Yes now, with what?" Laurel turned to watch Horsey rub her fingers together. "Oh, your big wads of cash."

"My five fingers. Idiot."

Laurel turned back to the sink. She fished out four forks, stuck them under the running water, and ignored the racket Horsey was making in the porch putting on her coat and boots.

"I'm going too," Bud said.

"You stay here."

"Furry Lewis needs cat food." Bud disappeared down the hall.

"You coming or what?" Horsey shouted.

Laurel dropped the wet forks on the counter. At least she could get the cat a flea collar. "What about Braya?"

"Bring her!"

They walked up Royal Avenue and cut across the parking lot behind Debbie's Video and the 104 Main. It was Friday. There'd be a lineup at the 104 later in the night. A mix of grown-ups and kids as young as Brax trying to get into the only dance bar in town. There were plenty of other bars. Stephenville's claim to fame was having the most bars per capita in North America. At least that's what Andrew and his stoner buddies said. Stephenville bars weren't famous, though. They weren't lined up along fancy cobblestones like George Street in St. John's; instead they were tucked around town like dirty little secrets. Holes in the wall that served yellow lager and single-shot highballs. They sported pool tables, dartboards, and in some back corner, a destitute row of slot machines. Andrew's dad had a thing for the slot machines. Laurel eased the stroller off the sidewalk and pushed Braya across Main Street. The cat loped after them.

Outside Foodland, Horsey whispered, "We could use the stroller." She gestured at the basket underneath Braya's seat.

"Not a chance. Bud can watch Braya out here."

"No way! This was my idea!"

"You'll just be in the way." Bud's face crumpled. "Listen. Furry Lewis can't come inside. And Braya's too little. I need you to stay out here and watch them." Bud looked around like he wasn't sure what it meant to stay out there. Laurel pushed the stroller to the curb at the far side of the entrance, sheltered and almost dry. "You can sit down and wait right here. Don't let go of Braya."

He took hold of the stroller's handle, pulled his coat down over his bum and sat beside it on the cold concrete. "Here Furry . . . pss pss pss."

"We'll be quick."

Horsey grinned at her and pushed open the glass doors.

The place was packed. Every cash register open. Carts lined up into the aisles.

"How're we gonna—"

"This is good. No one will even notice us." Horsey talked like a pro, but there wasn't a single store on Woods Road. She hadn't done any more five-finger shopping than Laurel had. She was completely full of shit. "Come on!"

Laurel followed her down an aisle with glass coolers on one side and boxed goods on the other. The coolers were stocked with milk and produce, packs of bacon. Laurel opened one and shuffled around frozen pizzas and boxes of chicken nuggets. She slid the door closed and followed Horsey around the corner to the next aisle.

"Like this." Horsey stopped in front of fruit snacks and granola. She grabbed a box of chocolate-covered bars and shoved it under the elastic waistband of her jacket. Held up her hands, spread her fingers wide, jerked her head at the shelf.

There were three other people in the aisle. A woman in a green trench coat and ball cap, her attention fixed on the various rice options. Another woman, stuffed in a short black jacket, pushed her cart as she read through a list. A man hurried past in squeaky boots. Horsey nudged her. None of the shoppers paid them any attention. Laurel walked a little farther, ignored the granola bars and fruit snacks, and focused on the cereal. She picked up a box of Cheerios and tried to stuff it up her coat.

"Too big!" Horsey snatched the box from her and put it back on the shelf. "Christ. Why don't you just take this?" Horsey grabbed a bonus family-sized box and pulled at the bottom of Laurel's coat.

Laurel pushed her away.

Horsey doubled over laughing. "Oh! Here you go!" She lifted a massive plastic bag from the bottom shelf—No Name puffed rice—and tried to shove it up her own coat. It looked like she was humping a pillow. More shoppers moved down the aisle. They all watched. One of them smiled, confused, as fat tears rolled down Horsey's face.

"Can I help you?"

Laurel spun around and faced a bearded man with heavy eyebrows. He wore a Foodland uniform and a red name tag on his chest: *Rodney*. "No?"

Horsey laughed louder. Rodney frowned.

"We forgot the . . . the . . . thing." Horsey grabbed Laurel; they sped down the aisle and past the checkouts and burst out of the store. They were breathless when they reached Bud.

"Oh my God!" Horsey shouted. "You could have nicked something small! A box of cereal?" She shook her head and doubled over again, hanging onto Bud who ducked his head and laughed along with her.

"Hey!" Rodney came through the glass doors, long-armed and pointing.

"Oh shit!" Horsey's voice cracked. "Go, go, go!" She batted at Bud.

Laurel shoved him out of the way, grabbed Braya's stroller and pushed her into the parking lot. Braya squealed with delight as the stroller bounced and rattled after Horsey, who skipped backward and waved at Laurel to run faster. Bud caught up and splashed ahead of them. His arms and legs pumped wildly. Mouth open in terror. Furry Lewis trotted at his heels, tail switching.

On cheque day, Maxine sent Laurel and Horsey back to Foodland with a grocery list. Horsey took empty grocery bags from the house, and when there was no sign of Rodney, they put everything they were supposed to buy in the cart and everything else in the bags.

"We already paid for these," Horsey said at the checkout. She indicated the plastic bags stuffed full of cookies, chocolate bars, and chips.

"When?" asked the cashier, a lady with fluffy grey hair and a face like a bird. It was a late Friday evening and hers was the only cash open. "I didn't check you out."

"We went to a different checkout. Down there." Horsey nodded down the store. "We forgot we had to get a bunch of other things, so we had to come back. The only thing we remembered was the junk food."

"You got a receipt?"

"Yeah, I must." She checked her coat pockets, then her pants. "Do you have the receipt?"

Laurel heaped groceries onto the conveyer belt. She paused to check her pockets, but came up empty.

Horsey checked hers again. "You sure?"

"I must have lost it."

The cashier's hair wobbled when she shook her head, but she pinched her lips together and scanned the groceries piled up on her belt.

Horsey's pinky touched Laurel's as they dropped the last of the bags in the cart. Laurel smirked. Horsey walked with a possessive finger hooked around a metal rung as Laurel pushed the cart outside. They made off with a large haul of food. Laurel gripped the handles of three bags at a time and lifted them out of the basket.

Horsey did the same, but four more bags, filled to bursting, still sat in the bottom of the cart.

"Cab?" Horsey looked wistfully through the doors at two phones affixed to a brick wall, direct lines to Blue Bird and Crown Taxi.

Plastic handles stretched and cut into Laurel's knuckles. She let go, dropped them on the pavement, then picked them back up one at a time and put them in the cart.

"Works for me." Horsey heaved all six of hers in at once.

The cart vibrated and skipped over the pavement. Laurel moved to the front to pull while Horsey pushed. When they reached the alley, the cart bumped and tipped in potholes and patches of gravel.

"Jesus," Horsey said. "This was a bad fucking idea."

Laurel's laugh sounded like an annoyed snort.

"It's not funny. My hands are freezing."

"Here, you pull for a while." Laurel took the handle and pushed. The wheels jammed up with dirt, wet and sludgy from the last two weeks of May drizzle. They had to push, haul and carry the cart the rest of the way home.

The apartment smelled of cigarette smoke when they got back. Maxine tapped ashes into a drinking glass. A pile of bills spread over the coffee table. She didn't look up as they carried the grocery bags to the kitchen. Bud helped them pack everything away, then worked at a can of Fancy Feast with the can opener.

"I'm trying to figure out what to do," her mother called out.

Laurel closed the cupboard door and helped Bud with the can opener. She carried the opened can to the living room and dumped the contents into Furry's bowl. "About what?"

Bud sat on the couch next to his mother and ate a Passion Flakie. Braya climbed up next to him and tried to snatch it for herself.

Maxine dropped the cigarette into the ashy water and helped

Braya into her lap. She cracked off a piece of Bud's Flakie and gave it to her. "About that." She jerked her head at the window that looked out on the driveway.

"Thought you were going to fix it. Get a new battery." Laurel stood in the doorway with the empty can. Bits of cat food clung to the sawed edge.

"Needs more than that. Transmission's gone. Brake pads. Starter. And then there's that." Her mother gestured to the bills, vaguely, as if they were too dismal to acknowledge. "The phone bill. Final notice. They're going to cut it."

"We need a phone."

"Of course, everyone needs a phone. And a vehicle. But we can't have both, apparently. I can try to fix the truck or sell it to pay the phone bill."

Laurel leaned into the archway.

"What's going on?" Horsey stood next to her and munched a Flakie louder than Bud.

"We need a phone," Laurel said. "I'm here by myself all the time, babysitting."

Her mother picked up her pack of cigarettes. "We won't have a vehicle." Bud dropped his wrapper on top of the bills.

"We haven't had one in ages."

"Might never afford another one." Her mother opened the pack, tapped out a cigarette and a tiny red Bic. She flicked the lighter a few times and puffed hard on the filter. Her face tilted toward the ceiling as she breathed out a thin cloud of smoke. "Guess I'll sell the truck."

Bud picked the wrapper back up, stuck his finger inside and swiped for traces of cream.

"I need a drink. Can you watch the kids for a couple hours?"

"How can you afford a drink if you can't afford the truck?"

Her mother's jaw tightened. "Either way, I have to sell the truck. So what's the difference?"

Horsey slid a glance at Laurel.

Laurel shrugged. "Sure. At least I can call for help if I need it."

"You okay?" Horsey raised her voice over Braya's shrill wails. Braya fussed every bedtime and her cries carried from her mother's room to Laurel's even with both doors closed.

Laurel shifted on the bed and tucked her hands under her cheek. "Mm-hmm."

"You sure?"

Laurel nodded as Horsey massaged tiny circles along the curve of her eyebrow. When they were little, they used to take turns massaging each other's eyebrows until one of them fell asleep.

"You must hear that all the time." Horsey moved her fingers to Laurel's other brow and Laurel adjusted her head to give her better access.

"Nah."

"You don't hear it?"

"I'm just used to it. I can block it out." Laurel rolled onto her back.

"You don't find it *hard* sometimes?"

"She's my sister."

"And?"

"What? It's just crying. Are you asking me if I have a problem with a baby that cries? Because babies cry."

"No. That's not—" Braya's wailing tapered off into sobby hiccups. Then stopped. Horsey's smile showed the tips of her teeth. She sat up and reached for the ceiling, waving her hands as if for a cheering crowd. Her ponytail flopped to the side of her head and she tugged the elastic free, let her curls fly wild around her face. She flopped back down on the bed. "Phew!" She rolled onto her side to face Laurel. "You know that's not what I meant, right?"

"What? Just forget it." Laurel closed her eyes.

"Well, I guess someone, someday, will have to tell her. You know? I mean, the earlier the better, so it feels more normal. Well, as normal as possible."

"*Forget* it."

"It's probably better to always know, than to learn—"

"Oh my God, stop."

"See? You're not okay. You keep way too much bottled up in there."

"You're driving me insane."

A quick knock on the bedroom door. Her mother opened it and poked her head in. "The kids are asleep. I'm going to head out now, okay? I won't be late." Laurel nodded and her mother pulled the door closed.

"Well." Horsey leaned over and picked up the phone. "If you got nothing to say, I'm calling Andrew." She punched in the number.

Laurel could hear the phone ring. Andrew picked up.

"We're bored." Horsey gripped the phone with both hands. The cord stretched to the floor.

Laurel shifted closer to listen to his response. "Oh yeah? What can I do about it?"

"I don't know. Maxine's going out. Get a ride over with someone."

"I could *probably* arrange that. Let me call Jason. He's got nothing on the go."

Horsey covered the receiver. "He's actually coming."

"Is he serious?"

She nodded. "Is that okay?"

Laurel's stomach panged. "Sure." She rolled over, away from Horsey, and let out a long, slow breath. Horsey chattered away to Andrew. Laurel slid her hand across the bed to touch the wall that separated her and Brax. Drummed her fingers gently, then made a fist and bit the knuckle of her index finger.

FIFTEEN

An hour and a half later, Andrew and his friend Jason showed up in a black Trans Am. Horsey held the door open wide and they clinked into the apartment, each with a case of beer. Laurel suggested they go down to the basement, where they wouldn't wake Bud or Braya. Horsey led the way, fingers trailing the walls of the stairwell, and the boys *clink-clinked* down behind her. "Welcome to the basement!" She jumped the last two steps and landed with her arms overhead as if she could transform the cement floor, brick walls, and metal support posts with sheer vibrance.

"Well." Andrew flicked his hair, streaked blond like James Iha's, and sized up the space. "Let's make it a tad more homey, shall we?" He set the beer on the floor, went to the boxes stacked against the far wall, chose one and pried open the flaps.

"You won't find anything interesting." Laurel folded her arms.

"I remember your house, man. Your mom is the queen of interesting." Andrew hefted out a volume of the *Encyclopædia Britannica*. "We need furniture." He carried the book to the back corner by the window. "Right here." He picked up two more books and laid them flat on the floor next to the first. "It's a table. Come on. Chop, chop!"

Horsey bounced into motion. She lugged books over and Andrew adjusted them to make a base. Laurel dragged out a large painting for the tabletop and Horsey used another book to hold it in place: Volume 14 "Lightning to Maximilian." Jason hauled out bins and tipped over five-gallon beef buckets for chairs and the four of them sat around the table drinking Blue Star.

"B'ys." Andrew's left leg vibrated. "We got a room with a view!"

Horsey laughed.

Jason fidgeted with his goatee. "Can I smoke down here?"

"Ahh . . . " Laurel glanced at the basement window. It was completely obstructed by grass.

"Your mom smokes in the house." Horsey cracked open her beer. "She wouldn't mind."

"I guess."

Jason pulled a pack of smokes from his front pocket and lit up. Andrew guzzled his beer, then tapped out a beat on the table. The painting wobbled, but Horsey caught the edge and held it. One beer down, Andrew got up and poked around the basement again. He found a twisted, gnarled stick and wielded it like a sword. A single leather stirrup that he swung like a lasso. And a lone moose antler that he held to one side of his head and walked around sideways. "You left Woods Road down here," he said. "All the fun stuff."

Horsey got up to join in the search. "You wanna see Woods Road, you should come out to the shack more often."

"Oh, I've seen plenty of the shack."

Laurel tipped back her beer to hide her eye roll.

"You've got to be kidding me!" Andrew hauled a wad of black fur from another bin. He held it up and shook it as if he needed everyone to confirm that he was really holding what he thought he was holding. The fur rippled in waves.

The smell hit her. Laurel tilted her head and inhaled. Damp earth and leaves, sour crabapples about to decompose. It was like catching a whiff of her own body odour.

"You got some burnt shit down here." Jason opened another Blue Star. Andrew draped the bearskin over his head. He made a show of trying to see through the small slits that had been the bear's eyes and stumbled around.

"ROOOAAAAARRRR!" He grabbed Horsey, bit her neck and growled. Horsey erupted in hysterics. She tried to run away, but he caught her and wrestled her down to the cement. The bearskin fell from his shoulders and he paused in his attack to tie the front legs around his neck, then he leaned over and kissed her. Laurel looked away. She made eye contact with Jason, who held out a pack of cigarettes.

"Smoke?" He slid one out, lit it and handed it to her.

Andrew rose to his full height again. "I got to piss like a racehorse. I mean a bear. I got to piss like a bear. I'm coming back for you!" He left Horsey sprawled on the floor and stood in front of the laundry sink, legs spread, and unzipped.

Horsey shouted at him not to do it. Laurel groaned her disgust. Jason laughed and lit a cigarette for himself. Andrew roared as a stream of urine pummelled the open sink.

Upstairs, the front door banged closed. Laurel jumped. "Mom's home!" She dropped her cigarette in an empty bottle and shook her hands at Jason to do the same. He dropped his smoke. Andrew's stream paused. Above them, someone walked across the floor. The basement door opened. Footsteps. Down, down, down. Brax came around the corner with his hands in his pockets.

"Oh man, Jesus!" Andrew bent double. "I thought it was Maxine."

"Sounded like you were having a party." Brax nodded at Laurel.

"You could hear us?"

He sat on Andrew's abandoned bucket and spoke to her as if she was the only one in the room. "I wasn't invited."

"Yeah, you were."

Brax smirked, ran a hand through his hair and pulled a pack of papers out of his back pocket. He stood again and patted his front pockets until he found a vial of hash. Sat back down, opened the vial and stuck the bent end of a hairpin into it.

Andrew left the sink without resuming his pee. He picked his beer up from the floor and hovered behind Horsey.

Jason tapped the neck of his beer. "I'm Jason."

Brax smeared a line of black-green oil down the paper. "What are you, some kind of superhero?"

Andrew untied the legs of the bearskin from around his neck and held it out.

"Ah, you're a bear."

Horsey snorted. Andrew frowned at her.

"You mind?" Brax took a cigarette from Jason's pack. He rolled it back and forth between his fingers and let tobacco catch in the oil like flypaper, then he tore a strip off the pack and coiled it into a filter. He hunched toward Laurel with the joint. "Just open the window."

Horsey sat down. "Ah—"

"Maxine won't even notice."

Laurel should have said no. She should have shut it down, but in her moment of hesitation, Brax lit up.

"All right, then." Andrew opened the window. Brax took a few puffs and handed the joint to Laurel.

Smoke slipped past her throat and smacked into her lungs. The shock of it made her cough. Her eyes watered. Someone laughed. Everyone laughed, except Brax. He watched her with an expression that was somehow patient and eager at the same time. She raised the joint to her lips and tried again. This time, she felt her tongue burn, but she let the smoke sit in her lungs before she blew it out in a coughing fit. Brax laughed, but it was a soft chuckle, and he shook his head like he was still impressed. Jason took the joint from her fingers. His turn.

The little window did nothing to ease the smoke that filled the basement. Laurel's eyes felt heavy. Irritated. She patted her lids. All swollen and puffy. Brax watched her with that stupid smirk. She laughed. He laughed at her laughing and she laughed harder. The joint was in his hand again. That meant she was next. Already. That's how it worked, right? Around and around in a circle. Puff, puff, give? Two puffs. She could do that. Brax stroked her finger when he passed her the joint. She held the smoke in her lungs for a count of one, two, three, and didn't cough when she let it out.

Jason slapped the tabletop and almost knocked it off the book stack. "You're wild!"

Horsey caught the painting and righted it. Laurel took one more quick puff and offered her the joint, but Horsey shook her head.

"That looks good and done." Andrew took it from her and tried to get another drag.

Pressure built in Laurel's bladder. How many beers had she had? At least two. Maybe three. A half-empty bottle sat in front of her. She picked it up and took a swig. If she could piss in the sink she wouldn't have to go upstairs, but she did have to go upstairs.

"Where you going?" Horsey asked when she got up.

"Upstairs." Laurel wasn't sure why that was so funny.

In the bathroom, she looked in the mirror at the tiny red slits that were her eyes. She ran a facecloth under cold water, then sat on the toilet with the cloth over her eyes and her feet on the edge of the bathtub. If only she had ice. Ice would be perfect. She heard someone moving around the house. Was Bud up? She couldn't deal with that right now.

Laurel crept down the hall to Bud's room and listened at the door. She turned the knob, quiet and slow, and opened the door to see Bud asleep in bed. Furry Lewis' head popped up from behind his knees. Maybe she was allergic to the cat and that's why her eyes were so puffy. Baker Dog, as usual, was tucked under Bud's arm. Laurel pulled the door shut and went to check on Braya in her mom's room.

There she was, a bump in the middle of their mom's bed. Her empty crib abandoned in the corner. Their mother was on the lookout for a second-hand bunk bed so she could move Braya into Bud's room. Until she found one, this was where she slept. As Laurel's eyes adjusted to the dark, she could make out her sister's round cheeks. Strands of fine hair that didn't quite reach her shoulders stuck to the drool around her mouth. Laurel tried to brush them away, but her hair had dried to her skin. She climbed on the bed and kissed her instead. Heat rose from Braya's body. Laurel closed her eyes and hovered with her lips pressed to her sticky hair for so long that she wasn't sure if she was trying to give something or take it away. A hitch in Braya's breathing. A pause, then a sudden, wheezy inhale. Laurel sat back. She watched her little sister until her soft breaths resumed their steady rhythm, then she pulled the blankets up, tucked them in tight around her and crept out of the room.

A cupboard banged downstairs and Horsey laughed, muffled, as if she had a hand over her mouth. Laurel found her and Andrew in the kitchen with a pot of water on the stove. "Shh! What are you doing?"

"Boiling spaghetti." Horsey clapped another hand over her mouth and bent forward, the ends of her hair brushed the floor.

Laurel tried to shush her again but her *shh!* stuttered into a laugh. She bit her lips to contain it.

"I love this stuff." Andrew whispered. He held up a block of foil-wrapped butter as he stirred the pot.

Laurel opened the fridge and surveyed the empty shelves. "We got butter, butter, and butter. Wait, wait, wait, no. There's options! Shortening. Margarine. And butter."

Horsey fell on her ass. She raised an imaginary bell and banged it. "Butter noodles! Come get your butter noo—" Her face contorted against the floor as she laugh-cried and silently kicked her legs up and down. She flopped onto her back.

"No." Laurel wiped tears from her own face. She tapped her friend. "Get up."

"What?"

"Get off the floor."

Horsey locked eyes with her. "Right. Sure." She scrambled back to her feet. "You okay?"

Laurel nodded.

"You sure?" Horsey called after her as she headed to the basement door. She nodded again and went downstairs. In the basement, she sat on the couch against the far wall. "Where did a couch come from?" Had she said that out loud? A bearskin rug was under her feet. She pulled her socks off and let the fur run between her toes. Her mom had shot that bear. There was a bullet hole in its neck. She searched the skin with her fingers. There, right next to a little shock of white fur. She poked her finger through it.

Brax sat on the couch next to her. Where was Jason?

"My eyes hurt. I think I'm allergic to Furry Lewis."

"Who?" Brax ran his finger across her eyes. "You're all puffy." He placed a hand on either side of her head and kissed each of her eyelids.

Laurel gripped the blanket she was sitting on and twisted it into her fist. "Did you make a couch?"

"Is it comfy?"

She nodded and Brax pulled her down next to him. Cardboard buckled and crunched. He slid a hand under her shirt and up her back, his face grew bigger as his lips landed on top of hers. Her head spun. Her stomach lurched. "I got to get up," she said into his mouth. "I need air." Laurel pushed at his chest, but he pinned her against the boxes. His hands squeezed her breasts. She pushed harder. "I got to . . . I can't . . . Stop!"

"Come *on*." His weight pressed into her pelvis.

The basement door opened and Horsey giggled down the stairs. Laurel shoved Brax and he sat up, red-faced and panting. He caught her hand and squeezed it. "Sorry," he whispered. "I'm sorry."

"I have to get up. I have to . . . I have to clean this place up." She picked the bottles off the table and stuffed them in the beer box. Papers littered the tabletop. Tobacco. Ashes. "Mom'll be home soon."

"Maxine won't care. Seriously," Brax said.

"You should go now. You too." She locked eyes with Andrew and his forkful of noodles paused mid-air. Butter dripped into the bowl. "Horsey?"

"Okay." Horsey set her bowl down. "Time to go." She clapped her hands. "Everybody out! Come on."

Laurel stomped upstairs and got a garbage bag to clear away the mess.

SIXTEEN

The prefect gig gave Laurel an opportunity to get her homework done. It was the only chance she had, now that she watched Bud and Braya after school. Horsey was there so often it was like she had decided to move in and people hung out in her basement all weekend long. It didn't seem to matter if her mother was home or not. Maxine let them pile downstairs. There was a CD player, a TV, and a VCR in the basement now. Compliments of Brax who was usually the first to arrive. He played AC/DC and Megadeth and Anthrax. It was like his new home-away-from-home. The box couch was piled high with blankets and pillows, and when no one else was around, she and Brax curled up on opposite ends and worked their way through his stack of Bruce Lee movies. As annoying as the movies were, they didn't bother her as much as his taste in music.

"Have you seen this one before? *Fist of Fury?*"

Laurel shook her head.

"Watch this part. See that? That's the one-inch punch." Brax slammed his fist into his palm. "One inch and he knocks a guy out."

"That guy just fell." Laurel adjusted her pillows so she could lie back and brace her feet on the wall. "It's called acting."

"No, no, he can do that though. The one-inch punch. He's won championships with that move." Brax turned back to the movie and pulled her legs down in his lap, worked her calf muscles.

She flinched, but he caught her leg and held it.

"It's just a massage. Come on, I like to keep my hands busy."

Laurel left her legs in his lap, and after a while, relaxed.

"Can I show you where it really feels good?"

She made a face at him.

"No, no, I don't mean that, but there's a spot. Let me show you." He raised his hands in the air, a gesture of innocence. "I can show you right here. I won't even move. I'm not trying to take your clothes off or anything."

Laurel lifted a shoulder.

"Okay." He grinned, raised her leg and reached for her crotch.

She squirmed away from him.

"No, no, just wait. Wait."

He touched a finger to the seam of her jeans.

"It's right here. Well. Let me . . ." He lifted her leg higher, ducked under it, so that her calf rested on the back of his neck. He found the spot he was looking for and rubbed with his thumb. A shiver ran up Laurel's abdomen. She hesitated, then let him do it a moment longer before she twisted away and pulled her leg back down.

"Yeah?" he said. "Feels good, right?"

Laurel shook her head. Chewed the edge of a fingernail.

"All the girls like that spot."

She adjusted a cushion under her hip and watched the screen for Bruce Lee's one-inch punch.

The next time Laurel and Brax were on the couch, Maxine came downstairs. "What are you watching?"

"*The Game of Death.*"

Her mother raised her eyebrows. "Sounds good." She crossed her legs and pulled her housecoat snug across her chest. "You got a cozy spot down here." She rocked a little, like she sat on a La-Z-Boy instead of a beef bucket.

Laurel and Brax watched the movie in dead silence. It was about halfway through when Maxine finally got up. She adjusted the belt of her housecoat around her waist. "Well, that's enough of that. I should get Bud to bed." On her way out, she did a ninja pose in front of the TV. "Hi-ya!" She chopped the air. "Don't pause the movie on my account."

As soon as she disappeared, Brax pulled Laurel's legs into his lap and started his massage. After he worked her calves for a few minutes, he lifted one of her legs, just a bit, and looked questioningly at her. Laurel stared at Bruce Lee dancing around in an orange jumpsuit and making praying mantis hands at his opponent, Ji Han-jae. Brax ducked his head under her leg and rested it across his shoulders. He reached for the spot and continued his massage. On screen, the fighters circled each other. Bruce Lee dove in and landed two sharp jabs to his opponent's face. Ji Han-jae caught him by the forearm and flipped him on his head, twice.

The feeling in Laurel's abdomen mounted and travelled up through her body. The two men railed on each other until Bruce Lee caught Ji Han-jae by the wrist and shoulder, and threw him across the mat. Brax's thumb pressed firm into the denim. Laurel pushed him away, squirmed onto her side and blinked at the TV.

Bruised and sweaty, Bruce Lee punched his rival in the gut, lifted him up like a piece of cut wood, and brought his back down *crack* across his knee.

Brax tried to lift her leg again, but the basement door opened and her mother shouted downstairs. "Friends are here! I'm headed out for a bit anyway."

Laurel kicked him away and sat up. "Okay!"

Brax squeezed Laurel's calf as Horsey, Jason, and some girl Laurel didn't know tumbled into the basement.

People she didn't know showed up in the basement all the time now. Most bought hash from Brax and left again, but some stuck around until the place cleared out. It was a blur of people that came and went all weekend long. Laurel sat on the box couch and puffed a joint. Through the slow cloud of her exhale, she watched Andrew come downstairs with Jimmy.

Laurel sat straighter and handed the joint off to someone else.

Jimmy nodded at her but hung around Andrew. Horsey gave him a beer. She offered him a smoke, but he shook his head. Eventually, Brax left to meet up with someone outside and an empty space opened up next to Laurel on the box couch.

"Hey," she said when Jimmy sat down.

"Hey." He picked at the label on his beer bottle. "So, this is what you're up to these days."

"What else?"

He shrugged. "Better than sampling Horsey's homebrew I guess."

She remembered doing that, years ago, out in Horsey's shed. Their first taste of alcohol. Moonshine they slurped out of a ladle. Laurel laughed but avoided eye contact.

He tried to look into her face. "Want to go outside? Get some air?"

She stood and held out a hand. He took it and his tall frame unfolded from the couch.

It was the beginning of June and still the night was chilly. They sat on the front step and Laurel pulled her coat down as far as she could to create a barrier between her jeans and the concrete. "Maybe we could sit in the truck."

"Yes! Please." Jimmy jumped up and blew into his hands. They climbed inside the truck, parked in the driveway waiting for her mom to sell it for parts.

The truck smelled of ashes and a stale evergreen air freshener that hung from the rear-view mirror. They jumped and twitched as they tried to sit on the chilly vinyl seat.

"It's colder than I thought," Jimmy said. "I'd offer you my jacket, but I think I'd freeze to death."

Laurel had grabbed a sweater that looked much warmer than his jean jacket.

"Maybe some body heat?" Even in the cold, Jimmy blushed. "I didn't mean . . ." He shifted and his knees bumped the steering wheel. "Just, it might help."

They shimmied around until Jimmy leaned his back on the door and Laurel rested against his chest. Her body curled around the gearshift that speared up from the floor. Jimmy shivered and squeezed her coat. "This is actually pretty damn comfortable."

"It is."

Someone walked past and Jimmy turned his head to watch as they receded past the ten-plex. His body shook as he laughed. "We probably look pretty strange."

"They think we're making out."

"We should rock the truck," he said. "Really get people talking."

No one in the Crown would give a shit, but she didn't say that. Instead, she just laughed. She searched for something else to say, but her head was as cloudy as the basement, hot-boxed.

"What?"

"Nothing. How's the farm?"

"The same. Quiet. Andrew's never around anymore, or Horsey."

"They're always here. Why are *you* here?" She looked up at him. "Tonight, I mean. Do you hang out in Stephenville much these days?"

"Nah. Andrew picked me up. I guess I wanted to see what everyone did all the time."

"This is it." Laurel wanted to ask if his parents knew he was on Royal Avenue, at the Crown, with her. But she knew they didn't. They'd never allow it. "You should come around more often."

"Oh yeah? Maybe I will."

"I won't hold my breath."

"What do you mean?"

"Nothing."

"What's wrong?"

"Nothing. Really." Laurel watched her breath frost in the air. The windows of the truck grew steamy around the edges. She stuck a finger in the tape deck to see if anything was in there.

"So," Jimmy said. "Brax Randall, hey?"

Laurel stiffened. "What about him?"

"You and Brax."

"There is no me and Brax. He lives next door. Right there." She pointed at the door adjacent to hers.

"Good." Jimmy nodded. "Not that he lives there. But that you and he aren't . . . don't . . . I mean, I can't even picture you and Brax."

"No." The word came out in a huff. Laurel's legs felt uncomfortable and she stretched across the seat. Jimmy squeezed her again, so gently she could barely feel it. He moved her hair out of the way with his nose and rested his head against hers. They stayed like that for a long time and she let her eyes close. She finally felt warm.

Jimmy said, "So, you're good?"

"Huh? What?"

"I just—"

"Why wouldn't I be good?"

"Just since . . ."

Laurel sat up and disentangled herself. Her knee hit the gearshift and she felt the cold metal through her jeans. "Since *what*?"

"You know."

"I have no fucking idea."

Jimmy shrugged and looked away. "Just, since . . . moving to Stephenville."

Someone banged on the truck door. Two loud blows. Laurel jumped and Jimmy twisted around.

"What's going on?" Brax cracked the door open.

"Fuck off, Jimmy." Laurel bounced across the seat, opened the passenger door, and climbed out.

"What the hell do you think you're doing?" Brax scowled. Jimmy climbed out of the truck, but Brax grabbed his coat and hauled.

Jimmy stumbled.

"This guy bothering you?"

"No, he's just my cousin from Woods Road." He wasn't her cousin, not even close. Jimmy's family had moved to Woods Road from Ontario when Jimmy was seven, looking for what, Laurel didn't know. The joy of rural life on a goat farm? Peace and fresh air and open, starry skies?

Brax gripped him by the shoulders and pushed him up against the side of the truck. Laurel shouted. Brax scowled into Jimmy's face, then let go with a shove.

Jimmy staggered away from the truck. "No you and Brax?" He caught his balance then strode down Royal Avenue without looking back. He shoved his hands in his pockets and faded into the shadows between street lights.

Laurel flipped her cigarette around to light another one off the cherry.

"You're an animal!" Jason said. "Look at you. A chain smoker!"

Brax passed her a joint. Laurel accepted it and Jason rocked forward on his beef bucket, eyes like paper cuts.

Laurel puffed hard on the joint, then on the cigarette. Jason fell from the bucket and writhed with laughter. He was the only one still there with her and Brax. A party up on base had called the rest of the kids away—even Horsey and Andrew were gone. Laurel had forgotten about the girl Jason came with until she clunked down over the stairs. Lana, that was her name. Lana stood at the bottom of the steps and wobbled. "You ready to go?"

"You don't look so hot," Brax said.

Lana looked like she was about to throw up.

Jason hauled himself up from the floor. "Let's go. You guys coming?"

"I can't." Laurel pointed at the ceiling. "Babysitting."

"Right." Jason shook his head. He opened his pack of smokes, took one out and handed it to her. "For later."

Brax sat back on the couch as Jason and Lana disappeared upstairs. "So," he said. "Want to watch a movie?" Laurel picked up the empties that littered the basement and put them in boxes. They had a pretty big collection of cases going. "What are you doing?"

The window wasn't even open. She went over, shoved it open—their room with a view—then picked up a pillow and waved it around until she felt dizzy.

Brax grabbed her. "What are you *doing*?" He pulled her up against him and she hung limply in his arms. He guided her to the couch and sat her down on the boxes. He sat next to her and kissed her neck. His mouth travelled to hers, and as he kissed her, his weight pushed her down. Laurel closed her eyes. Her head spun as his hands roved up and down her body, then one slid inside her pants. Brax's fingers bumped and prodded around inside the tight spaces of her underwear.

"Don't."

He tugged at her jeans, until he wedged them down to her thighs.

Laurel bent her knees so he couldn't haul her pants down any farther. "Don't."

He let her pants go, but his hands continued to explore. His knuckles grated the bones of her pelvis. She shifted away. The edge of a box ground into the base of her spine. Brax gripped her knees and pushed them up.

"Come on," he said. "Just once."

Brax pushed her knees toward her chin, exposing her, like a baby about to get its bum wiped.

"Just once, I swear." He twisted around and pulled his own pants down.

She thought he meant he would put it in once, just once, to feel what it was like, and take it out again. Then he would stop and it would be over. It might not even be so bad. At least, not as bad as the hard knuckles of his fingers grinding her pubic bone.

She relaxed a little and let her knees come up to her chest.

Brax pushed into her.

It didn't hurt. Horsey told her it would hurt, but what she felt most was a cramp in the back of her knees as his weight crushed her. He wrenched her knees to one side and tried to push in deeper.

Laurel tried to move her legs but he held them tight, her body twisted at the waist. The fog in her head suddenly cleared. His face sharpened into focus. She braced both hands on his shoulders and shoved, but he was a solid wall of muscle. The air in the basement was thick with smoke, and the smell of beer and sweat. Laurel whacked his jaw with the heels of her palms. "No."

Brax looked down at her and smirked. Flicked a curl from his eyes.

Laurel let her knees fall to the side.

He leaned forward to kiss her.

She clenched her hands into fists and snapped her head up. His nose crunched against her forehead.

Brax jumped up with his hands over his face. "What the fuck!" Blood poured down his chin and dripped to the floor. "You broke my nose! You fucking bitch!" His pants fell halfway down to his knees. His penis flounced behind his T-shirt.

Laurel hauled up her jeans and redid the button. "You have to go."

Brax kept one hand to his face and tried to pull his pants up with the other.

"Go. Now!" She got up and waved her hands at him, shooing him.

"Fuckin' fuck!" Brax held his pants to his waist and made for the stairs. Blood dripped as he pounded up the steps. Laurel followed him to the porch. He paused to shove his feet into his boots, but she kicked them out the door. "FUUUCK!" he shouted as he chased after them in his socks. She slammed the door and locked it. Laurel looked at her hands. They were clean, but specks of bloods stained her shirt. Brax cursed and stomped around outside until his apartment door smacked shut. The walls rattled.

She pulled her shirt off over her head and balled it up. Tied it in a garbage bag. Then inspected the floor for drops of blood. She crawled from the porch to the basement door, wiping each drip. Then she worked her way downstairs. Checked the steps. The walls. The rail. She examined every surface from different angles, tilting her head, letting the light catch on changes in texture. Laurel made her way down to the basement, where she scrubbed the cement on her hands and knees, back and forth from the stairs to the box couch. Again and again. The blanket in a heap on the floor was stained too. Laurel stuffed it in the garbage bag, along with her shirt, and tied the bag closed in triple knots. She crawled around on the cement, scanning for spots one last time. Just to be sure.

SEVENTEEN

Maxine shook her awake early the next morning. "What the hell, Laurel?" She yanked the blankets off the bed.

Laurel groaned and reached after them, head pounding. Next to her, Horsey rolled over to face the wall.

"There's puke all over the house!"

"What . . . ?" The blankets sat in a heavy pile on the floor. Laurel tried to tug a bedsheet free to cover herself.

"Outside!" Her mother smacked her bare thigh, then went and opened the bedroom window. "Look."

"Laurel puked out the window." Horsey's back shook with laughter.

"I did not." Laurel rolled out of bed and stuck her head outside. The cold air soothed her face. She closed her eyes and stuck her head out farther.

"Well?"

She looked down at the brick siding. Vomit fanned out from the window in streaks. "That wasn't me."

"It was totally you." Horsey turned back over, covered her shoulders with the thin sheet.

Laurel couldn't remember being sick, or going to bed. But she remembered Brax. His weight on top of her. The crunch of his nose against her forehead.

"Are you all right?"

She folded her arms across her chest. "It wasn't me."

"Oh, for God's sakes." Her mother put a hand to her head. "I can't deal with this right now. Get up." This time she gave Horsey a sharp whack on the thigh.

"Ow! Jesus."

"Follow me." She left the room, then waited in the hallway, toes tapping, as Laurel pulled on a sweatshirt and Horsey dragged herself to her feet. The girls followed her downstairs. Bud sat at the coffee table eating a bowl of cereal. He looked up as they passed the living room. Braya was splayed on the floor with a gummy-looking toy shoved in her mouth.

In the kitchen, Maxine lifted the kettle off the stove. "Take those." She indicated a stockpot and saucepan, shuddering on the back burners as they steamed. "Come on."

Laurel chose the stockpot. They carried pot after pot upstairs and poured boiling water out the window, splashing the brick siding until the dried puke softened and washed clean. Horsey let her pot clatter to the floor and collapsed on the bed. Laurel curled up next to her. Her mother barked out a laugh. "You're not finished."

Downstairs, her mother opened the basement door and the smell that wafted up from the bowels of the apartment almost sent Laurel running to the bathroom. Horsey coughed and cleared her throat. Laurel gripped the rail and took slow, shallow breaths as she descended. Her mother turned the light on at the bottom of the stairs. Laurel and Horsey crowded behind her and took in the wreckage. Beer bottles. Ashes. Cigarette butts. A pizza box with mouldy crusts. Papers and tobacco scattered across the encyclopedia table. Open tinfoil with scraps of pot. Vials of hash oil scraped clear to transparent green. Bent bobby pins.

"I knew you were smoking down here. Maybe having a few drinks, but this?" Her mother shoved a garbage bag into Laurel's chest, then Horsey's. Horsey grunted and stepped back. She lowered her gaze to the floor. Maxine crossed the room and pushed the window open. "This is out of control. *Way* out of control." She glared at the book table. "You got an hour. Clean it up." She stomped back upstairs. "I want it spotless."

Laurel picked through the debris on the table. "I don't know if I can do this."

"I can't." Horsey sat on the box couch and flopped to one side. She folded a jacket someone had left behind and tucked it beneath her head. "Get me a smoke."

"There's not much. A couple of butts."

"Perfect."

Laurel pinched a filter between her fingers, lit the burnt end and passed it over.

Horsey took a puff. She coughed, chuckled, then smoked the rest of it.

"There's no way I puked out the window." Laurel took Horsey's garbage bag from her and flicked it open.

"Nah." Horsey dropped the butt in a beer bottle. "Must have been that missus with Jason. Hannah. Rihanna. Banana. She was such a state. She showed up at the party too. Laurel! Be glad you didn't go to that party." Horsey put both her hands to her forehead.

Laurel brushed the mess on the table toward the open mouth of the bag.

Horsey pointed. "Save the butts." She sighed and pushed herself to her feet. "This is going to hurt. Real bad. Like, I might die."

The back of the painting was stained with ashes and oil smears. The book on top equally soiled and with charred corners where someone had idly burned it. Laurel filled a beef bucket with soapy water while Horsey picked up beer bottles, slow and long-armed, and dropped them into their corresponding cases. In the past month, the box couch had grown in size, each end extended by cases stacked up and hidden under blankets. Laurel carried the bucket over to the table and scrubbed at the mess, but the wet rag only ground ashes deeper into the fibres. The back of the painting, what Laurel had thought was some kind of wood, was dense cardboard and the harder she scrubbed the worse it looked.

Horsey peeled the blankets from the end of the couch and added new cases to the stack.

"No." Laurel dropped the encyclopedia on the floor and lifted the painting off the base. "That thing's being dismantled."

"I love our couch."

"This all has to go." She shoved the painting behind a plastic bin and left it jammed up against the wall, more or less where they had found it in the first place.

Horsey stood back when Laurel hauled the blankets off. "You okay? I don't think your mom—"

"I'm fine." Laurel opened box flaps until she found one with the encyclopedia, then grabbed two volumes in a death grip, carried them over, and slid them inside. "It's just, yeah, way out of control." She returned for two more books, then again, until the table base was gone and the boxes were full. Rows of rich burgundy spines from one end to the other. She folded the flaps and closed them up.

Horsey swept the floor while Laurel took the couch apart, box by box. When only cases of empties were left, she covered them with a blanket and threw the rest of the blankets in the wash.

"Hey." Horsey scrunched her nose and sniffed. Her eyes grew wide. "Your mom's cooking."

They raced upstairs. Her mother had made bacon, eggs and toast and was plating it. Bud kicked his legs back and forth under the table and Braya fisted scrambled eggs into her mouth.

"Maxine!" Horsey gave her a hug from behind and kissed her cheek. "You're the best."

"There's coffee."

"Oh my God."

"How's the basement?"

"Clean." Horsey spread her hands. "Spotless."

"Good. That's what I thought."

Laurel piled up her plate and sat at the table. "What's up?"

"I can't cook breakfast for my favourite girls?" Her mother poured a cup of coffee and set it next to Laurel's elbow.

"You *can*, but what's going on?"

"Tina's coming." She poured another cup for Horsey. "Thought you could use some energy to help me clean the rest of the house."

Laurel groaned and picked up her coffee.

After breakfast, Laurel helped her mother clear away the table and dropped dishes into the sink. Horsey called her mom to pick her up. She didn't want to be around for Tina. It was just as well—Laurel and her family had to put on a good show for the social worker and Horsey wouldn't know how to play along. It was just one day. One day acting like they were a normal, happy family. One day alone together, pretending they were fine. Horsey sang out, "See ya later," as she disappeared out the door. Laurel picked up the towel to dry the dishes her mother washed.

Tina sat on the couch with her notebook on her lap. She opened it and reviewed a page. Her review looked more like a way of getting comfortable than an actual memory refresh. It's not like she could forget their family. Laurel, the girl who killed a man at the back end of Woods Road when she was fourteen. A man who happened to be her little sister's father. Braya sat in her mother's lap and sucked her fist. Bud sat cross-legged on the floor in front of them and Laurel perched on the couch, far away from Tina. Tina licked her finger and turned another page.

Over the course of Tina's visits, once every four months for the past two and a half years, her inquiry had plateaued into pretty much the same series of questions. She directed her questions at Maxine and Laurel and centred them on situations. *How's the money situation? How's the job situation? How's the situation at school?* Their answers now a recitation: *Fine. Good, good. Oh, great.* Bud chewed the inside of his lip until Tina made her inevitable last query. "And how's our little man?"

"Terrific." His usual gap-toothed response, but this time he insisted she meet Furry Lewis, their newest family member. Tina said that was a wonderful idea. Bud grinned and called for the cat. When she didn't come, he jumped up and looked all around the house. Tina closed her book and slid it into her satchel, then waited with her hands in her lap. "Fuuurryyy, pss pss pss!" Tina shifted on the couch and smiled from Maxine to Laurel. Braya, impatient with the whole process, bobbed up and down and head-butted her mother in the chin. "She must be outside." Bud opened the back door and yelled into the yard.

"It's all right!" Maxine shouted from the living room. "Tina can meet Furry Lewis another time."

The couch creaked relief when Tina stood. Laurel got up and waited for Tina to lead the way past the coffee table. Her mother set Braya down and the three of them followed the social worker to the porch.

"Wait! You need to meet Furry." Bud shoved on his shoes and went outside. He left the door open as he stomped around the backyard and smacked a tin of cat food with a spoon. His shouts grew frantic. "Jesus Christ, Furry!"

The sides of Tina's mouth twitched downward.

"Sorry." Maxine wrung her hands together. "I can tell him you had to go. You can meet Furry Lewis next time."

Bud came back inside. "I can't find that stupid fucking cat anywhere!"

"Bud! Watch your mouth! Apologize to Tina for your language."

Tina adjusted the bag over her shoulder.

Bud shoved past Laurel. He still had the tin of cat food and the spoon in his hands as he pounded upstairs to his room and slammed the door.

Maxine sucked in a breath and closed her eyes. "I'm sorry." She blinked at Tina. "I'll talk to him."

Laurel hunched her shoulders and shrank into herself.

"Maybe it's time I had a session with him one on one." Tina held the doorknob.

"That must be normal though . . . ? At that age? He's a good kid. He just . . . really likes that cat." She laughed. It sounded forced, but it was a laugh.

Tina stared at Laurel's mother for what felt like a moment too long, as if she was trying to process the word *normal* in relation to this particular family. "A session would be good." She adjusted her bag again and opened the door. Her chin bobbed as she said, "I'll set it up."

EIGHTEEN

"You can't come over this weekend." Laurel banged her locker closed and tucked her math book into the crook of her elbow. She had avoided Horsey all week. She had avoided everyone all week and spent recess time as well as lunch huddled at the back of the library. It was only now, on Friday, that Horsey seemed to notice.

Horsey made a face. "Why not?"

"I'm busy."

"Doing what?"

"Just busy. I got stuff to do." The flattened coil of her notebook pinched her arm as she stormed down the hall. She'd already missed homeroom and was getting later and later for math.

"What stuff?"

Laurel walked faster but Horsey easily kept up. "Just, stuff. Don't you have class?"

"I'm coming over. Stop being weird."

"I'm not being weird. I don't want you over, okay?" She said it a bit too loud and her voice rang in the empty corridor.

Horsey stopped. Sneakers squeaked. "What the hell is wrong with you?"

"Nothing." Laurel spun around. She lowered her voice to a hiss. "I don't want you coming over and screwing Andrew in my house anymore."

Horsey's mouth fell open, then she clamped her jaws shut. Her face twisted into an ugly expression. "Fuck you, Laurel."

"That's the only reason you come over anymore. Andrew's using you. And you're using me. For the same thing. To get fucked. So, fuck you." Her voice echoed.

Horsey shoved Laurel one-handed, then stalked off in the opposite direction. Her head jutted forward as if she couldn't get away from her fast enough.

Laurel carried Horsey's shove in the centre of her chest for the rest of the day. She thought about skipping off and going home, but she felt too heavy to leave the building and ended up back at her locker again and again, standing in front of it, surveying the halls when she had no reason to be there. At the end of third period, she finally spotted her at the far end of the corridor. Horsey, taller than every other girl and most of the guys, she claimed space as she moved. Everyone naturally bent out of her way. She never bothered with makeup. Never fussed with her hair. But her hair was wild with curls and her eyes huge and dark.

"Laurel?"

"What?" Laurel snapped. Mrs. Harding stood behind her. Her teacher frowned. "Sorry, I mean. What is it?"

"Do you have a minute?"

Mrs. Harding led her to an empty classroom and gestured for her to sit in the front row. Laurel squeezed into a chair as her teacher leaned her backside against the desk at the top of the room. "Your grades are slipping. I know you get some homework done in the library, because God knows you haven't been doing the prefect duties I assigned you."

Laurel folded her fingers together and rested her chin on the giant fist they made. She stared at her knees.

"Miss Best tells me you're skipping class. You're always late for homeroom and that's when you bother to make it all. She also tells me that she's talked to you about it, but her words aren't having any effect. Well, I didn't think that sounded like you at all. That's not Laurel Long, my library prefect. So here I am." She clapped her hands together in her lap.

Laurel let her chin sink behind her hands until her nose rested on her knuckles.

"You're a smart kid, Laurel, but exams are coming up. You'll need to hunker down and study. Next year's your senior year. This isn't the time to give up."

"I don't have any money."

"What?"

Laurel lifted her chin to her fingertips and looked at her teacher. "It's not like I can afford university or something."

"My girl, student loans will pay for everything: tuition, housing, food." She ticked each item off on a finger like it was as simple as that.

"Then I have to pay it all back. I'll end up worse."

"You have to pay it all back. Most of it anyway. But isn't it better to have the chance? Isn't it better to try?"

Laurel tiled her head down the steeple of her hands.

"I'm still paying off my student loans, but I have a job, a home that I love. And all of you to worry about." She spread her arms as if to encompass the whole school. "I'd do it all again if I could. Exactly the same. Well, I could have spent less money on beer in my first year, but besides that . . ."

Laurel shifted in her seat and forced a smile. "I want a job. I mean, a real job for the summer, not like . . ." She gestured in the general direction of the library.

"A real job that pays real money." Her teacher laughed. "Come by when I'm not on duty. I can help you with a resumé. That's no trouble. As long as you think you can get your focus back on school. Make that your priority."

Laurel nodded and bit the inside of her lip.

Mrs. Harding cleared her throat and leaned back on her arms. "I hear you're spending a lot of time with Brax Randall."

Laurel shook her head. "He's just my neighbour."

"Brax Randall's bad news. The worst kind of news. I highly, highly"—her voice rose several octaves—"recommend you keep your distance from *him*." Mrs. Harding stood up straight.

Laurel slid out of the desk. "Are there any prefect duties that I need . . . to . . ."

"Just make it to class, show up on time, and we'll take it from there. Okay?"

Laurel slipped back into the hall and headed to the library to eat her lunch.

Buses idled at the curb, spewing exhaust. At the back of the line, with the high school kids, Jimmy stood off to the side. He frowned and shook his head when he caught Laurel watching him as she hiked past, and pretended to be absorbed by something on the pavement.

Horsey picked her way down from the smoke hill. She would pass Laurel on her way to the bus. Laurel looked back at the school, as if she'd forgotten something, but Horsey would never fall for it. Laurel flopped out a wave at waist-level and slowed her pace. "Hey."

"Hey, what? Hey, Horsey, I'm sorry? Hey, Horsey, I'm an asshole? How can you ever forgive me?"

"I didn't mean—"

"Didn't mean what?" Horsey bent forward and leaned into Laurel's face. Laurel knew she'd be mad. She knew Horsey would need some time to cool off, but maybe this was it. Maybe she had crossed a line that couldn't be uncrossed. After everything with Rick. After everything with the move. And the babysitting. And the no food. Maybe all Laurel had to offer was a scummy basement where you could do whatever the hell you wanted. Maybe they were done.

Laurel took a step back. "Nothing. I didn't mean . . . I didn't mean anything."

"Hey!" Brax slip-slid down the dirt hill in a T-shirt. He raised his hands as he approached them on the sidewalk, stopped and flicked a finger under his nose. "Nothing broken. Thought you'd like to know. Just a bloody nose."

"You gave him a bloody nose?"

"Oh yeah." Brax bobbed his head. "A bad one."

"No, I—"

"No harm done though. I'm not mad." He fake-punched Laurel in the arm.

"You're out of control, Laurel. Like, seriously fucking homicidal."

Horsey marched off and joined the last of the kids boarding the bus. She gripped the open door and swung inside. The door whooshed closed and she was gone.

"That's harsh," Brax said, "I wouldn't say homicidal. I get bloody noses all the time. I'm prone to them. I mean, you're just a shrimp."

"Go fuck yourself, Brax."

He laughed, high-pitched and exaggerated. "Go fuck myself?"

"Go. Fuck. Yourself."

"Everything okay over there?" Mrs. Harding's arms swung half-moons as she strutted down the sidewalk in her thick heels.

"We're fine!" Brax shouted.

"You're not supposed to be on school grounds. You've been expelled for the rest of this school year." She pointed a finger up at the smoke hill, her cheeks flushed. "If I catch you down here again, harassing our students—"

"I'm not—"

"I'll call the police." She pushed a finger into his chest. Brax looked at the finger like he wanted to grab it and bend it backwards until it cracked. He jerked his head to one side, shook it off, then headed back up the smoke hill.

Mrs. Harding turned to Laurel. "You all right?"

"Yeah."

She puffed out a breath. "Oh! I get so mad!"

"Me, too." Laurel turned and continued across the lot, then paused. "Thanks."

Mrs. Harding waved and headed back down the line of school buses as they pulled out of the loop.

Laurel crossed her arms over her chest as she walked home. She spotted Bud in the distance trotting toward Royal Avenue, but she continued by herself to the ten-plex. The shared front step for apartments five and six was exactly as wide as it had to be. Grey cement from one end of her door to the other end of Brax's door, without an inch to spare on either side. She stood on the step, rested her forehead on the glass in the screen door and sighed a heavy cloud of condensation. Stamped her foot. Stamped it again. Groaned deep in her throat, then let it out. "Aagghhh!" She stepped back and flung the door open.

The fresh paint smell had long ago faded into the general musk of the building. Braya was waiting to be picked up at apartment one, but Laurel dropped her bookbag on the floor, hauled off her boots, and ran upstairs to her mom's room. It was empty, of course. Bed unmade. Clothes heaped on the floor. Laurel stepped over a T-shirt tangled in a bra and crawled into bed. She hauled the covers over her head, curled onto her side and breathed the warmth of her own breath. When she ran out of air, she wiggled and made a hole in the blankets for her mouth.

Downstairs, the door cracked open. It closed, then opened again. Laurel dropped the covers from her head.

"Laurel?" Feet scuffed up the steps. Her mother walked past the open doorway.

Laurel sat up. "In here."

Her mother spun on her heel. "What are you doing in here?"

"I just . . . I had a headache."

"Oh." She leaned against the doorframe. "You should drink some water."

"What are you doing home?" Laurel swung her legs over the side of the bed. Swallowed the dryness in her mouth.

"I . . . ah . . . got off early. Is Braya here? I can go get her."

"I was just about to."

"That's fine. You okay?"

Laurel nodded. "Just a headache."

"Okay." Her mother pursed her lips and left the room.

The blankets shaped a perfect oval where Laurel had been. She adjusted the covers, crumpled them up around the pillows until the bed looked the way it had before. She closed her mother's door, but it jammed and she had to tap the lock in the centre of the knob to haul it shut. Next door, Megadeth pounded to life. "Symphony of Destruction." Laurel rolled her eyes and ran downstairs. She met Bud in the porch.

"Where you going?" he asked.

She shoved her feet into her sneakers and pulled her coat out of the closet. "Not far. Mom's home. She's just gone to get Braya." Laurel shrugged into her coat and pushed outside. She passed the ten-plex, cut through the alley, and continued onto Main Street.

Home Hardware looked empty when she went inside. The store owner looked up from some paperwork on the counter. "Can I help you?"

"I'm just going to look around."

He stuck his bottom lip out when he nodded, adjusted his glasses and returned his attention to his work.

Laurel watched her reflection as it fish-eyed above her. She walked past the mirror and headed down the farthest of four quiet aisles. Baskets of nails. Screws. Nuts. Anchors. Bolts. Each basket marked with a paper label. The organization ended at a shelf stuffed with heavy cords. Bungee cables in every colour. Ratchet straps. Next to that, a carefully stacked triangle of round tubes. Laurel inched her way around the tubes and down the next aisle. This one filled with fuses, wires and lamps. Finally, in the next aisle, doorknobs, hinges, locks. She picked out a brass padlock. A latch sat in the plastic behind it and a little ring with two keys. They jingled when she shook the package. Laurel checked to make sure she couldn't see the mirror at the front of the store, then shoved the kit up under the elastic waistband of her coat.

NINETEEN

Food scanners beeped out of sync with each other, cash registers rang in totals and a cashier shouted across the store that she needed a void. Everyone buzzed with purpose, even the customers lined up with their grocery carts. Rodney, a familiar face, dressed in his Foodland uniform and red name tag, led Laurel up a tiny flight of stairs that opened into an office. He gestured at a chair pushed up against the far wall and told her Marge would be there soon, as if Marge was someone she should already know. The room was all desk. The top of it cluttered with coffee cups and papers. A ceramic mug with the face of a sailor stuffed with pens. Laurel navigated past, careful not to disturb the Post-its stuck to the sides or the notices tacked in layers to the walls. She sat down and surveyed the room as if the secret to working at a grocery store was hidden somewhere in the mess.

A woman who must be Marge charged in, broad as the barrens, coffee in hand, and immediately began to go through papers.

Laurel shifted in her chair.

"So." Marge opened a drawer. "Looking for a job are ye?"

"Yes. I—"

"You ever work before?" She pulled out a fistful of papers and flipped through them.

"I'm a library prefect at school. And I babysit at home." Mrs. Harding had insisted she include babysitting. She said it showed maturity. "And I've done some fundraising, in school." Laurel pictured the fundraising forms she handed back every Christmas with one line filled out. A single ornament purchased by her mom.

"I saw that." Marge held up Laurel's resumé, looked over the top of her glasses and read from the paper. "Hard working and determined. That it?"

Laurel picked at a hangnail.

"It's a hard summer for work, with the moratorium. You're bold, I'll give you that."

Laurel's dad had been a logger. Her family had never had any connection with the fishery. Its closure nothing more than white noise to their already hard summers, winters and every grizzled day in between.

"How about we start you off on a trial?"

"Yeah?"

"Next Saturday. Can you handle that? We can start you off on weekends. You can work more when school lets out."

"Yes. Absolutely."

"Okay. Go see Joselyn. Jos, we calls 'er. You'll find her in the break room. Tell her to write you into the schedule for weekends. Starting this Saturday. Go on." She waved the resumé at the door.

The metal chair screeched when Laurel got up. She nudged it back into place so it looked the same as it did before she sat down. "Ah, thanks."

"We'll see you next Saturday." Marge tucked herself behind the desk and searched for a spot to place her coffee cup.

At the front of the store, Rodney paced back and forth like he was on patrol. He was in motion, like everyone else, but he was the only one who didn't seem busy. Laurel made her way back to him. "Hi? Again. Ha."

Rodney clasped his hands behind his back and peered down at her.

"Marge told me to see Jos. Do you know where I can find the break room?"

He squinted through his eyebrows at the beige bricks next to the main entrance. A slim white door that she had never noticed before suddenly revealed itself. Laurel crept around customers and rattling carts and paused in front of a sign that read "Staff Only." She looked back at Rodney, but he was already on the move again. She squared her shoulders and pushed the door open. Two women and a man, all in uniform, played cards at a table. None of them looked up when she came in. Laurel pressed herself against the wall.

"Something I can do for you?" a woman with long grey hair said into her cards.

"Sorry. I'm looking for Joselyn."

"Jos. You found her."

"Marge sent me. She wants me . . . She wants you to write me into the schedule. Starting this Saturday."

Jos set her cards face down on the table and got up. She stared at a schedule tacked to a pegboard on the wall. Columns and rows filled with names and days. She ran her finger along a row, then paused and started over.

"It's your turn." The man twisted toward Jos, cards to his chest.

Jos counted across the columns under her breath, then ran her finger along another row. "By the Jesus!" She tore the schedule from the wall. "If that's not last month!"

The staff at the table chuckled.

"Wha?" Jos laughed, flipped the page over, then jabbed it back on the wall with a thumbtack.

"Here." She pointed at the last Sunday in June. "We'll start you on Sunday. It's not so busy. You'll do the following Saturday, if you works out. You'll train with Doreen here." She pointed a thumb at the other woman, who looked up at Laurel over the rim of her glasses. Laurel gave what she hoped was a formal nod.

"What's your name?" Jos sat back down and picked up her cards.

"Laurel."

"Right on, Laurel. We can work you to the bone over the summer. I'll write you in later when I finds a pen. We'll see you Sunday."

When Laurel got home, she found her mother on the back step. She sat with her knees up to her chin, cigarette in hand. Bud played hide-and-seek with Braya. He crouched behind an abandoned washer and moved from one side to the next as Braya peeked around the corners.

"You know what I'd like?" Her mother asked as she watched them. "A barbeque. This entire stretch of backyard and not a single barbeque. Or picnic table. Or swing set. Isn't that strange?" She exhaled a stream of smoke.

Maybe she'd buy her mom a barbeque, or maybe she would save every cent for school. "Mom? I can't babysit anymore. I got a job."

Her mother smiled. Then her head tilted back and she laughed, loud and hardy. She paused to puff her smoke. Laughed again. This time it sounded as thin and sour as the raspberry jam she used to make. "Well, I quit *my* job. Turns out we're better off on welfare, but I guess it's all right for you to work."

"I don't want to babysit at night either. Not all the time."

"Fine, fine. I get it. Don't worry about me. I'm just fine." Braya squatted in a patch of dandelions and Bud pretended it was hard to see her through the new growth. She giggled when he stomped past. *Braya? Where are you?* Maxine stubbed out her cigarette on the side of the step and dropped it in the dirt. "We're all fine."

Laurel was propped up on an elbow, working through math equations in bed, when her mother knocked on the door, three trademark taps, and opened it.

"You're in bed already?" Her mother folded her arms in her bathrobe. Rested her hip against the doorframe. "I know you said... But it's Saturday night. And... do you have plans to go out?"

Laurel stared hard at her. The latch she had screwed into the door hung open and the brass padlock dangled from a metal hoop on the wall.

"If you're just studying anyway..."

"Studying is *work*. Babysitting is *more* work. Getting up every day—*work*. But sure, go on out and have a good time." Laurel was determined to get her grades back up during finals. Mrs. Harding's disappointment had been crushing, and if university was a ticket out, she'd make sure she'd be able to take it.

"It's more like taking a break from all the work."

"Any sign of Furry?"

"No. Poor Bud. It's not even his cat. It might already have a home somewhere, but I can't say that to him."

"It's his cat."

"Yeah, well... we'll keep looking." Her mother backed out of the room. "I'll just be a couple hours."

Something clattered to the floor on the other side of her bedroom wall. Laurel flinched. "Fuck you, Mom."

Maxine whipped the door back open. "What'd you say to me?"

"I said, don't forget your key. And lock the door." Laurel turned back to her book and worked her way through a page of linear equations, problem by problem.

It was late, hours later, when someone banged on the screen door. Laurel sat up. She'd fallen asleep with her textbook open, the light still on. She shoved the book aside. Another bang. She leaned over and peered out her window, just in case her mother had forgotten her key. The top of someone's bleached-blond head peeked up at her from the step. Three more bangs. Sharp. Loud. *Bang! Bang! Bang!* "Laurel?" A woman's voice. Laurel sighed and dragged herself out of bed.

Lynne, from apartment one, stood on the step in a tightly belted trench coat. The synthetic fabric shone in the porchlight. Her lips, rivered with old lipstick, thinned when she said, "I think it's your cat." She pointed down the road, into the dark.

Laurel shoved her feet into sneakers and headed out in her pyjamas. Lynne's heels echoed down the driveway, then they sank into the ground as she cut across the grass toward a small lump on the corner of the road and the driveway of apartment one.

"Oh my God." Laurel rushed forward. She fell to her knees next to Furry Lewis. The cat sprawled on the pavement. Its belly heaved with quick intakes of breath. She tried to get her hands underneath its body, but Furry Lewis let out a long, low snarl.

"Poor thing," Lynne said, hovering close to her. "Must have took off on a cat vacation and got hit by a car on her way home."

"Was Mom with you?"

"She was."

"Where?"

"At the Redwood."

"Can you go fucking get her please?" The Redwood was only a five-minute walk. In normal shoes.

"You want . . . ?"

Laurel tried again to slide her hands under the cat.

"Okay. I . . . I can do that." Lynne backed up, then clattered away down the road.

The cat hissed and growled. Laurel left the animal there and ran back to the apartment.

"What's going on?" Bud came out of his room rubbing his

face.

She rummaged around the hallway closet, clutching a towel. "Go back to bed."

Braya appeared behind him. Her little head didn't reach his shoulder.

"Now you got Braya up." Laurel closed the closet and ushered the two of them back into their room. "Sleep together if you want. Right here." She patted Braya's bottom bunk. "Go on. You need your sleep, or you'll be tired in the morning."

Bud frowned at her, but he crawled into bed. Braya scrambled up next to him. Laurel pulled blankets up to their chins. Quick kissed foreheads. "Night night."

She left the room at a slow, controlled pace, then ran downstairs. She found a box under the kitchen sink. An old banana box filled with glass bottles and jars that her mom liked to paint and place around the house with a dried flower stuffed in the mouth, or a thick, freshly cut cattail. She dumped the box and guided the bottles out onto the floor of the cabinet, as quietly as she could. Laurel dropped the towel inside. On her way back out, she paused in the porch, unsnapped the dustpan from the broom handle and added it to the box with the towel.

Furry Lewis hadn't moved. The cat's chest was still. She crouched close and laid her hand on its side. A slow rise underneath her palm. Laurel set the dustpan aside and slid her hands underneath its body. She held her breath and lifted the cat from the pavement, wincing when its head flopped sideways. Steadily, but quickly, she transferred the animal to the box on top of the towel. The cat kicked its hind legs and showed its teeth, then quieted. Laurel tucked the fabric around its fur and sat back. Royal Avenue stretched into the dark. A vehicle whispered down Main Street and illuminated the empty alley. Laurel picked up the box by the bottom and carried it to the apartment.

Bud waited with his face pressed to the glass. Laurel kicked the door and he pushed it open for her. "What's wrong with Furry?"

"Furry's okay." Laurel noticed specks of blood on the beige towel.

"Lemme see."

"No. Bud. I'll take care of Furry. But you don't want to see." She carried the box at chest level, down the hall and into the back porch.

"Let me see."

"No." She lifted the box higher.

"I want to see Furry!" He raised his voice and Laurel heard Braya thump down the stairs, one step at a time on her bum. Thump, *slide*. Thump, *slide*.

"Listen. You can see Furry Lewis later. In the morning. But right now, I need to fix her up. Okay? And I need to do that by myself. You need to go to bed so I can help Furry. Take Braya. Furry's hurt. And Braya shouldn't see." She clamped her lips shut, but her chin pulled and wobbled.

Bud took a step back. Laurel bit her lip as she turned around, blocking the entryway, and set the box on the floor. Her fingers were bloody, too. She pushed her little brother out of the porch and pulled the door closed. "Come on." Hand at his back, folded into a fist, she forced him forward down the hall.

"Fur Fur?" Braya came around the stairs.

"Back to bed." She herded them both up to their room.

Laurel promised Bud she would fix his cat. She promised him that first thing in the morning, he could see her. She promised that Furry Lewis would be up and running around and looking for a can of Fancy Feast. When Bud and Braya finally settled, she went to the bathroom and washed her hands. The bar of soap turned from white to pink as she rolled it over her palms. She closed her eyes and let Furry's blood rinse down the drain. Then she picked up the soap and washed her hands again.

Downstairs, Furry had moved a little inside the box. Instead of lying on its side, the cat had shifted partway onto its back, neck exposed, teeth clenched and visible. Its underside—the side Laurel had touched, the side she had lifted and held—was matted with blood. The towel underneath sopping and red. Standing there, Laurel couldn't tell if the cat breathed or not. She reached out a hand, but it shook as it hovered above Furry's body. Laurel lifted her face to the ceiling and tried to haul in a breath, but the tiny porch sucked her in and wouldn't let her back out.

The back door bumped her legs.

"Laurel? Are you on the floor? I can't . . ." The door bumped her again. "I forgot my key."

"Mom!" Laurel shot up and the door swung open. "Furry Lewis—"

A man, a stranger Laurel had never seen before, stood behind her mother. He had a six-pack and a half-grin on his face. He smiled at Laurel like he expected her to welcome him inside.

"Who's that?"

His smile faltered.

"Who the hell is that?"

"Laurel! We just came back for a game of cards."

"Right. Cards."

"Laurel, honey. We had a nice chat at the bar, and the bar closed, so—"

"You closed the fucking bar? Nice. What time is it?"

"It's late. I'm sorry. I didn't mean . . ."

"Is this your drag-off?"

"Laurel! It was just cards and a chat. That's all."

"Maybe I should go." Drag-off's mouth came way too close to her mother's ear when he spoke. Her mother nodded and he stepped into the porch, snaked an arm around her waist.

"Get out."

His head snapped up. An eyebrow raised.

"Get out!" Laurel's voice rose to an uncontrollable pitch. "Get out!"

"Go." Her mother pushed him, but he was already moving. He held out a hand as if trying to escape a feral creature as he backed down the steps.

Laurel shoved past her mom and slammed the door. "Furry Lewis is dead. She must have been hit by a car and Lynne . . . I think Furry's dead."

"What?" Her mother dropped her purse and went to the box on the floor. She touched the cat's belly and waited. "Oh no. No, no, no." She moved her hand to its neck, then laid it on the cat's side. Gently, she adjusted Furry Lewis's head so it rested into the towel. "Oh, honey. Oh, no."

Laurel moaned into her fist.

"Honey, I—" Her mother got up and gripped her by the shoulders. She tried to pull her close.

Laurel smacked her arms away. She twisted to look at the clock. "It's . . . it's three in the morning, Mom." She shoved passed her mother and into the kitchen. "Three a.m.!" Laurel yanked the clock off the wall. The screw that held it up came free in a spray of plaster dust. "What the *hell* is so important at the Redwood?" She fired the clock at the floor. It bounced and cracked. A sharp split from midnight to the bottommost apple seed. "Why weren't you here?" She stomped until the clock cracked in half and the arms fell off. "Why are you *never* here?"

"I'm so sorry."

Laurel's feet stung. She smashed the clock again and the centre peg stabbed into her heel and stuck there. "I had to deal with . . . *everything!* I had to—" She kicked and the clock flung free of her foot.

Her mother jumped back.

"Bud saw." Laurel kicked the broken halves around the room,

feet burning. "What do we tell Bud?"

"I'll tell Bud."

"What are you going to tell him? What?"

"I'll deal with it." Her mother held her gaze and didn't blink. "I'll deal with it. Okay?"

"Braya saw. Braya."

Her mother closed her eyes.

"She had to see that. A dead body." She spit it out. "There was so much blood. On the . . . on the floor. On my hands. I tried to clean it up but . . . No one should have to see that. No one. Not Bud. Not Braya."

Her mother took a step closer, reaching. "I'll tell Bud. And Braya. I'll tell them."

Laurel's mouth hung open but nothing came out. The room heaved away from her and she shrank to the floor.

"Shh." Her mother crept close. She crouched next to Laurel and touched her back. "Shh, shh, shh." Her mother's hands slid down to her tailbone, then up her shoulders. The heat of her palms reached Laurel's muscles. Her nerves. Her rocking slowed.

"What do we tell Braya?"

Her mother paused. She sighed long and deep. Moved her hands again, slower. "I don't know." She relaxed forward, stretched an arm around Laurel, and rested her head on the back of her shoulder.

Laurel straightened her legs. Flinched her mother off. "I don't know either." She pushed up from the floor. "No idea." Laurel stormed out of the kitchen and down the hall. At the bottom of the stairs she called back. "Maybe you'll find the answer at the Redwood."

TWENTY

In the backyard, Laurel helped Braya poke a fistful of dandelions in a jar. The jar tipped and Laurel dug a little hole in the ground, pressed the jar inside and packed dirt around it to hold it in place. Bud sat rigid on the step while his mother stroked his hair. Braya stood and brought him a bunch of stemless dandelion heads. He opened his palms on his lap and she dropped them inside.

Their mother had told them Furry Lewis was hit by a car and didn't make it. Laurel had listened in bed as they wailed. She'd rolled over and stared at the wall as they covered a shoebox with messages and drew pictures of their best memories of Furry. Her mother had dug the grave. Washed out a jam jar. Encouraged flowers. Laurel joined them just before she placed the box in the ground and they took turns pouring dirt on top of it until the hole was gone. When they stood back and looked at the raw patch of earth, Laurel reached for Bud, but he pulled away.

"Furry Lewis is still with us," her mother said on the step as she brushed Bud's cheek. "She'll always be with us." She tapped his heart. "Right here."

Bud nodded. He sniffed and pressed his lips together, but there was no help for it. His face crumpled.

In the basement, Laurel hauled the blanket down and counted twenty-six and a half cases of empties. Molson. Blue Star. India. And four clear strawberry cooler bottles. She stacked two cases on top of each other and lugged them upstairs to the front porch. Esso took empties, and it was only a short walk away, but it would take forever to cash in two cases at a time. She set her cargo on the floor next to her mother's flopped-over knee-high boots in the porch. She returned to the backyard, where her family had spent the full afternoon. The grocery cart she and Horsey had dragged home from Foodland was still parked next to the cement step. Laurel tugged it free from its resting place.

"What are you doing?" her mother asked.

"Cashing in empties."

Her mother blinked at her, then tore up another clump of flowers. The little patch of dirt invisible now under dandelions, dandelion heads, and grass.

The cart cut through the grass as Laurel pushed it to the front of the building. She rattled onto the driveway and Brax strutted out of his apartment with a girl. Blond hair, round-nosed. Brax smirked at Laurel, put his arm around the girl and they swaggered down the steps together. The girl muttered *slut* under her breath as they passed Laurel. Brax laughed his stupid smug laugh and said, "nice wheels." But besides that, Laurel got by unacknowledged. She parked the cart, transferred the two cases from the porch, then made six more trips to the basement. Beer boxes towered above the handle and the cart refused to move under the weight of the bottles. Laurel shoved with her back and shoulders until it shrieked and lurched forward.

She had to stop and shove with her back again when the cart landed lopsided in a pothole, but eventually she caught a good stride. Wheels turned with a shameless screech as the cart shuddered and clinked up the back road behind Main Street. She rolled alongside the gas station, parked at the entrance and carried cases inside two by two.

At first, Bud resisted Laurel's attempt at a movie night, but after she covered the coffee table with chips, soda and sour candies, he gave in and sat down to watch *The Lion King*. She sat next to him and tucked blankets around his knees. He shifted, rearranged a pillow, and settled a tiny bit closer to her than he had before. Maxine curled up on his other side and Braya squeezed her butt in between them.

Bud's eyes didn't leave the screen as he ate the entire bag of candy, one piece at a time. Furry Lewis had been in their lives for such a short while, maybe Bud would be okay. Crumbs fell from Braya's hands into her mother's lap as she stuffed chips in her mouth. She'd be okay, too. They were certainly better off without Laurel's friends in the basement all the time. One more year, and with a bit of luck, Laurel would head off to university. Her mother watched Bud as much as she watched the movie. She reached over and ruffled his hair, picked the empty bag from his lap and crumpled it up. Her mother would be okay, too. They'd all be okay. They had to be, because Laurel had to go. She couldn't wait to go.

Bud stiffened. Mufasa, the daddy lion, plunged backwards from a cliff, screaming his son's name as he fell. *Simbaaa!* Laurel jumped off the couch. She hit fast forward as the lion was trampled by a stampede of wildebeest in the gorge. Simba sobbed all over his dad's lifeless body in muted, rapid movements. "Should I turn it off?"

"Stop!" Bud's little spine arched. "I want to watch it."

"You do?"

"Stop," Braya said into her chips.

Laurel waited until the scene ended before she hit play. She wedged back into her spot on the couch, picked up the two-litre of soda and poured a glass full of pink fizz. The bubbles washed away salt from the chips and coated her throat with sugar. She coughed and tried to clear it, but the sweetness clung. Bud sniffed and Laurel looked over to see quiet tears slide down his face. She put her glass back on the table.

"I miss Dad." A forgotten nub of sour candy fell sticky from his mouth and his cheeks turned red as he sucked in his lips.

"Dad," Braya echoed.

"I know." Her mother's eyes welled. But her jaw set. She let her head fall back against the couch and stared up at the ceiling. "I know." In a jet stream of breath she said, "I do too." A sigh erupted from somewhere deep inside her. It grew louder and louder until she clamped her lips together and shut it off. She adjusted her bangs and turned her gaze back to the TV. Bud wiped his tears away and rested his head in her lap. Braya scootched around and settled her head next to his. Laurel swallowed. Tongue heavy. Saliva thick with syrup. The four of them watched the movie in silence as a lion prince, a warthog, and a meerkat danced around, slurped bugs and sang.

At bedtime, Bud said he wanted a family cuddle. They piled into the bottom bunk and their mother read a Mickey Mouse story. Pure silliness with zero emotion. Braya was asleep before the story was over, Bud not long after.

"It'll take him a while to get over Furry." Maxine moved Bud's hair off his forehead and Laurel thought she would get up then, but instead, she wiggled closer and curled around him. "I miss this. A big, old family cuddle. Someday, you'll all be grown up and gone. I can't even . . ."

Laurel shifted, her hip jammed between Braya and the wall. Outside, a car crept slowly down Royal Avenue. Rocks crunched under tires. "I'll probably go to university."

"Oh yeah?"

"I need to get my grades back up a bit. That's all. Mrs. Harding said student loans will cover everything."

"What'll you do?"

"What do you mean?"

"What will you study?"

"Oh . . . I don't know."

"I always liked biology, back in high school. I would have loved university." She closed her eyes and burrowed her face in Bud's hair. "It sounds . . . it sounds very far away."

Laurel drew her knees up under her sister's feet and rested her chin on top of her head. Corner Brook was only an hour away. Memorial University had a small satellite campus there. She could go, and still come back home whenever she needed. Laurel imagined herself walking the tree-lined streets of the city, enjoying calm, sunny days in the valley. "I'll visit."

Her mother nodded, a slight movement though the mattress. The room was quiet except for Bud's deep sleep-breaths and Braya's snores. Laurel and her mother two fetal-shaped bookends.

"Well. Goodnight." Her mother leaned in under the metal laths of the top bunk and pecked Laurel on the cheek. "I'm done with this day." She eased out of bed, tightened her housecoat, and shuffled out of the room, switching off the light before she shut the door.

Laurel blinked until her eyes adjusted to the street-light glow through the window. Bud and Braya cast in pale blue. Cheeks shiny. Eyes dark little hollows. A brush of lashes. She reached across Braya and pushed Bud into the space their mother had left behind. He flinched and muttered in his sleep, then folded into place. She shoved Braya closer to Bud, making enough room to roll onto her back. Stretched her toes to the bottom of the bed. Folded her hands across her chest.

Above her, a series of shapes came into focus. Drawings scratched into painted metal by other kids who had lain awake in this same bunk. Kids who had grown older and either held on to each other or let go and drifted apart. Straight-edged hearts. Stars. Sunbursts or snowflakes or asterisks. A jumble of initials. She reached up and traced them. The edges rough under her fingertips. Almost sharp.

PART FOUR
1997

TWENTY ONE

SEPTEMBER

The pay phone hung inside a booth at the end of All Girls West. The booth also held a bench, a fold-down desk, and a hard plastic binder that dangled from a metal cord with every phone book for Newfoundland and Labrador jammed inside. For the forty girls on the floor, the phone was the only means of communication with the outside world. Isolation that also signaled empowerment. The outside world could call in, but the caller had to be given the unlisted number and wait as the phone rang against the brick wall until someone bothered to answer it. Laurel's room was the closest to the phone booth, but she spent the first few days at Grenfell Campus in student loan lineups in the gym, lineups at two different banks, then back on campus and in line at the bursar's office to pay tuition. She waited until morning on the first day of class to use the phone. Laurel shoved the binder out of the way, sat on the bench and slid her phone card into the slot.

Her mother sounded groggy when she picked up the line. She yawned as she spoke. "You're up early." It was the first day of Laurel's new life. She had spent most of the night in her bunk, wide awake, staring at the ceiling. Bright white tiles, snug in cool metal frames, blinking down at her like a checkerboard of clean slates. "How's it going?"

"Good. It's going good."

"You all settled?"

"Getting there. How's Bud? And Braya?"

"Fine. Everyone's great. I got to get them up now for school."

Laurel explained the phone situation and waited for her mother to find a pen. She could picture her in her bathrobe rummaging through the clutter stuffed in her jewellery box, the dresser top, the bedside table, then giving up on the room and going downstairs to the kitchen, where she would open drawer after drawer until she finally settled for a crayon or a pencil with a cracked lead. Laurel gave her the number. "Put it on the fridge or something. Somewhere where you won't lose it. It's free to call me, but I have to pay to call you."

"Of course," she said. "I won't lose it."

Residence was arranged into two-person units. Laurel had a single room all to herself and shared a kitchenette and bathroom with her roommate, Haley, a girl from St. George's she'd only seen a few times. Haley's mom had spent the weekend somewhere in Corner Brook and whisked her off every morning to shop and lunch and walk the trail around the pond. A note scrawled on their message board indicated her mom had finally left. *Miss you already! Have a great first week!* Laurel's new keys jangled as she unlocked the unit.

"Hi!" Haley's cheer pushed her back into the hallway. Laurel blinked and tried again. The shared kitchenette had exactly enough room for two girls, a mini-fridge, and a small counter that held a toaster and microwave. Haley's ponytail bobbed as she made toast. "Want some? Mom's homemade jam. Raspberry. It's, like, the best."

Laurel's stomach clenched against the smell. She ran a hand over the front of her shirt. "No. Thanks." She let her fingers drum the bones of her chest.

"Seriously?" The word came out, sir-yus-ly? A St. George's accent, or Haley's way of expressing mild annoyance.

"I don't really do breakfast. Thanks though."

"Do you do tea?"

Laurel hadn't noticed the electric kettle crammed behind the toaster. "Yes, but I'm good. I'm just going to take a shower." She carried her towel and bottle of Finesse 2-in-1 into the bathroom. Pulled her T-shirt over her head and stepped into the shower. The pipes clanged when she wrenched open the tap and cold water blasted her in her face.

Thirty minutes later, Haley met her at the door, ready to go. "What's your first class?"

"Chemistry." She had chemistry, then math, then history, then English. She had no idea what courses she should do in her first year of university, so she'd basically replicated her last year of high school.

"Ugh, science. I'm in V.A. You know, visual arts? I think my first class is more of a meet and greet, with the whole group? I'm not really sure." She hopped a little as she shut the door behind them. "You're on the way though. I'll walk you."

"Great!" Laurel forced pep into her voice as Haley linked an arm through hers and pranced down the hall. "I miss home already, don't you?"

"Yeah, totally."

Haley beamed *Hi!* at every girl they passed and Laurel smiled along, even when her face started to hurt. Their residence wing was attached to the Arts and Administration building and Haley guided her through the doors and into the clamour of student lockers in the main corridor. A line of students in lab coats stretched along the brick wall and obstructed classrooms. Laurel tried to peek around them at the room numbers.

"That's not my class, is it? I don't have a lab coat."

"Do you have a class or a lab? I have no clue about sciences."

Laurel pulled her schedule from her bookbag and ran a finger down the columns as Haley hovered over her shoulder. "Chem. Room 324."

"That's upstairs. This way." Ponytail swinging, Haley led her to a wide stairwell that echoed with the marching feet of students Laurel didn't know or recognize. A thrill grew in her belly as she climbed. She clung to Haley and pinched her lips together to stop her grin from spreading across her face. At the top of the steps, Haley pointed. "You're that way, I think. I'm this way, in the Fine Arts Building. I can walk you if you want."

"I can find it."

"Okay. Happy first day!" Haley squeezed her hand, spun around and bounded off.

Laurel waved after her, then joined the flow of students headed in her direction. She sat at the back of every one of her classes. From that vantage point, she could watch the room as it filled with unfamiliar people and inhale the freedom of anonymity like fresh air. She didn't know anyone. And they didn't know her. They didn't know about Rick Warren. They didn't know about Brax Randall. They didn't know about the Crown, or the box couch, or the book table, or the basement. Every single one of them a clean slate. An opportunity for Laurel to reinvent herself. In English 1000, the last class of the day, Jimmy Patey ducked through the open doorway. He spotted her and headed straight to the back of the class. They sat at long crescent-shaped tables, seats attached by swinging metal arms, and Jimmy pulled out the seat next to hers.

Laurel stared straight ahead and watched as her professor wrote her name on the board, *Dr. Mary Hollis*.

"Small world," Jimmy muttered.

She shrugged. This was her world, and until two seconds ago, it had felt wondrously enormous.

"How you been?"

"Fine." Laurel opened her notebook and scribbled the date across the top of the page.

"It's good to see you."

"Sure."

Jimmy's chair creaked back and forth. He leaned in closer. "Why the hell are you like this?"

Laurel blinked at him.

"Why are you always so pissed at me?"

"I'm not pissed—"

Dr. Hollis stopped talking. A student in front of them turned around and glared. Jimmy sat up straight. Laurel pretended to write in her book. Their professor resumed speaking to the class. Laurel remembered Jimmy on that cold night in May, up against the truck, chin tucked into his neck as Brax snarled in his face. She'd told him to fuck off. Called him her cousin. Laurel wrote *Sorry*, and slid her book over. Jimmy flicked a glance at her note, slid the book back.

He rested his forearms on the table. His elbow a bony right angle as he leaned forward. Wrists as thin as hers. Soft freckles along narrow triceps.

She wrote: *It's good to see you, too.*

He ignored her and kept his attention on the board. Laurel pushed his book aside, replacing it with her own, then fidgeted with her pencil. Dr. Hollis passed stacks of papers to students in the front row, told them to take a sheet off the top and pass them on. The handouts worked their way around the auditorium. Laurel reached for her notebook.

Jimmy's hand landed on the page and pinned the book to the desk. "All right," he said. "Just this once."

She raised her eyebrows and almost smiled as he gave her notebook back.

A dwindling stack of papers reached Laurel and another reached Jimmy. She took a class syllabus and traded Jimmy for the course introductions. They each took another page and sent the stacks off down their row.

A hush settled over Laurel when she left the clamour of the Arts and Administration building behind and walked down the empty residence hall. In the kitchenette, she gathered the few groceries she'd bought at Sobeys and carried them down to the lounge. Spaghetti noodles. Ragu with beef. A can of mushrooms. An onion. The lounge had two stoves, a fridge, cupboards and a long table for dining. It also had a floor-model TV with three comfy-looking couches arranged in front of it. Laurel dropped her supplies on the table and searched through the cupboards for a pot. She found cookware overhead that looked old and standard issue.

The lounge door slapped open and a girl bounded in. "Buffy, Buffy, Buffy, Buffy!" She squeezed past the couches and turned the TV on. "Do you watch Buffy?"

Laurel looked around, but there was no one else in the room. "Ahh..."

The door banged open again. This girl wore a headband with little black cat ears on it. "Are you looking for Buffy?"

The girl in front of the TV nodded excitedly. She had the remote pointed at the screen two feet away. "Uh huh."

"Channel 42."

She flicked faster through the channels.

Another bang. Another girl. "Buffythevampireslayer?"

Laurel didn't watch TV. They had two channels in apartment five and she'd only ever used them for babysitting purposes and movies. She stirred the noodles as girls poured up bowls of chips and piled onto couches. Cat Ears stuck a bag of popcorn in the microwave, then rummaged around the cupboards. "Are there any more pots?" she asked Laurel.

"Oh . . . I'm not sure."

She leaned in to see what Laurel was doing.

"I'm almost done with these."

"Are those your pots?" Her nails were long and pointy. "Are we supposed to bring our own pots?" The question was directed at everyone in the room.

One of the heads on the couch popped up and turned around. "I brought mine. Up there. Above the microwave."

Again, the door banged open. This time Haley shuffled in wearing a fuzzy bathrobe and matching slippers. "Please tell me that's the Space channel." All the heads nodded and Haley wrapped her fuzzy arms around herself. "Oh my God, I love you. I love you. I love you."

Laurel flashed a smile, but her roommate didn't notice. Haley jumped onto the nearest couch and squeezed herself between two other bodies. Before the door fully closed, someone else caught it and two more girls came in, both armed with blankets and pillows. "We're ready for BUFFFAY!"

The loaded couches erupted with laughter. Cat Ears dropped two Pop-Tarts in the toaster and rescued her bag of popcorn from the microwave. One of the Blanket Girls had a box in her hands. She dropped it on the coffee table and tore the flaps open. "There's cookies." She tossed a bag of cookies and a random hand shot up to catch it. "There's cheese." Another toss. "Crackers." Toss. "Those are the best crackers. Oh, oh, oh, and crack. Mom makes the best crack."

Laurel peered over. It looked like some kind of peanut brittle.

"It's basically graham crackers and butter. And chocolate. And peanuts."

Water bubbled over the sides of the pot and hissed on the burner. She flicked on the range hood and the fan rattled to life. Someone turned up the volume on the TV. Laurel pulled a wad of spaghetti out with a fork, snagged a noodle between her fingers, and popped it into her mouth. She carried the pot over to the sink and dumped the water out in a cloud of steam.

"There's a colander under there." Cat Ears flicked a finger and munched her popcorn.

"Thanks." Laurel wasn't quite sure what a colander was, but she finished draining the noodles with the lid held open at the edge of the pot, then put the pot back on the stove.

All the plates and bowls in the cupboards looked new and purposely bought. One set had cats on them, another the Eiffel Tower, another tiny stars. She could see her mother now, browsing around Walmart for a set of dishes with the perfect print to match Laurel's personality. Laurel dumped the sauce from the jar directly into her pot of noodles.

"Ahh . . . do you need a bowl?" Cat Ears slumped past with a plate of chocolate Pop-Tarts and her bag of popcorn.

"Nah, I'm good." She waited until the sauce bubbled, then wiped down the counter and stove one more time. Nobody had used the table, but she wiped that too, big wide swipes across the laminate. Finished, Laurel turned off the fan, took her pot of spaghetti and carried it back to her room.

TWENTY TWO

All Girls West transformed from a quiet sanctuary of study and primetime TV to a bubbling den of hormones and drinks on Saturday night. Music pooled into the hallway: Toni Braxton, Daft Punk, Smashing Pumpkins, and Aqua. Girls shouted the innermost details of their closets and stripped off in open doorways. Laurel weaved through them in her new Sobeys uniform and made her way toward her room where she could hear Great Big Sea spilling through the open door.

"Arrwoo! Arrwoo!" Haley shouted along to the music, a hoot that sounded like something between a dog's howl and a drunken whoop. "Laurel!" She raised a beer. "You have to come out with us!"

Cat Ears keeled over into the Blanket Girls and *Arrwoo*-ed out of sync with the song at an even higher pitch.

Laurel stood in the doorway and unzipped her coat. The smell of rotisserie chickens and baker's bread wafted from her body. Her left eye twitched with exhaustion. "Sure." She unclipped her name tag.

"Get dressed! Come ooon!" Haley pointed her fingers like guns and pulled the triggers. "Hey, hey, hey, above the knee, drinks for free!"

A shower and a makeover later, and Cat Ears showed her how to tamper with the birth year on her MCP card to use it as a fake ID. Hunched over Haley's desk in a hot-pink tank and super-short mini, looking as comfortable as if she wore flannel pyjamas, Cat Ears scratched at the number 9 with a razor and turned it into a 7, making Laurel twenty, instead of eighteen. Just before midnight, the five girls squeezed into a taxi. Knees bared. Laurel had managed a quick swipe with Haley's Gillette, but stray hairs on her kneecaps caught the traffic lights. She covered her knees so they wouldn't brush against her roommate, who was squished up against her in the back seat. Haley pumped her fist in the air and shouted their destination at the cab driver: "The Studio!"

The taxi pulled up at the entrance on Broadway. The double doors were heavy, wooden, and vault-like. The girls tumbled out of the car in a tangle of legs. Laurel passed her ID to the bouncer, but he barely glanced at the altered card. He raised an eyebrow and handed it back, as if by making the effort, breaking the law was her choice and he was just happy to do business with another college student. Lights pulsed and flashed. Bass thumped through the soles of her feet and scaled her spine. Haley's teeth flashed fluorescent when she shouted, "Come on!" She took her coat from her and disappeared. Laurel, in Haley's halter top and spandex skirt, scrambled after her, but the room opened up into a crowd of flickering bodies. She craned her neck toward the dance floor. Metal cages hung on either side of it, and inside them, short-skirted girls ground against the bars and each other. Suddenly, she wasn't sure if her floormates were ahead of her or behind. She looked back in the direction of the door and they swept her up on either side: Haley, Cat Ears and the Blanket Girls. They made straight for the bar.

"Tom Collins!" Haley nudged her elbow.

"Who?"

Drinks landed in front of her, one after the other. The girls snatched them up and sucked on straws as they headed to the dance floor. Laurel's drink hadn't arrived. "A Tom Collins?" She waved a finger at the bartender as if trying to order champagne for the table. He nodded and Laurel leaned in, urging him to hurry with the force of her stare. Lights pulsed as her floormates drifted away. Cat Ears' tank bobbed like a buoy into a sea of bodies and disappeared. Laurel tugged at Haley's skirt. It actually went past her knees, but Haley had folded it so it landed halfway up her thighs. She rolled it back down. A tall pink drink landed in front of her. "Thanks!" It tasted like syrupy lemonade.

Laurel dodged slow bodies on her way to the dance floor. Under the flashing lights, everyone bobbed like a beacon. She walked the perimeter with Cat Ears' top firmly in her mind. Haley's high ponytail. A crowd of girls pushed past and Laurel was shoved back. She stretched and leaned and tried to see over heads, then gave up and retreated to the bar.

The song didn't end. It changed a little, then a little more, until it thumped into a whole new song altogether, but her floormates didn't come back. Laurel had a second drink, and was partway through her third when a stubbly guy in an undershirt shouted at her in a cloud of hard rum. "Can I get you another drink?"

"They're free."

"Not in that skirt." He swivelled his empty glass. His bare, sweaty shoulder bumped hers. Laurel shoved off from the bar and went in search of a bathroom.

She threaded through the thumping, gyrating crowd until she found a hallway. The music changed into a muffled *whomp, whomp, whomp* as the hall turned and narrowed. It ended at a rusty metal door, propped open with a crushed beer box. Not the bathroom, but Laurel pushed the door open anyway. It opened to the outside. The air cool and damp on her bare arms. She recognized the circle of people standing behind the building. Not the individuals themselves, but their shape. Their slow movements. The dank smell of burning grass. She stepped closer. A girl with double piercings in her lip made eye contact, then looked away. A joint passed in front of Laurel. She tried to put her hands in her pockets, but she didn't have pockets, just a tiny slit in one side where she'd stuffed her cards. She folded her fingers in front of her ribs, cracked her knuckles, and took half a step closer to the circle. Three guys. Two girls, both with multiple piercings visible. The guy closest to her flicked a glance up and down her body. He wore a camel brown jacket, long, fuzzy on the inside, and almost classy for someone smoking a joint in an alleyway. "Where you from?" he asked.

"Stephenville."

The girl across from her made eye contact again. "You in school here? College? University?"

Laurel nodded and adjusted the straps of her halter top. Sequins folded over each other along the neckline.

"I've been in Stephenville. I almost got jumped at the 104." Camel Jacket exhaled smoke and offered her the joint. "Rough town, oh man."

Laurel took it and stepped closer. "Hash?"

He laughed. "I told you. Everyone in Stephenville smokes hash. Pot." He nodded. Sniffed. "You live up on base, too?"

"No." Laurel took one puff and handed the joint off, but another came to her from the other direction. She helped herself to a few hauls of weed before passing it to her new friend. "Downtown."

"You been to the 104?"

"Nope."

"Ahh. You're a good girl."

Laurel lifted her shoulders to her ears. "Sometimes."

He smiled and let smoke dribble from his lips as he offered the joint back to her.

"The other way."

He grinned wider and passed it in the other direction. "Vincent," he said.

"Laurel."

Laurel did shots at the bar with Vincent—salt, tequila, lemon—while he lost track of his friends and she kept watch over the dance floor for hers. The lights grew brighter. Sharper. Electric red and orange and yellow. People danced with their arms swaying over their heads, fingers fluttering. Vincent held her forearm and licked salt from her wrist. "What was in that?"

"What?"

"What did I smoke?"

Vincent shot his tequila. Slammed the glass down. Cringed into his lemon. He shook his head. "That shit's always laced." He grabbed her and pulled her away from the bar.

Laurel tugged free. "What do you mean laced? With what?"

"Nothing bad. Relax."

"What did I smoke?"

"I have no idea! Nothing bad, I swear. Just enjoy it." He guided her onto the dance floor. He'd shed his jacket somewhere and she felt the heat of his body as he moved close, arcing over her as he danced. He took both her hands and held them. Hips touching hers as he swayed.

Laurel scanned the floor. Bodies throbbing and jerking in brilliant, stop-motion flashes of light. Razor-sharp cheekbones. High, snubbed noses. Mouths opened in laughter. Teeth like static. No sign of Haley, Cat Ears or the Blanket Girls. She numbly copied Vincent's movements, in sync with the beat pounding through her muscles. He threaded his fingers through hers and raised her hands above her head. She looked up past his sharp cheeks. Squinty eyes. Up at a kaleidoscope of lights, swirling above like a portal to another world. All she had to do was reach. Higher. Taller. She spread her fingers, letting Vincent's hands go, and let them dance. Her heels lifted off the floor. Vincent's arm around her waist. Bass thrummed up through her toes. Her feet. The backs of her knees. She reached higher and let her hands sway. Someone bumped her from behind and she stumbled against Vincent.

"You okay?"

"Fine!"

He bent into her neck and kissed her behind the jaw. Spoke into her ear. "Want to get out of here?"

Laurel nodded and he led her off the floor, back to the bar, where he retrieved his jacket and draped it over her shoulders.

In the taxi, Vincent leaned back against the seat and gave the driver his address. "Stop at the Ultramar on the way," he added and dropped a hand on her thigh.

Laurel blinked as the car started to move, then closed her eyes against a sudden wave of dizziness. The car lurched into traffic and she snapped her eyes back open. Sat up straighter and gripped her seatbelt like it might have the power to stop her head from spinning. She stared out the window and tried to find a distant, fixed point to focus on through the passing lights. Vincent's hand found the bottom of her skirt, hiked it up and settled back on her thigh. His thumb stroked her bare leg. A crack spiderwebbed the bottom corner of her window and a single cut ran diagonally across the glass, distorting Laurel's reflection. Cheeks flushed. Eyes bright with mascara. Shiny dark brown hair. Laurel leaned toward the driver's seat. "Grenfell Campus, please."

"Ultramar first?" the cab driver asked.

"No." Laurel responded at the same time Vincent looked at her, incredulous, and said, "Yes. I thought you were coming to my place?"

Laurel shook her head. "I need to go back to campus."

The taxi pulled into the gas station and Laurel rested her face on the cold windowpane and waited until Vincent came back with a dozen beer. "You should come to my place."

She shook her head against the glass. They were almost there. A straight shot up the hill.

"I just got beer." Vincent slumped and planted his forehead on the back of the driver's seat. Laurel took off his coat and dropped it over the beer on the seat between them. When the taxi pulled up in front of residence, she opened the door before the car came to a complete stop.

"Hey! Wait." Vincent opened his door, but he didn't chase after her. Instead, he tore the flap from his cigarette pack, pulled a pen from inside his coat and scribbled down his number. "Here. In case you change your mind later, or just want to hang out sometime."

Laurel snatched the paper and headed toward Arts and Admin. Through the front glass, she saw the security guard, his elbows resting on the booth, watching her.

TWENTY THREE

The next few weeks slipped by in a blur of classes, homework and shifts at the grocery store. In Stephenville, except for a few young boys who bagged groceries and wheeled them out to old ladies' cars, the staff at Foodland had been much older than her and had worked there for years. At Sobeys, there were other students working the checkouts. One of them, Susan, spent their Friday evening shift together sending Laurel secret looks of disgust whenever she had a customer buy the big bag of turkey necks, vacuumed sealed blood puddings, or little tubs of something called head cheese. Laurel did the same in return, the highlight of her day being a massive bag of No Name puffed rice that reminded her of five-finger shopping with Horsey. Susan didn't get it, but Laurel giggled to herself for the rest of her shift, and again at the mall, as she deposited her cheque in the bank machine. Laurel stared at the deposit slip. She had known her student loan was in there, but that money had felt distant, abstract somehow, until she looked at the total printed on the bank receipt: $942.96. Almost a thousand dollars.

Laurel trotted through Sears pushing a cart stuffed with a new comforter for her bed, a new pillow, a Fiona Apple poster for her wall, a set of plastic dishes in bright rainbow colours, notebooks, felt-tipped pens, fake leather gloves, fuzzy ankle boots, jeans, and a cozy new sweater. She'd lugged her giant shopping bags back to residence in a taxi. The next day, she sat at her desk with her notebook and new felt-tipped pen, and tried not to think about everything she'd bought.

The math didn't make sense. To get through Christmas and have enough money to last over the holidays she needed to pick up extra shifts at Sobeys. But she had already missed classes for shifts that week, and she could only make so much money before her income was deducted from her student loan. She'd have to work even more shifts next semester to make up the difference, leaving her with an even greater deduction from her loan after that. The pay phone rang in the hallway. Shrill rings that bounced off brick walls and dug into her nerves. She dropped the pen and sat back.

The phone was incessant.

Since her room was the closest to the phone booth, she was often the one to answer it. At first, she didn't mind. She knocked on doors, poked her head in the lounge, and when she couldn't find the recipient, she wrote messages on their whiteboards. Any of the other girls would do the same for her. Except they never had to. Her mother had probably lost the number five minutes after she wrote it down. If she had ever written it down. Someone finally answered the phone, then knocked on her door looking for Haley. Laurel snatched her bookbag and keys off the desk and headed to the library.

The campus library was made up of two storeys that made her old high school library look as small as a classroom. Her favourite spot was a little nook she'd found in the reference section tucked underneath the stairs with two cozy seats and a low table. When she situated herself just so, nobody could see her behind the heavy volumes on the bookshelves: *The Book of the Year*, *The World Book*, and several editions of the *Encyclopædia Britannica*. They were studying *Emma* in English class, and Laurel curled up in one of the chairs, determined to read it cover to cover.

"Hey. Laurel." Jimmy ducked under the stairs in a rustle of windbreaker vinyl. "I hoped I'd catch you."

She put her book down as Jimmy sat in the other chair. "Hey."

He opened his bookbag and hauled out a sheaf of papers. "Notes from class. You missed a few. We have a paper due soon."

Laurel took the messy pile of looseleaf and flipped through it.

"I tried to drop by your room, but residence is always locked. I felt like a creep just standing there, waiting for someone to let me in."

"That's what it's like to call."

"Call?"

"The pay phone. It just rings and rings, and whoever's calling just has to wait for someone to answer."

"What's your number?"

"Oh. Ah . . . I don't actually remember!"

Jimmy laughed and re-zipped his bag. He got up.

"You're going?"

"Yeah. It's Saturday night." He grinned. "Don't you have something to do?"

She fanned herself with the notes as if exhausted by all the somethings she would do later. "I'm just taking a breather."

He adjusted his bookbag across his shoulders. Straightened his jacket. His hair was longer than usual and it curled away from the tips of his ears. "See you in class."

Laurel nodded and Jimmy disappeared back behind the book stacks.

The notes were organized by date. Handouts from Dr. Hollis and a few lined pages in Jimmy's handwriting. Perfect blocks of text with underlined topic headings. She skimmed the writing, looking for a comment from Jimmy himself. Something he'd written just for her. She checked each page, but everything was copied directly from the board. Laurel tucked the notes away, picked up her book and found her page. Read the same paragraph three times. She sighed. Stared at the back of the steps that led to the second level. The sturdy curve of the staircase as it wound overhead. Laurel dropped the book in her lap, stretched out and put her feet up on the table.

The different encyclopedia editions that lined the bookshelves and kept her hidden were marked by different colours: dark green, navy blue with a beige stripe, burgundy-brown. Her mother would love to pick through them and point out the differences. Laurel closed her eyes and rested her head back on the chair. She had only been six or seven when her parents got their set. She'd been confused by the extravagant purchase and her mother had said that every good family needed the encyclopedia because it was full of information about anything. Whenever you had a question, you could look up the answer.

The books had arrived in four neat boxes and her parents had cleaned the entire house before they opened them. Her father took all their old books off the bookshelf and dusted. He packed some away in boxes, reshelved the rest and left the two bottom shelves clear for the new volumes. Her mother had cleaned the clutter off the coffee table and swept the floor. Quick hard strokes that lifted dirt from the carpet, swept it across the canvas and out the front door. Laurel had listened from bed as her parents opened the boxes late into the night. They lifted each book out, one at a time, and read the spines out loud. "Volume 1 'A to Anno.'" Anno? What do you think that might be?"

"Excuse me? Hi? I'm sorry. The library is closing." The woman had a warm face that smiled at Laurel's confusion.

Emma fell from her lap when she sat up.

"Oh, you're not the first to fall asleep in here with a good book on a Saturday night." A silver name tag on her chest said *Liz*. A librarian. She stepped away and gave Laurel space to wake up and wipe drool from her chin.

The bold clock face above the library entrance told her it was ten o'clock. She'd been there for three hours. Her face grew hot under the low hum of electricity as she followed Liz to the door. The librarian unlocked it, let Laurel out, then waved at her through the glass.

That night, when everyone had gone out and the floor was quiet, Laurel called home.

"Hello? Longs' residence."

"Bud! Hi, Bud."

Her little brother laughed.

"Miss you, buddy." He told her he missed her, too. "Well . . . um . . . how's school?"

"Good."

"Grade four. That's a big one." Laurel ran through a series of boring questions about school until Bud handed the phone off to Braya. She started over and asked the same questions again, but it was less awkward with a four-year-old on the other end of the line than a nine-year-old. "You're going to pre-school, huh? That's big!" Braya's answers quickly tapered off from full sentences to single words to babbles, then her mother got on the phone.

"It's about time you called."

"You were supposed to call me!"

"I know. I meant to. I was going to call and then I got busy with the kids. Getting school supplies and shoes and . . . you know. Then I went to call and the number wasn't on the fridge where I put it and . . . I got a job!"

Laurel tightened her grip on the receiver. "Doing what?"

"In home care. Like before."

"Who's watching Bud and Braya?"

"I got a sitter. It's only part-time."

"What about rent? Won't it—"

"I can't—" Her mother inhaled. It sounded like air being

sucked from the receiver. "Especially now that I got Braya in preschool three days a week. Being home all day. Not working. It's *depressing*. I can't do it anymore."

"Do you pay the sitter?" Laurel's voice raised a notch.

"Don't worry about it. I got it covered." Her mother cleared her throat. "September was rough. I had to wait three weeks for my first paycheque, but I should be able to catch up now in October, if I can make it through to next week." She paused, cleared her throat again. "I'm just worried about the phone."

"You mean the phone you don't call me on?"

"I meant to, and I will. I will call, but I'm behind on the heat, and next week I'm going to have to choose one bill over the other . . ."

Laurel waited for her mother to say whatever it was she was about to say.

She sighed loudly. Laurel moved the receiver away from her ear. "I can't ask you. I know. You got enough going on."

"You just did."

"Laurel—"

"You just asked me!"

"No. Forget it. Forget I said anything. It'll be fine. I promise. I'll just pay enough on each bill to keep the wolves from the door. And I'll get caught up next month. You got your own thing now. Don't even think about it. Forget I brought it up."

"You sure? Because I can—"

"No. It's fine. I swear. So. Anyway. How's school?"

Laurel stared at the wall. The texture of the bricks smooth and muted under layers of yellow-beige paint. Along the hard edge of the pay phone, paint peeled away into ribbons. "Good. School's good."

TWENTY FOUR

Jimmy sat in the same spot every English class. There were plenty of other seats, especially now that the weather had turned. Residence students sat comfortably around the room in regular clothes while everyone who lived off-campus shed sopping coats and toques, or didn't show up at all. Laurel watched as he sat down and tried to pull his arms out of a jacket and fleece liner without making any noise.

She turned her attention to Dr. Hollis at the front of the class. She'd missed a lot of classes that week and had to catch up.

Jimmy swivelled his chair closer. "You missed a lot of classes this week."

Laurel bit the inside of her lip.

Dr. Hollis smacked the board with a piece of chalk. "What do these women have in common?" She had scrawled *Mary Ann Evans* and *The Brontë Sisters* across the board.

Someone raised their hand. "They were all writers?"

"Of course they were all writers. Anyone else?"

Jimmy slid a note across the table. *Hike tomorrow?*

Laurel slid it back without answering.

When no other hands went up, Dr. Hollis turned back to the

board and spoke as she wrote. "They are all women who published as men."

Another note: *the gorge, 9am.* Jimmy pushed the note over, bumping her notebook.

The gorge sounded like a good place to toss a dead body. She didn't hike. She walked. To get from one place to another. Laurel ignored him and listened to the lecture.

At the end of class, Dr. Hollis placed a stack of papers on her desk and told them to find their assignments on the way out. Laurel waited in her seat for the line of eager students to dwindle. Jimmy folded his arms on the table and sighed as he rested his head on his crossed wrists. He looked at her sideways. "Fresh air," he said. "Sun. Trees."

Laurel got up to join the queue.

Red marks covered her paper, and in the top right corner, her grade: 54 per cent. She had expected to do better than that. Much better. She flipped to the last page and read a note scrawled underneath her final paragraph. *This isn't meant to be an opinion piece. Do research. Periodicals. Websites. Try a search engine. Learn how to back up an argument. This is barely an essay.*

Laurel crumpled her paper into a ball. Dr. Hollis snapped her head to look in her direction, then looked away again. Other students stepped around her as they left the room with their own grades clutched to their chests.

"Come on." Jimmy ushered her out of class. "What's up?"

"Nothing." Laurel shoved her paper in her bookbag.

"Here." He rubbed his fingers together, but when Laurel ignored him, he jammed his hand in the bag and pulled out the wadded-up assignment. He held it in front of his face. "I did better than you? In Lit? What happened? You know how to run a search right?"

"I'm not an idiot." Actually, she was, and the instructions taped on the computers in the library hadn't helped. She'd entered her topic "Emma," in the search bar at the top of the screen, like the instructions said to do, but got a message that said *Page Cannot Be Found*.

Jimmy read one of the comments off the front page. "This is not an introduction." He guffawed, jaw cranked open.

Laurel pushed past him.

"Sorry." He thrust her paper back at her. "I'm sorry. I didn't mean—"

"It's just a paper, Jimmy. No big deal." She threaded through the students in the crowded hallway. "Byeee! See ya later." He followed her into the crowd, but eventually he must have given up and let himself drift away, because when she looked back from the top of the stairwell, he was gone.

Someone tapped, very lightly, on the unit door at exactly 9:00 a.m. Laurel fell out of bed and answered it before Haley woke up.

Jimmy whispered into the opened crack. "I didn't think you'd be up."

"I'm not."

"You coming? No pressure." He stepped back. Hands raised. "Just thought I'd check before I left."

"Gimme a minute." Laurel pulled the door closed and crept back to her room.

A hike. Like a walk that was hard core, only not hard core like trailblazing through the woods, but on a trail. In hiking gear. Laurel rummaged through her clothes on the floor. Gear. A water bottle. And sneakers. Hiking boots? A jacket that wasn't a winter coat or a jean jacket, but something in between and ideally made out of colourful vinyl. Snacks. A backpack for the snacks.

Laurel pulled on a hoodie and her loosest pair of jeans. The only pack she had was her bookbag. She dumped out the books and threw in a roll of toilet paper. Haley had apples in the fridge and she threw one of those in next to the roll. She found a box of granola bars above the toaster and took one of those, too. She couldn't find a water bottle, but Haley had fruit punch juice boxes. Laurel didn't judge her roommate for having the lunch items of a fifth grader as she added a juice box to her bag. She'd have to splurge on groceries later to return all the stolen goods. There was nothing she could do about her shoes—fuzzy brown ankle boots—but at least they had rubber soles and a low heel.

Jimmy didn't comment on what she wore, he just strode down the quiet hall with his fingers looped in the straps of his backpack. A water bottle tucked in a side pouch rode just above his hip. A carabiner jangled from the zipper. "You go home since school started?"

"No. You?"

"Yeah. Last weekend. I drove the truck back." He pushed the residence doors open and they headed to the main entrance.

"You have the truck? And we're going for a hike?"

"Yeah. Why?" Jimmy laughed. "You don't want to go for a *drive*. Like a Sunday drive around the big city. That'd be pretty lame."

Laurel looked at her booties as she stepped out into the cool October morning. "I don't know."

"Anyway, feel free to catch a ride anytime. Anywhere you want to go."

They talked until they hit the trailhead and started up a steady incline. Laurel found it hard to talk and breathe as she climbed, so their conversation tapered off and she followed quietly behind as the trail narrowed. Trees pressed in tight on either side of them. The sky a lattice of branches. Maple dominated in the valley. And birch. Pine. Tamarack that turned electric yellow before needles dropped and snapped underfoot. Spruce and fir knitted into patches of green that smelled of sap and wet moss and black tea boiled over an open fire. Laurel adjusted her bookbag over her shoulders and watched her step as she made her way over damp roots and leaves.

The gorge was a massive hole in the earth hidden behind the Corner Brook golf course. The trail skirted along the top of it, then climbed to a lookout where they peered over a rail down inside the hole.

"Have you ever done the sinkhole?"

Laurel was out of breath and it took her a minute to answer. "The what?"

"The sinkhole. It's up on the Northern Peninsula, around Lomond. It's kind of hard to find if you don't know where it is, but it's a legit sinkhole. People throw all kinds of stuff in there. Sofas, couches, washers, old dirt bikes. What about Cedar Cove?"

"What about it?"

"That's a nice hike."

Laurel squinted into the glare of the clouds. "No."

Jimmy stopped. He plucked his water bottle from his pack, spun the lid open and offered it to her.

The thought of sucking Haley's fruit punch through a straw turned her stomach, so she accepted Jimmy's water bottle, tipped it up, and chugged.

"It's not like blazing your own trail through the woods, I guess, or scaling the riverbank." He took the bottle back. "I remember you going barefoot all the time, running all over the rocks like it was nothing." When she didn't say anything, he went on. "Remember the old hay barn? How we used to make tunnels and little caves?"

Laurel nodded and looked down into the gorge. They could hike down there if they wanted to. Work their way along the steep ridges until they reached the very bottom.

"Search engines are easy to use, once you know what you're doing."

"You read *all* the notes?"

"No. Well, I mean, yes. But I had to ask the librarian for help before I knew what to do. I could show you. If you put the topic right in the URL bar it doesn't work. That's what I did first."

Yeah, that's what she'd done. She'd tried a bunch of different topics, and every single time, *Page Cannot Be Found*. Where the hell were all the pages?

"You need to find a search engine first, like Yahoo. You got to type out: h t t p, forward slash, forward slash, w w w dot yahoo dot com. Then you put in the search topic, like Jane Austen's *Emma*, or whatever."

Laurel stared at him in mock terror.

"What? I memorized it! I thought you were the library nerd! They hire students there all the time, by the way. I always see kids reshelving books. And since you have all that prefect experience."

Laurel laughed, but it sounded more like an irritated huff. She hadn't really meant to sound like that.

"Fine, fine. I'll back off."

"Whatever."

"Right. Whatever." Jimmy leaned over the rail and shouted into the gorge. "WHATEVER!" The gorge echoed back at them, growing louder before fading to a distant *er er er*. "Want to hike down there?"

"I kinda do actually." Laurel leaned forward and shouted "AARRGGHH!"

Jimmy raised his eyebrows, impressed.

"Not in these shoes."

"Just take them off."

Laurel looked at jagged shale that led down into the hole. Her feet would be sliced to ribbons.

"Another time." Jimmy opened his pack and took out a sandwich. White bread with some shaved meat on it, probably fancy Black Forest ham. Crisp lettuce poked out around the sides. He offered her half.

"I'm good." Laurel opened her bookbag and took out the pilfered apple and granola bar. The juice box.

"There's caves here, too." Jimmy talked as he chewed. "Up on

Massey Drive. You can hike in for a good stretch. You need a headlamp though. It gets dark as shit."

It occurred to Laurel that after she moved to Stephenville, Jimmy grew up on Woods Road alone. Horsey was always in Stephenville with her, then she was always with Andrew. Laurel, Horsey and Jimmy had been the steadfast Woods Road kids, and Andrew had been Jimmy's sidekick whenever he visited over holidays. They had enjoyed all the freedom that came with their world. She pictured Jimmy out whacking trails and swimming in the swimming holes by himself. He must have done other things. He'd played basketball at school and she'd heard he was pretty good. But after the shooting—after *that* night—Laurel's world had broken. Jimmy's had gotten caught in the cracks.

Laurel sat down on top of her bookbag and stretched out her legs. A shiver travelled up her back and she pulled her hoodie around her chin.

Jimmy threw the crust of his sandwich into the gorge and shouted after it. "WHATEVER!" He shoved his hands into his pockets and danced around on his toes, then he pulled his hands back out and moved through a series of stretches. Laurel threw her apple core over the rail.

"You remember . . ." Jimmy spread his legs apart and bent to touch the ground between his feet. "You remember that night? You know . . ."

The pit of Laurel's stomach went cold.

"You asked me if I went in." Jimmy twisted from side to side.

Laurel got up and brushed off the back of her pants. She picked up her bag and shook it out.

"I saw the lights the night before. The cop cars. The ambulance. When no one answered the door at your house the next morning, I went in."

Laurel slung the bag over her shoulders and started to hike back down the hill.

"Laurel! I didn't mean to. I didn't know. But once I saw . . . I couldn't unsee, you know?"

She sped up. The soles of her crappy shoes slipping over rotting leaves. Jimmy caught up and his long strides effortlessly kept pace with her.

"I'm sorry. I just wanted to tell you."

She moved faster.

He paced her easily, like a long, relentless shadow. "I just . . . I wasn't okay after that. So, I can't imagine how you . . . I just wanted to tell you, that I know."

Laurel stopped. Jimmy almost smacked into her. He flung out his arms to find his balance.

"Know what? What is it that you think you know?" His eyes widened, but he just stared at her, like he'd gone mute. "Hey?" Her voice echoed back at them. "That I'm . . . that I'm a fucking disaster." Spit flew from her lips and Jimmy took another step back, like that's exactly what she was. She took a step closer. "Is that what you know?"

Jimmy held his ground.

"Because I am." Her chin quivered. She spun around and ran down the trail.

"Laurel!"

She heard him shout, but she didn't hear him behind her. He was probably cowering in the trees or bounding off in the opposite direction like a scared little rabbit. Her feet flew out from under her when he grabbed her elbow. She flung out a hand to catch herself and her knee struck a rock that jutted from the trail. "Jesus Christ! What the fuck?"

"I'm sorry! Ohmygod. I didn't mean—"

"Just leave me alone."

Jimmy helped her up. Laurel flicked her hair out of her face and strands of it slapped across Jimmy's. He wiped it away. Something about that—the way her hair stuck to his face. The way he wiped it off—struck her as funny. "I'm okay. I'm fine. I mean . . ."

"It's okay if you're not. I don't mean your knee. I mean . . . if *you're* not. It's okay. Maybe you are, but . . ." Laurel pushed the rest of her hair from her face. Jimmy brushed a few strands off her forehead. "You're not a disaster. You're just . . . you're just . . ."

"I just fucking killed somebody." That was it. Her face fell apart and she couldn't catch it in time to put it back together, all she could do was cover it up. She bit her palm and tried to swallow it back down, but she felt her chest split. A sob bubbled up through the crack. She bit harder.

Jimmy pulled her into his shoulder. "No. That's not how I see you at all." She sniffed into his jacket. Bright green with a blue stripe across the middle.

"I'm fine."

"You're amazing."

Laurel laughed.

"I don't think . . ." He squeezed her tighter. Laurel wiped her nose and waited for him to go on. "I don't think *what happened* diminishes you in any way. I think it makes you brighter. Like you just burn it up . . . or something." He rested his chin on her hair.

"Brighter." Laurel shook her head. She patted his chest and pulled back. "I have to move." Her toes were numb and cold stung her fingertips. "I'm freezing." Laurel scrambled up off the ground.

They finished the rest of the trail out of the gorge in silence, but when they hit pavement at Margaret Bowater Park, Jimmy cleared his throat like a car changing gears and talked about his apartment. He lived in a basement apartment with Andrew on Coronation Street. Andrew and Horsey were still a thing, did she know that? Andrew had a car. A Sprint, the smallest kind of beater, but it got them around town. Andrew practically had to duck his head when he drove.

Laurel's feet hurt and she felt both too hot and too cold at the same time.

"We can cut through the park, take the trail back to Grenfell." Jimmy pointed in one direction, then another. "I can go that way, or I can go that way. It's all a circle. It's probably the same distance to walk through campus."

In the park, kids bundled into hats and mitts and colourful splash pants ignored the playground equipment and slid down wet grass or chased after each other. Overhead, the last of the season's leaves fluttered orange and yellow. They crossed a steel bridge that clanked beneath their feet. The spaces between the laths offered a clear view of the river rushing below them.

"You should come to our place tonight." Jimmy raised his voice over the sound of the current.

"What?" She didn't mean to sound shocked at the invite, but she didn't know what he meant. Should she go over to hang out and watch a movie, just the two of them? Should she go over because they were throwing a party? Or was it just like old times and they would sit on the living room carpet and play *Super Mario Bros?*

"We're having a few people over."

A few people likely included Horsey. "I don't know, I have a hot date with a search engine."

"Fine. Whatever."

"Whatever." Laurel's calves burned with the day's effort. They reconnected with the trail on the other side of the bridge and started back up the hill to campus. She let Jimmy pull ahead when the trail narrowed again.

"Horsey'll be there." Jimmy looked back over his shoulder.

Laurel's boots were soggy. Water stained. Her feet squelched inside them, warm only from exertion.

"She'd like to see you. She might give you shit but—"

"Why would she give me shit?"

"I don't know. It's been a while."

Laurel leaned into the trail as it grew steeper. "I never heard from her."

"Yeah, but. She's Horsey. And you're . . . *you*."

"What's *that* mean?"

The trail widened again and Jimmy slowed until Laurel panted beside him. "She'd like to see you. That's all."

Exhaustion took over. Everything hurt. Her legs. Her lungs. Her tailbone. Most of all, her nerves felt raw and fraying. Campus came into view. The side parking lot dotted with cars. They crossed the lot without a word. Jimmy stuffed his hands in his pockets and his pace slowed again, but Laurel veered toward the footpath that cut across the campus lawn. She paused when her feet left the pavement. "Thanks. For the hike."

He stopped. His face mottled red with cold. "Sure. Anytime."

"Well." Her nose itched. A thin trickle of snot worked its way out of a nostril. She sniffed and turned away. "I'll see ya."

"What about tonight?"

"Maybe."

Inside the main entrance, Laurel wiped her nose and looked back through the glass doors. She was pretty sure that walking through campus meant Jimmy had a longer walk home. A much longer walk home. Jimmy waved. Pavement stretched behind him, then dropped off like a cliff. The rest of the city below, scrambling between steep hills and the Bay of Islands. A steady plume of smoke rose from the mill, white against grey cloud as wood ground into pulp, into paper, relentlessly working. The whistle blew. A long, low drone that marked a change in shift. Jimmy stuffed his hand back in his pocket and carried on. Gaze steady, fixed on the road ahead of him.

TWENTY FIVE

Laurel climbed into bed, curled up with blankets around her cheeks and waited for her body to warm. She closed her eyes, but they drifted back open. She stared up at the ceiling. Hot water pipes clanked and hummed as someone in the next unit got a shower. She tossed to one side, then turned to the other. Checked her alarm clock at regular two-to-three-minute intervals. Rolled onto her back. Stared at the ceiling again. Counted tiles. Checked the time. Laurel flung the covers off and got up.

She carted her dirty clothes down to the residence basement and did laundry. Cleaned her room. Ate. Managed some homework. Showered. Then agonized over what to wear for the second time that day. She was dressed and ready before she decided to go. Coronation Street was a steep, miserable hill and her shoes were already soaked. Her feet ached. Her freshly washed jeans felt too tight in the ass. With every step, she considered turning back, until she stood at the bottom of a stairwell, under a pasty dome light that trembled and buzzed.

Music played inside. She couldn't decipher what it was, but it was something low and steady. Acoustic. She took a deep breath and pushed the door open. Stepped down onto a mat covered in about twenty pairs of shoes. Sturdy boots, skinny knee-highs, low-heeled booties and wet sneakers. A cloud of smoke and voices hung in the air in front of her. She hesitated to close the door. No one had actually seen her yet.

Someone with a bottle of vodka in one hand and a smoke in the other passed through the fog and froze. Laurel recognized that stance. That hip jut. That head cocked to one side.

"Laurel?" Horsey padded closer in her bare feet. "Laurel fucking-Long-time-no-see." She paused when she noticed her hand on the door. "What, are you leaving?"

Laurel shoved the door closed. "No, I—"

Horsey rushed at her. She jabbed her cigarette in her mouth and it dangled from her lip when she hissed, "You're not going *anywhere*."

"No. I—just got here." Laurel popped off her shoes as Horsey dragged her into the apartment and through the living room. She recognized Andrew. Jason. But for the most part, she was being hauled through a room full of strangers. She caught a whiff of hash or weed. It all smelled the same to her.

"Laurel!" Jimmy hopped off a couch. "You came."

"Observant as always."

He cut Horsey off. Laurel stumbled into her and Horsey pushed her back with her hip. "What's going on?"

Horsey took the cigarette from her mouth and squinted as she exhaled a long stream of smoke over her shoulder. Laurel raised her eyebrows at Jimmy in a plea for help, but he lifted his hands in defeat and stepped out of the way. Horsey tugged her to the kitchen and pulled out a chair. "Sit."

Laurel sat.

The bottle landed in front of her, followed by a shot glass. "Don't move." Horsey opened a cabinet and rummaged through glassware. The tiny kitchen looked like it was from a different era. Mashed-pea-green countertop. Cupboard doors inlaid with black and white tiles. A cat-faced clock hung on the wall, whiskers ticking. Shellacked wooden pictures. One of a boiling pot that said, *Simmer down*. Another of two strips of bacon: *You are the bacon to my eggs*.

Another shot glass landed next to the first. Horsey snatched up the bottle and filled each to the brim. Vodka poured over the sides and pooled on the table. It dripped from the glass when she picked it up, tilted her head back, and threw the shot down her throat. Horsey gritted her teeth as she breathed, jerked her head at the table. "That's yours."

"I think you're drunk."

"Drink."

Laurel picked up the shot and tossed it down. The vodka knocked out her breath. She clenched her jaw, picked up the bottle and filled both their glasses to overflowing. She slid Horsey's to her in a stream of booze, picked up her own and raised it. Horsey's eyes narrowed, but she raised her glass in return. Bottoms up. Slam. Laurel gagged, but she picked the bottle up again and poured.

This time, she had her shot gone while Horsey stared at hers, eye level. "I *may* be a little drunk." She downed it, coughed, then plunked into the chair across from Laurel. A column of ash fell from her cigarette. Horsey licked a finger, picked the ash off the table and dropped it in the shot glass. She brushed the tabletop where the ash had been, then shifted on her seat and sat with an elbow propped on one knee, tapped her thumb to her temple. Cigarette aloft as it burned. She looked the same as she always did. Makeup free. Wild hair. A flush at the uppermost part of her cheekbones. "It's been a while."

Laurel looked down at the hangnail she'd been picking. "Sorry, I think I just lost . . . track of . . . time."

"Lost track of time." Horsey craned her neck toward the living room and shouted over the music. "You hear that, Jimmy? She lost track of time!" She turned back to Laurel. "Like what, a year? Two? But who's counting?"

Laurel looked at the clock. "One year, seven months, four days. And . . . twenty-seven minutes."

Horsey blinked at her, stunned.

Laurel tried to keep her expression serious, but the vodka loosened her up. She pinched her lips together.

Horsey pointed at her. "You fucking . . . you fucking forgot weeks." She dropped her cigarette butt in the shot glass.

"Too long," Laurel admitted. "I didn't mean . . . I didn't know you wanted to hear from me. I was a bit of a mess back then."

"I know."

"You knew where I lived."

Horsey nodded and bit the tip of her thumb. "Yeah. I was a bit of mess back then."

Laurel remembered Jimmy's sinkhole. She pictured sofas, couches, washers, and old dirt bikes being sucked down into the earth, never to be seen again, just like her childhood. Their childhoods. Maybe the problem was trying to get something back that was gone. Maybe the problem was drinking too much. "Do you live here too, or is Jimmy the bacon to Andrew's eggs?"

"I pretty much live here." Horsey pushed up from the table and got two glasses from the cupboard. The freezer door opened and closed. Ice clinked. "Andrew's obsessed with this apartment. And he's always collecting weird shit. I blame your mom for that." She pointed at the cat face on the wall. "Apparently, those eyes are supposed to tick back and forth." She returned to the table with two tall glasses of ice and a jug of orange juice.

Laurel rubbed her forehead. "I need to quit drinking." She rubbed her eyebrows as Horsey poured a drink and placed it in front of her. "I quit smoking."

Horsey snorted and slid her pack of Du Maurier kings across the table. It got stuck in the puddle of vodka. Laurel picked it up and took out a smoke. Horsey poured a drink for herself. "I've had alcohol in my blood since I found Dad's homebrew behind the hot water tank in the shed. At the ripe old age of twelve."

"I was with you. I was ten!"

"Ten! You might have been *eleven*?"

"Ha! Maybe."

"What else is there to do in the woods?" Horsey lifted her glass to Laurel. "Cheers."

Laurel took a sip of her drink. She coughed at the ratio of vodka to orange juice, then took a good long chug to keep up with Horsey.

"We should have talked more." Horsey put her glass down.

"We talked all the time." Laurel exhaled a lung full of smoke. She watched it gather in the air between them and dissipate. Horsey suddenly looked farther away. Laurel blinked to bring her back into focus.

"You know what I mean." Horsey stretched her arms across the table. "Our childhoods weren't normal. I grew up in that shack. And you . . . I helped you . . . Sorry. Jimmy said you guys talked."

Laurel flicked hair from her eyes. "It was a long time ago."

Horsey drummed her index finger. "Too long."

The room spun for a moment. Laurel shook her head and Horsey settled back into place, face pale in the low light.

"What'd you do to her?" Andrew filled the doorway. He was bigger than Laurel remembered. His shoulders wider and more muscular, but his face was still the same, making the proportions of his head and body look strangely out of sync.

"Nothing she didn't have coming."

"I'm fine. I've just been sitting in the same spot for too long." Laurel took her drink and got up. "I need to move around." She walked into the living room, stood inside the entryway, and sipped. Jimmy sat on the couch next to Jason, talking to some girl. He was animated. Head bobbing as he spoke. The girl laughed. Eyes heavily made up. Lips red. Jason made eye contact with Laurel and she went and sat on the carpet, close enough to talk to him but out of Jimmy's immediate line of sight. "Hey."

"Still double-fisting it I see."

Laurel looked at her hands. She had a cigarette in one and a drink in the other. "Yeah, and you're still saying shit like 'double-fisting it.'"

Jason laughed.

Laurel reached for an ashtray on the end table and stubbed out the cigarette. Clutched her glass in her lap.

"Heard you're in college."

"Yeah. University."

"Up on the hill." Jason raised his blond brows. His goatee replaced now with a full beard. "You *and* Jimmy."

She took a drink, but her glass was empty. The music had changed to a dance remix of an old song. Something by the Pixies. A little blond girl in cut-offs fell in her friend's lap next to Jimmy. She jumped back up and tugged on her friend who tugged Jimmy in turn, trying to haul him off the couch. Laurel slumped over and put her head on the floor. Cheek to the carpet. She looked at Jason sideways. He'd said something. "What?"

Jason shook his head. "I said, 'You and Jimmy.'" He hunched forward, elbows on his knees.

"What about Jimmy?"

"Nothing, man."

Horsey sat next to her and pulled her up. She handed her another vodka and orange juice. Laurel sniffed it before taking a sip. The room was already spinning. She peeked over the top of her glass. The girls were dancing now. They began a two-girl conga line around the living room. Jimmy still sat on the couch. An empty spot next to him. He leaned into Jason and said something.

"I babysit for your mom sometimes," Horsey shouted.

"Serious?"

"I mean, Bud's old enough, but your mom doesn't want to

leave them alone all the time. I can see why." She laughed. "Not that she pays me. Sometimes she tries, but I don't take it. Not usually."

"*You're* the sitter."

"Do you go home much? Or call? I haven't heard from her lately." Horsey handed her a half-smoked cigarette.

Laurel took it and adjusted her legs underneath herself. Other girls were dancing now, a small cluster on the linoleum by the kitchen. A girl landed in the empty spot next to Jimmy. A girl with black hair that swung. Legs that crossed. A drink that balanced on her bare knee at the end of her fingertips. "I've called a few times."

"They're sweet, you know? Bud and Braya."

"I know."

Horsey rested her chin in her hand. "But do you know . . . that Braya thinks her dad died in a hunting accident?" Laurel's head tipped back. "I know she's only four, but how can anyone tell her the truth, now?"

Laurel kept her mouth clamped shut. If she opened it and breathed, the room would spin out of control.

"She'll hear rumours, Laurel. You can't keep her from knowing who she is."

"That's not who she is."

"It's a part."

"Maybe she doesn't need to know that part."

"This isn't just your story. You don't get to decide what happens. What if what happened to Braya's dad sets everything else in motion? How could it not? What if it's the one thing that pushes her to be . . . something more." Horsey raised her hands to encompass the whole of the living room. "Something amazing."

"What if it doesn't?" Laurel's gaze jumped around the room. The carpet. The end table. The couch. Everything was spinning now. There was no fixed point to focus on.

"You need to love the dark parts too, Laurel. You need to love the dark parts most of all."

Laurel moved her hand in a slow, deliberate motion and dropped the cigarette in the orange juice. She tried to focus on Horsey. Gripped her shoulder and stumbled up from the floor. The conga girls bounced past, bare hips jangling over low-rise jeans.

"Come on, I gotcha." Horsey helped her up, wrapped an arm under her armpits and turned her around. "Bathroom's this way. I knew you were still a lightweight."

Laurel woke up in Jimmy's bed. She had a vague memory of Horsey helping her into it. Her head pounded and she rolled over, but her bladder ached as badly as her head and her tongue had swollen to the roof of her mouth like a parched slug. She eased herself up and stumbled around the room in the dark until she found the door.

A ring of light outlined a door across the hall. When she opened it, the sudden brightness seared straight to the back of her skull. Fluorescent on porcelain. She gripped the sink and shut her eyes. Tapped a finger on the hard curve of the bowl. Her stomach clenched.

Laurel breathed in slow and deep through her nose. Squinted her way to the toilet. She undid her pants and sat down. Her underwear was bloody. The crotch of her pants, too. She cleaned everything as best she could with toilet paper, then checked under the sink for supplies. Nothing but the sink's sharp U-pipe and a jagged hole cut through the vanity floor. Her hands shook as she opened the mirrored door of the medicine cabinet. Empty save for a rusted-out razor.

Laurel wadded tissue into her pants, then bent over the toilet. Nothing came up. She crouched closer. In the long run of the day ahead, it would be much better to throw up now, but her headache was unbearable. She unfolded herself from the floor, closed her eyes for another minute, then turned on the tap and let the water run cold. The soap on the ledge was worn down to a splinter and she washed her hands until it cracked apart and dissolved. Laurel splashed her face then sucked water directly from the tap until her tongue softened and shrank back to its normal size.

Back in Jimmy's room she checked the bedsheets for blood stains. She smoothed the clean flannel and closed her eyes. The blankets were half on the floor and she tugged them back over the bed, replaced the pillows and left the room.

In the dim light through the windows, she could make out the shape of someone asleep on the couch as she crept through the apartment. A knee bent to the sky. Jimmy. She found her coat hanging off the back of a kitchen chair. Her shoes flipped upside down on the doormat. Laurel quietly zipped her coat, shoved her feet in her boots and slipped outside into the raw morning.

She slept the rest of the day. It was almost midnight when she finally climbed out of bed and found All Girls West was quiet. Phone card in hand, she slunk down the hallway to the phone booth. She punched in her number and sat down. Waited. But it didn't ring. Instead, a metallic click. Three obnoxious beeps. Followed by an automated voice that spoke to her from a million miles away: *We're sorry, the number you have reached is not in service.*

TWENTY SIX

Laurel dropped a six-pack of Molson XXX on the counter at Ultramar. She slipped her student card with her photo ID, and her MCP card with her birth year, next to the case.

The cashier picked up the medical card. "What's this for?"

"That's my birth year right there. I just don't have my driver's licence."

He inspected the photo, then looked at her with bored, tired eyes.

"And a pack of Du Maurier? Kings."

He sniffed, slid Laurel's cards back, and scanned the case of beer into the sales system with a little beep. Muffins sat under a glass dome by the register. Laurel lifted the lid.

"You can have those." He grabbed the pack of cigarettes from the back wall.

Her hand hovered above the last banana chocolate chip.

"We close at two. I'll just have to throw them out. Here." He pulled a paper bag from behind the counter. Snapped it open, picked up the remaining four muffins and dropped them inside.

"Thanks." She paid for the beer and cigarettes, wedged the six-pack into the bottom of her bookbag, and placed the muffins on top. "Have a good night."

Outside, snow landed on pavement under street lights and disappeared. Her sodden footsteps and the light clink of bottles the only sounds as she crossed the intersection and started up University Drive. She was too rough on her footwear. Her new boots already had a crack in the side where sole met shoe. A spot where water seeped in faster and colder. She was too rough on everything. She'd gone too fast, seeing Horsey so soon after Jimmy. And what did Horsey know anyway? Why would Laurel's mother say that to Braya? To what end? Fuck you, Horsey. Laurel plodded uphill. Face tilted into snow that turned to drizzle.

It was the end of October and the beginning of that time of year. A season between seasons. No longer fall, but not yet winter. When snow turned to sleet turned to snow turned to sleet for a solid month, sometimes two. Sometimes, the snow didn't stick until December. It was a season as long as the summer, but too ugly and miserable for anyone to acknowledge as a season at all.

Laurel squelched past security. The booth empty. She left a trail of wet down the hall and into All Girls West. Every door on the floor was closed. Whiteboards a mash of messages. New colours. Words scrawled on top of words. All the girls asleep or secretly studying. The messages on Laurel's door were all for Haley: *Love ya Hay* ♡. She dropped her bookbag in her room and headed to the lounge.

Butter sizzled. Noodles bubbled. Laurel turned off the lights and ate her pot of spaghetti in front of the TV. The empty lounge felt less hollow in the dark. The TV glow almost warm. She watched a black-and-white movie without ever catching the storyline. When it was over, she cleaned up her mess and returned to her room, where she put on a mixed CD. Portishead, Liz Phair, Ani DiFranco. She cracked a beer. Smoked a cigarette out the window. Cracked another beer. Smoked another cigarette.

Light crept over the bay. The smoke from the mill, a shadow on the horizon. An alarm went off somewhere down the hall. The floor slowly woke up around her. She pushed her cigarette into the screen, daring the mesh to burn, then dropped the butt in an empty bottle, closed the curtains and crawled into bed.

Haley pounded on her bedroom door. "Visitor!"

Laurel's room smelled sour. Empty bottles cluttered the top of her desk, their insides ashy. She got up and straightened her pants that were twisted sideways on her body. Tucked her T-shirt into the front. Smoothed her hair behind her ears and stepped out into the kitchenette.

Jimmy stood in the open doorway of the unit. He held out a fistful of notes. "You missed class."

"Thanks." Laurel shuffled barefoot across the tile, took the notes, then pulled the door halfway closed. "How'd you get in?"

Jimmy shrugged. "I waited. What have you been up to?"

"Not much." She doodled. Drank beer. Listened to music. Read sometimes, but nothing for school. One day had bled into the next without her noticing. She wasn't sure if she had missed one English class or two. If it was Tuesday or Wednesday. "I'm kind of in the middle of something right now." Laurel closed the door as much as she could without bumping Jimmy out of the way.

"What did Horsey say to you?" He leaned into the doorframe.

"Nothing." Her hair escaped and she swiped it behind her ears again. It felt matted and dry. Her fingers snared a tangle. Laurel tucked the notes under her arm and looked closely at the knot. She tried to pick it apart.

"I asked *her* and she said she didn't say anything that wasn't the truth. What's that mean?"

The knot pulled tighter. It was the kind of tangle that needed conditioner or a pair of scissors. She pinched the hair just above the knot and tore it out. Brittle strands cracked and broke in two. "What do you think it means?" She rolled the freed knot of hair between her thumb and finger.

"She wouldn't say."

"I have to go."

"What'd she say to you?"

"Thanks for the notes." She tried to pushed the door closed, but Jimmy caught it.

"Laurel?"

She sighed. "Jimmy. Just leave me alone. *Please?*"

A muscle in his cheek twitched.

"I just . . . can't do this right now."

His tongue rolled around inside his mouth as if searching for the right thing to say. He sucked the side of his cheek. "Good enough. Let me know when you can. If ever." He bowed his head and stepped back.

The door clicked shut.

The weight of everything sat on her chest. Braya's father bleeding out on the kitchen floor. His legs spread apart and twisted. The rifle kicking back into her shoulder. Lights from the ambulance flashing across the driveway. Her mother collapsing against Una. Paramedics running with a stretcher. Blood dripping from Brax's fingers. *You fucking bitch!* Bud's cat in the porch, teeth clenched and straining. Braya dropping dandelion heads into her brother's palm. A lion prince, a warthog, and a meerkat dancing. Singing. Her mother smoking a joint out the window. Gran Keane shouting, *Rum!* Braya, a newborn in her arms. Her face as squishy as a peach. The automated voice over the disconnected phone line: *The number you have reached is not in service.* Laurel sank into her mattress and worked to breathe.

She spent days in bed listening to the residents of All Girls

West. Doors banged open and closed. Shouts. A peal of high-pitched laughter. The clang of old pipes. Sounds came to her muffled, as if she had sunk to the bottom of the river. She remembered lying on the shore. The lone crow flying up to the crooked tip of a spruce. The roar of the water. Snow turned to hail pelting her face. Her cheeks. Her eyelids. Jimmy emerging from the trees. Laurel pulled the blankets over her head and lay in bed all day, every day. Unmoving. Awake. Or asleep. She didn't know. It didn't matter.

Some evening later that week, Cat Ears knocked on her bedroom door. "Laurel?"

Laurel counted the water stains in her ceiling tiles. Faded patches of brown that oozed out from the corners. She listened as Haley came out of her room next door and said she hadn't seen her all week. Maybe she'd gone home.

Cat Ears knocked again. "When you see her, tell her I was by, will you?"

Laurel shuffled deeper under the blankets and let herself drown.

She left her bed at night, when everything was quiet, and pushed through the same routine. Beer at Ultramar. Free muffins. A 3:00 a.m. trip to the lounge. By adopting the habits of a nocturnal animal, she could avoid everyone. Well, almost everyone. One of her floormates liked to watch TV with her boyfriend in the dead of night, but they ignored Laurel. They pawed at each other on the couch. Platinum-blond hair draped over some guy's face as if his identity needed to be protected for being on the floor past visiting hours.

Laurel missed another week of classes and a math test. She could try to make up the test, but she had to keep on top of her shifts at Sobeys or end up broke. On Saturday at 4:00 a.m., she searched her room for her work schedule. She scoured the insides of her desk. Her bookbag. Piles of papers on the floor of her closet. She flipped through textbooks. Stumbled over a beer bottle and knocked it over. Soppy ashes pooled on the floor. She flopped back on the bed.

At 6:00, she threw on her coat and boots and walked down University Drive. She sat on a wet guard rail and smoked cigarettes until the manager showed up and unlocked the door just before seven.

"Must be the new look," he said when he saw her. "Your hair." He held the door open and she walked inside.

"It's not . . ." Laurel let her sentence trail off. She went to the break room and checked the schedule. In the block where she had expected to find her name, she found *Susan* instead. She ran her finger down the column, double-checking the rest of the shifts for that week. Laurel flipped the page over and searched the other side.

"You missed two shifts in a row," the manager said behind her. "We didn't hear from you, so I took you off the schedule."

"What? I—"

"Don't worry about it. Not everyone's cut out to be a cashier."

The kindness in his voice made her eyes burn. Laurel shoved past him and pushed out through the door. She had no intention of being a cashier forever, but she was most definitely *cut out* for the job. She even liked her job, most of the time, and she never let on when she didn't. She had chatted with customers. Carried on conversations with old men. Smiled as she scanned blood puddings. Laurel stomped up the sidewalk with her face twisted into a scowl. Her arms swung wildly. Despite the damp and the cold, she was in a sweat when she reached Ultramar.

She stood in front of the cooler and panted on the glass. Through the condensation, her reflection scowled back at her. Pale. Hollow-eyed. Dreadlocked. Laurel slammed the cooler open and snatched a six-pack of Triple X.

"No."

Laurel dropped the case in front of him. "You can't refuse my business."

"It's seven-thirty in the morning."

"On a Saturday."

"It's Sunday."

Laurel stared at him over the top of the box. He didn't blink. She shoved the case at him. He caught it, lifted it, and put it on the floor behind the counter. He folded his arms and raised his eyebrows. She opened the lid on the muffins, took one out, shoved it in her mouth. And left.

Halfway up the hill, the wet sidewalk froze. Laurel had to widen her stance and walk with one foot dragging on the crusty edge, or she slid backward. She balanced with her arms extended and moved slow. Thighs stiff. Back straight. A car sped past and the last of the wet in a frozen puddle flicked across her face. She stopped. Wiped ice crystals from her cheek. The edge of her mouth. She shoved her damp hand in her coat pocket and continued upwards. The soft edge of a piece of paper prodded her index finger. When she stopped again to rest, she took out the worn flap torn from a cigarette pack.

Vincent's phone number. *In case you change your mind later, or just want to hang out sometime.* She'd almost forgotten about Vincent.

The paper burned too fast on one side. Laurel felt the heat of it in her mouth. She took another haul and watched the burn flare. The run crackled close to her lips. It was probably laced with something.

"Here." Vincent took the joint from her fingers. Touched his tongue to the scorched side to moisten it.

Wendy, his pierced friend in the driver's seat, cracked the window open. "You going in?"

"Yeah." Vincent sucked in the word. Laurel leaned forward to give her hips more room on the seat. She was squished between Vincent and another guy in the back of Wendy's small hatchback. Vincent pinched the joint between his thumb and forefinger, took two quick puffs and handed it off up front. He opened the door and Laurel crawled out behind him in a cloud of smoke.

The lights in the Ultramar were much too bright. Overexposed, Laurel shielded her eyes and followed Vincent around the store as he grabbed beer and chips and packs of cherry-red Twizzlers. A lollipop dangled from the cashier's mouth like an unlit cigarette. He frowned at Laurel. Vincent piled his goods on the counter and the cashier popped the lollipop from his lips, pointed the candy nub at her. "You owe me for a muffin." Laurel stuffed her hands in her pockets and inspected the magazines in the rack while Vincent paid.

The door rattled open. Wind gusted and Jimmy came in. He stamped slush from his boots. Blaze orange toque down over his ears. Mitts halfway up his forearms. He stopped when he saw her. The brown of his eyes almost as dark as his pupils.

Laurel pushed her hands deeper into her pockets, as if she might disappear inside the linings.

"Looks like you're up for something." He took his wallet out and stepped up to the cash. "Pump . . . ah . . ." He looked back through the glass doors.

"Pump two," the casher said.

Laurel took one of Vincent's cases of beer and carried it out of the store. Jimmy's truck, a brown Tacoma, was parked at the pumps. She rushed past, opened the car door, and tried to wedge the beer on the floor of the hatchback. There wasn't enough room for feet, legs and a twelve-pack, so she climbed inside and held the case in her lap. Vincent slid in next to her. Bottles clinking into place.

"What's this guy doing?" Wendy said, smoking a cigarette now that the joints were finished.

Jimmy peered in through the windshield as he walked around the front of the car. Toque blazing. He spotted Laurel, came to the back window and knocked on the glass. Sharp raps with his middle knuckle.

Vincent's buddy rolled the window down. "What's up, man?"

Jimmy kept his eyes on Laurel. "You okay?"

"Yeah." She sank into her seat. Beer box to her chin.

"You're sure?"

Air caught in her chest and expanded. Her eyes stung from the smoke in the car. She nodded.

"Come on." Vincent hit the back of the passenger seat. "Let's go."

Jimmy glared, but he turned toward his truck and walked away. Wendy started the car.

Laurel shoved the beer at Vincent. "I need to get out." She scrambled over his friend and reached for the door handle.

"You've got to be kidding me." Vincent grabbed her arm, but Laurel yanked free and opened the door. "Laurel!" She stumbled out of the car.

Jimmy stopped next to the truck, under the fluorescent lights of the canopy.

Laurel stomped after him. "You know . . ." She stumbled, the pavement a rutted mess of half-frozen slush. "It'd be nice if you invited me to your place when there wasn't a big fucking party."

"What?" Jimmy shook his head, laughed.

"It's not funny."

"No?"

"Laurel!" Vincent called from the car.

"Let her go," Wendy shouted. "She's a total snob."

"Forfucksakes, Laurel." The car rolled past, then sped out of the parking lot.

Jimmy pointed up the hill. "You want a ride now that your friends are gone?"

She shook her head.

"Well, what do you want, Laurel?"

Lights buzzed overhead. Jimmy's face sharp in the glare. Laurel's eyes were probably bloodshot. And she definitely smelled like weed. She looked down, shifted her weight from foot to foot to steady herself. Took a step closer. "You can ask me to go on a hike again. Sometime."

"The weather's kinda shit right now."

"Well, invite me over when there's not . . . when it's just . . . us."

"Just you and me?"

Laurel nodded.

He adjusted his hat. "Anything else?"

She rubbed her neck. Worked cold fingers into an ache deep in the muscle. "Maybe. You could do something nice."

"Oh yeah? Like what?"

She dropped her hand to her side. "You'll have to think of that."

Jimmy stepped closer.

Laurel closed the distance. Her head reached his collarbone. She leaned forward and rested her forehead on the cold vinyl of his chest. His arms reached around her and his chin settled on top of her head.

"I could cook?"

She nodded into his jacket. "I really hate cooking. So that'd be good."

"I can do that."

"Well, you haven't actually asked me yet. If I want to."

His hands were firm against her back. Laurel relaxed and breathed in the smell of exhaust and gas and Jimmy's coat. A car pulled up behind the truck, idling for the pump. He squeezed and let go. "You want a ride to campus?"

Laurel stepped back and shielded her eyes from the headlights. "I think . . . I need to walk."

"I'll walk you. Are you going to remember this tomorrow?"

"I have no idea." She waited on the other side of the pumps as Jimmy climbed into the truck and moved it out of the way. The car pulled forward, fan belt rattling. Inside Ultramar, the cashier watched through the glass. He raised his lollipop in salute.

TWENTY SEVEN

"Laurel!" Cat Ears. "Laurel, are you alive in there? If you don't open up, I'm calling security." Laurel kicked the sheets off her bed and waited to see if it was a bluff. Keys jangled outside her room and she heard Cat and Haley in the kitchenette. Their shadows moving under her bedroom door. One of them pounded the door with a fist. "Haley! Go get security. Now!"

"I'm up! Okay? I'm up." Laurel jammed her hair behind her ears, slumped across the room and opened the door.

"For God's sake, Laurel." Cat stood in the doorway. Haley frowned behind her. "You have a package. At security. Apparently, it's been there forever so it better not be food." She scrunched up her face. "And you seriously need a shower."

Laurel shoved her feet into a pair of slippers and left her room during daylight hours for the first time in over a week.

Haley stepped back out of her way, but Cat Ears followed her into the hall. Laurel glared sideways at her.

"*You* need an escort."

"I know how to get to security."

Cat Ears walked next to her like she was in a cat costume, hands to her chest, fingernails pointed at the floor, and her hips swaying an imaginary tail. "Have you just been hiding in your room for the past two weeks?"

"I've been busy."

"Huh."

At security, Cat Ears grinned at the security guard. "Found her!"

"ID?"

"Please tell me you remembered your ID?"

Laurel slid it over.

The guard disappeared into the back room and returned with a banana box, though this one was printed with oranges and said *Florida* in tall, skinny cursive. Duct tape covered the holes on the sides of the box, and a sheet of lined paper stuck to the top with her name and address scrawled across it in thick black marker: *Laurel Long, Universitay*.

Cat Ears squealed and folded her hands together. "Uni-ver-si-tay! Meow!"

The guard dropped the package in Laurel's arms.

"Education doesn't equal intelligence, you know?" Cat Ears sashayed next to her as they headed back down the hall. "That's what my dad says. Neither of my parents went to university, or my grandparents." She tilted her head to the side and rumpled her nose. "Or my aunts, or uncles, or cousins. I'm the first! Uni-ver-si-tay! Wait, one of my cousins did, but I'm the first girl. I think. That still counts. Right?"

"It counts. For sure." Laurel balanced the box on her forearms, then wrapped her arms around it.

"Your hair's a wreck."

Cat Ears unlocked the door to All Girls West and held it open for her. Laurel hugged the box to her chest. Sweat trickled down her spine. She was hot and thirsty, and a headache niggled at the back of her skull. When they passed the lounge, Cat Ears stopped, pointed a long nail at the double doors and cleared her throat.

"I'll open it in my room. Just in case."

"In case of what? Do you know what's in there?"

"No idea."

"Show me later?"

Laurel balanced the box against her hip as she unlocked the door to her unit, then to her room. She searched for something to cut the tape, but the only sharp object she had was a pen. She stabbed the tip of it into the duct tape over and over until she'd made a perforated line all around the lid.

The smell of it hit her.

Fresh air. Damp earth and leaves. Decaying crabapples.

A knock on the unit door. Laurel ignored it. Duct tape stretched into gooey strands and tore as she pried the lid free. She inhaled the smell of the bearskin. Fur unfolded in ripples when she lifted it out. She hadn't seen the skin since she'd dismantled the box couch and shut down the basement two years before. She'd stuffed the bearskin away somewhere. In a bin or a box or a garbage bag. Laurel sat on her unmade bed and held it to her chest.

Another knock.

Laurel closed her eyes, stroked the fur.

"Laurel! I know you're in there. I was just with you!" Cat Ears shouted. "Security called. You have a visitor at the front. If they haven't already left!"

Laurel dropped the skin on the bed, snatched her keys off the desk and rushed out of the room.

"What was in the box?" Cat called after her down the hall.

"Nothing!" A visitor at security meant a non-resident. A non-student. She couldn't think of anyone who would show up on campus like that, unannounced, except someone from home. Her mom or Bud and Braya. Their phone line was cut. Maybe they'd been booted from the Crown because they couldn't make rent. How did they get to Corner Brook? Laurel had enough student loan money left to help out with an apartment. For the first month, but that was it. She needed a job. A new job, but she wouldn't get a reference from Sobeys. Probably not from Foodland either, since they had recommended her to Sobeys in the first place. Laurel pushed out through the entrance into Arts and Admin and ran to the security booth.

She leaned in close to the little hole in the glass. "I have a visitor?"

The security guard tucked his chin and gazed toward an old woman sitting on the bench next to the main entrance. Laurel caught her breath and waited a second for her heart to calm.

The woman snorted. Phlegm hocked in the back of her throat and rattled when she cleared it.

"Gran Keane?" The grated floor rang under Laurel's feet.

Rheumy eyes looked up at her from the bench. "I was in Corner Brook." Her voice was slow and wobbly. "At the hospital. Thought I should visit my granddaughter at the university. My great-granddaughter. Still." She thumped her walking stick on the floor and leaned into it. Skin hung from her face in grey folds. Tugged at her eye sockets. The hard jut of her cheeks matched the shape of her hairless eyebrows. Her knobby hand shook. "I don't have long left, you know."

Laurel stepped back as her great-grandmother pulled herself upright. "Should I call someone?"

"I told myself I would come see you." Her shoulders hunched. Her right arm trembled. "I've done it now. Time to go."

"Go where?"

"The hospital." A cab idled at the curb outside. "I did my best by your mom. It wasn't . . . *good*. But it was my best. Considering." Gran tapped her way across the metal grate, *tap-step, tap-step*. She paused at the doors. Laurel hit the activation button and the doors buzzed open. Gran inchwormed outside. "I told myself I would say that, too."

Laurel walked next to Gran Keane with a hand outstretched,

just in case the woman toppled over and died before she reached the car. Patches of ice spotted the pavement. Wind pushed at them. Did the old woman expect her to pass along that message? After all these years? After a lifetime. *Oh, hey Mom, Gran dropped by to tell me she did her best by you.* Laurel reached ahead of her and opened the cab door, then held it as the old woman made a rickety climb inside. Gran Keane groaned when her rear landed on the seat. She rested her hands on the cane in front of her. "Should I call someone for you?"

"There's no one to call."

"I could call Mom."

She snorted. "I'm fine."

Dead leaves, frozen and curled into themselves, scattered across the road in a gust of wind and *tick-tick-ticked* on the pavement. Laurel resisted the urge to fold her arms across her chest and stood with her hand on the door as Gran adjusted the seatbelt over her shoulder and across her lap. She shivered.

"Wait." Gran let the seatbelt go. It retracted back into its holder. Her fingers stuttered down the side of her coat. She leaned sideways and searched her pocket. Whatever was in there caught in a fold and Gran frowned as she tugged. Froth clung to the corners of her mouth. "Forfucksakes," she muttered under her breath and freed a tattered envelope from the fabric. "Here." Spittle flicked on the card as she jabbed it at Laurel.

MOM was printed on the front of the envelope in clumsy capital letters.

Gran hauled at the seatbelt again.

The envelope, soft with age and speckled with mould, smelled faintly of mothballs. "What's this?"

The buckle snapped into place. Gran reached for the door.

The door bumped Laurel's tailbone. Laurel carefully opened the flap of the envelope, clamped her teeth together so they wouldn't chatter from cold, and pulled out a card that showed a child's artwork on the cover. Two stick people with big round heads. One tall. One short. The tall one had a red heart in the middle of her chest. They held hands and were surrounded by little squiggly lines. The squiggles looked like butterflies or birds. She looked closer. Flowers. The door bumped her again. "You never sent it."

"To Iris? Your grandmother? I never heard from her." Gran Keane tugged the door, aggressive this time. Laurel jumped out of the way and the door banged shut. On the other side of the window, Gran looked straight ahead, mouth set, and tapped the driver's seat with her cane. The car rolled forward, but Laurel pounded the glass.

"What the hell is this?" she shouted.

Gran stared back at her. Bald eyebrows raised.

The taxi stopped and Laurel opened the door. "Where were you all my life?"

The woman waved a veined hand at her.

"Why are you here? Now?"

Gran brought her hand to her mouth and shook her head. Quick, tiny shakes as she spoke into her fingers. "I shouldn't have come. It's too late."

Laurel stepped back and slammed the door. She stared at her own reflection in the window, then leaned forward and the old woman came back into focus behind the glass. Gran Keane closed her eyes and clutched her seatbelt with both hands. The cab pulled into the road and circled around the loop. It whooshed past. Then disappeared down the hill.

Something fell from the card when Laurel opened it. Something that had been tucked away all these years, scrap of paper, pressed flower? It flitted across the road and into a cluster of trees. The little scrap caught in a V-shaped fork at the base of a young maple and flickered there. Laurel dashed after it, but it was hopeless. A gust of wind and it was gone.

The letters on the inside of the card were big and colourful. The words split onto different lines: HAP-PY5 BIR-THDA-Y!

Laurel stood in her bedroom doorway and surveyed the state of it. Bedsheets and blankets hung off the bed and knotted on the floor. A patch of cigarette ash dried to the tile. Beer bottles. The skeleton crusts of toast left on plates and napkins and toilet paper squares. Empty mugs stained with the dried remains of tea. Books and CDs she'd once organized along the shelves above her desk were jumbled and flopped on their sides. Textbooks open and discarded on the floor. Dirty clothes everywhere. She opened her window as wide as it could go and fresh air rushed in. Laurel picked the bearskin off her bed and put it back in the box, then pulled the fitted sheet from her mattress and dropped it in the hamper.

She spent the day doing laundry, climbing up and down the stairs to the basement, basket balanced on her hip. She rinsed beer bottles and stuffed them in cases. Scrubbed every surface in her room. Reorganized CDs and books in order from her most to her least favourite. She couldn't decide where to put Tori Amos so she dropped the disc into the player and listened to *Little Earthquakes*. Gran Keane's visit to campus looked like it had taken a great deal of effort. The way she shook and trembled. *Tap-step, tap-step* across the threshold. *I told myself I would come see you.* Laurel pulled the last load of clean clothes from the dryer and lugged it upstairs.

"Laurel. You're back." Haley intercepted her in the doorway.

"I never left." Laurel carried the laundry basket inside her bedroom and closed the door, grateful for the campus's single-room layout. Haley had barely spoken to her since that night at the Studio, except to give her a lecture on leaving the bar alone.

Laurel's room had grown cold, but she wasn't ready to shut the window. Wind rattled the door in its frame as shirts and sweaters came free from each other in crackles of static. She folded shirts into the drawers under her bed and hung sweaters in the closet. When the basket was empty and her room was spotless, she returned to the banana box. She lifted the bearskin out and smoothed it across the top of her bed. She sat down. *I've done it now. Time to go*. Was her great-grandmother about to die and Laurel the one relative she'd chosen to see? Surely the woman had other people in her life. Other people besides Laurel. She must have visitors at the hospital. Her words. Her manner. Her whole visit was too cryptic to take seriously, and yet Laurel's stomach knotted at the knowing of it—there was only her. She got up and dug her phone card from the desk drawer.

Laurel sat in the phone booth, untwisted the metal cord and lifted the binder into her lap. She flipped through the book until she found the number for the Corner Brook hospital. An automated voice sent her in a wide circle before she landed back at *Option 1: Reception*.

"I'm looking for a Mrs. Keane. Is she there? At the hospital?"

"What's her given name?"

What *was* her given name? Iris? No, that was her grandmother. Rose? That was it. "Rose. Rose Keane."

Rose Keane was on the surgery ward. Visiting hours were every night from seven to nine p.m. and one to three in the afternoon, but she was scheduled for surgery in the afternoon. There was no private line to her room.

Laurel hung up and tried her mom again. *Beep-beep-beep. The number you have reached is not in service*. She slammed the phone in its cradle. Picked it back up. Slammed it again.

Back in her room, Laurel sprawled on top of the bearskin and stared at the ceiling. Tiny holes perforated the tiles, crusty, like the surface of snow after a blast of freezing rain.

Doors slammed up and down the hall. Girls shouted and laughed as they made plans to make supper in the lounge or order takeout.

At seven p.m. Laurel got up and turned off her bedroom light. Her room was freezing, but she stripped off her clothes and crawled into bed underneath the bearskin. The skin crinkled whenever it moved—bits of tissue dried hard. She caught the scent of it. Just there. Wind at the cusp of winter. It swept across the bog, through dense, skinny spruce trees. It blew past the farm and the crabapples and the goats in the pasture. Along the West River.

The curtains billowed out across her room, then settled back against the brick walls. Goosebumps raised on her arms as she ran her hands through the bear's fur, searching in the dark. Her fingers snagged the ragged edge of the bullet hole. She slid a finger into it. Another. Her mother had killed that bear when her dad was away in Labrador. Laurel had been outside one morning, playing with Bud in the snow. Her mother yelled at them to get in the house. She never yelled at them. Not like that. Not urgent and terrified, but Laurel wasn't strong enough to carry Bud. Her mitts had slipped on his snowsuit when she ran and she dropped him on his face in the snow. Her mother picked him up by the back of his suit, one-handed, and ran as he wailed. Her other hand, at the back of Laurel's neck, pushed. Forced her to move fast through the crusted snow. Her knees burned, cracking the surface.

Laurel hadn't known why her mom was so mad, she'd thought it was because she'd dropped Bud, until she heard her on the phone with Uncle Rol. *There's a bear*, she'd said, *its tracks are all over the garbage bin*. Laurel listened from the carpet. Bud liked it when she swung his feet back and forth by his socks. One of his socks slipped off and his heel bumped the floor. Whatever Uncle Rol said upset her mom. She screeched into the phone that it wasn't a dog. Slammed the receiver down. She slammed it down over and over, until Bud started to cry, then she ran over and scooped him up.

"But Mom." Laurel tried to put Bud's sock back on his wriggling foot. "It's winter." She'd been playing on top of the garbage bin and hadn't seen any tracks.

"It's not impossible for a bear to wake up. Goddamnit!" She took the sock from Laurel and shoved it onto Bud's foot, sat back and sighed through her nose. "I'm sorry." She lifted Bud from the floor. Pressed him to her chest. "It's rare," she said, "but it happens.

And a winter bear is hungry. Sometimes, it's a little mad."

They spent days boarded up in the house. Her mother would go out onto the verandah and bang a spoon against a metal pot, then scour the yard for tracks while Laurel watched with her face pressed to the window.

"I think it's gone," her mother said after what had felt like an endless amount of time stuck indoors. She unlocked the hunting rifle from the gun case, then stood on the top step and fired a warning shot into the air. Finally, she ushered Laurel and Bud, bundled in snowsuits, outside to play.

Laurel breathed in so fast her nostrils stuck together. Her mother shovelled little walking paths for Bud, and Laurel dug a cave into a snow pile. It was hard work to make a snow fort. She needed a shovel or a bucket to dig it deep enough to sit inside. There was always something like that lying around the garbage bin. Laurel made her way over to the old deep-freeze and spotted a stick spearing up from the snow. The same stick they used to prop open the lid. Laurel hunched down and worked it back and forth. The snow crunching as she tried to tug it free.

Her mother's shout sounded like a crow. Ragged. Piercing. "Don't move! Laurel! Don't. Move. You hear me?" Her voice rose to an impossible octave. She shoved through the snow with the rifle in her hand. The gun swung in wild arcs. She wasn't carrying it properly. Not the way Laurel's father had shown them. There were all sorts of gun rules. The rifle was always locked in the case. It was only for shooting practice and hunting. You could never touch it unsupervised. You always had to move it slow. With purpose. You never, *ever*, pointed it at a person.

Something huffed on the other side of the bin—a deep, guttural breath. The bin shook. A growl sent a cold shot of fear into Laurel's gut. She froze.

Her mother crunched to a stop in front of her and raised the rifle, legs spread wide, shoulders braced. Laurel had never seen her look so tall. So strong. She cocked the lever and locked it into place. Leaned her shoulder into the gun.

The garbage bin bumped Laurel's back. The bear snuffed and snarled. Laurel couldn't breathe. Her mother's face had a sheen, like ice when it starts to melt. Her eyes narrowed.

Thump. Thump. The freezer rocked.

Her mother's lips pursed. She pushed out a breath that rolled and coiled along the barrel. The brown of her eyes turned almost black. *Bang!*

Nine p.m. Laurel kicked the blankets off her bunk. The bearskin fell to the floor. She pulled clothes from the drawers under her bed and got dressed. Haley shouted at her when she banged out of the room. "It's freezing in here!"

Laurel rushed down the hall and picked up the phone. Her phone card was out of money. She dropped it on the floor, listened to the dial tone, then dialled "o" for the operator. "I'd like to make a collect call, please?"

The voice on the other end of the line sounded tinny, impossibly remote. "The number?"

Laurel remembered the number as clearly as if it had been her own. She turned her back on Haley, who hung out the doorway glaring at her, and gave the number to the operator.

TWENTY EIGHT

Daylight suddenly drifted through the window. At some point during the night, Laurel had awakened to see her breath frost and had gotten up to close it. The phone rang in the hall. She jumped out of bed and rushed out of her room.

"Security. For Laurel Long."

"This is me."

"You have a visitor . . ." He cleared his throat. "You have *visitors*."

Bud and Braya leaned into the security counter. Their faces pushed into the hole in the glass. The guard stood behind it with his arms folded, a book of crosswords rolled up in his hand.

"Hey!"

"Laurel! 'Bout time!" Bud turned and ran toward her. All arms. Skinny legs. Floppy hair. He crashed into her and she stumbled backwards. She wrapped her arms around him so she wouldn't fall. "This place is cool." Bud looked back at the booth. "You got security."

"Sorry I haven't come to see you yet."

"You've been busy, I'd imagine." Maxine clacked down the hall in her knee-high boots. Hands in her pockets. A flourish of leather fringe. She turned to Braya, who trailed behind in oversized purple mitts and a scarf that dragged on the floor. Braya grinned wide and sped ahead of her mom. Una followed at a distance.

Braya took Bud's place and Laurel scooped up her little sister. "How you doing, chicken nugget?"

"I miss you!"

"I miss you, too!"

Her mother untangled a few strands of Braya's hair. "Look at you," she said around the top of Braya's head, "in university."

"It's been a while." Una caught up. She smiled at Laurel. Laugh lines etched around the sides of her mouth. Una pulled Laurel in for a quick hug. Braya squished between them. "I'm glad you called."

Laurel put Braya down, then stood and brought her hands together. "Right. Okay. Ready to go see Gran?"

"No," her mother said.

"Well, I need to get dressed. Come see my room. You can all meet my roommate, Haley."

At the hospital, visiting hours were closed except for immediate family members. They huddled around the nurse in the waiting room. Maxine was about to go in and see Gran Keane alone, when she paused and grabbed Laurel's arm. "Come in with me."

Laurel hesitated. She looked to Una, who shrugged as she sat down in a chair and pulled her purse into her lap.

"Please?"

"Don't you want to see her alone?"

"No. I don't really want to see her at all."

"Okay." Laurel nodded. "I'll come with you."

They followed the nurse down the hall. She stopped at the door and gestured into the room. "Last bed over there."

Gran Keane was asleep in a curtained-off back quadrant of the shared hospital room. Laurel's arm brushed against a scratchy blue curtain as she squeezed past the foot of her bed. Someone coughed, long and loud, on the other side of it. There was just enough space between Gran's bed and the exterior wall for two waiting-room chairs. Laurel hovered by the first chair and flattened herself against the bricks, forcing her mother to move past her to the head of the bed. Her mom pursed her lips as she squeezed by.

"It's not quite a private room." She looked around at the curtains. "But it's not too bad."

Laurel sat down, leaned back and pulled an ankle over her knee. A TV was mounted in the corner on an adjustable metal arm. A phone sat on the bedside table. Neither was connected.

Maxine blew out a sigh. Her lips quivered. "I guess I'm supposed to say something nice?" She put her hands on the metal rail by Gran's head. "But I don't know what."

"She liked *Jeopardy!*"

Her mother's wedding ring clinked the rail before she let go. She left the bedside and sat in the chair next to Laurel. "That woman watched a hell of a lot of TV."

"She's not dead yet."

Her mother barked out a laugh, then looked at the ceiling and fussed at the corners of her eyes.

"I can go. I just thought someone should . . . see her."

"No." She caught Laurel's hand and squeezed it.

Laurel shifted in her seat. A monitor beeped at Gran Keane's side. An intravenous line ran into her arm. A tube up her nose.

"I hated her." Maxine let go and her boot heels struck the tiled floor as she got up. She strutted back to the bed, gripped the rail with both hands. "I didn't want to, but I really, really hated her. You know?" She clicked the floor, as if keeping time with her heel. "She made it impossible for me to feel anything else." Her gaze flitted around the room. She let the rail go and swung her arms back in a snap of leather. She shook her head and her chin wobbled. "I can't forgive her."

Laurel leaned forward. "But just being here. Maybe there's something in it for you?"

"She's got nothing I want." Her mother shook her head. Quick little shakes. Her lips trembled. "No." Her mouth settled into a hard line and the head-shaking, the lip-trembling stopped as abruptly as it had started. Her gaze landed on Laurel. "I tried. I'm sorry, baby." She squeezed past the curtains and pushed out through the door.

Laurel flopped back in her chair and sighed.

"Da fuck is all that racket?" A whisper rough as smoke.

Her chair creaked as she peered over the top of the bed.

"Who's there?"

"We came to see you. Before your surgery." Laurel stood to reveal herself.

"Iris?"

"No. It's . . ."

"Maxine."

"It's me, Laurel." She moved to the spot where her mother had stood. Put her hand on the bedrail.

Gran rolled her head from side to side on the pillow, thin wisps of hair plastered against her skull. She raised a forearm, spotted with age, and inspected the IV. She fidgeted with the oxygen at her nose and settled her gaze on Laurel. "I don't want to be buried."

"What?"

Her Adam's apple bobbed when she swallowed. "And don't leave me in a jar. I want my ashes scattered across the ocean." A shaky hand reached for the bedrail and tripped along the metal until it bumped into Laurel's. "On the wind."

Laurel caught her hand and held it. The sensation of her great-grandmother's fingers spiny like a long-legged insect. Gran's eyes slid closed again. She'd come to see her on campus in an attempt to appease some sense of guilt, or to settle affairs. Laurel might have imagined it, but for a moment, the old woman had looked proud. The expression could have been a trick of her deep wrinkles. Her hard-set mouth. The fierce glaucoma in her eyes. Or it could have been a manifestation of Laurel's own hopeful brain. But she leaned on the rail and held the cold, brittle hand until the nurse came in and wheeled Gran Keane off to surgery.

Laurel returned to the waiting room. Horsey was there now. She sat in the back corner with one foot on her seat, knee up. The other leg stretched into the aisle.

Una kicked her in the shin and Horsey moved her leg out of the way. She pulled her coat from the chair next to her, indicating she'd saved Laurel a seat. Laurel gave Una a nod as she sat down.

"Hey," Horsey said. "Sorry about . . ."

"It's fine. I'm glad you're here."

Horsey nodded and slumped down in her chair. "Well, now what?"

"We wait, that's what," Una said.

"Yep." Maxine shifted to get comfortable, chewed on her pinky finger and squeezed Braya's knee. "We wait."

Braya settled in her seat and rested her head on her mom's shoulder. Bud sucked the inside of his cheek and let go with a loud popping sound. Una picked at a tear in her purse. Horsey tapped her fingers on the sides of her thigh. A little girl pulled a *Cosmo* magazine off the top of a stack on the table. She looked about two or three. A kid with a crooked haircut and a runny nose. She climbed into her seat with her magazine. Next to her, a woman who was probably her mother, stared straight ahead at the hospital walls. The magazine pages opened with a sloppy crinkle. "How to Please Your Man in Five Steps."

A vending machine hummed in the opposite corner of the room and Bud got up to check the offerings. "One twenty-five for a pack of chips," he said when he came back. "Anyone got any money?"

A chorus of "No, sorry," and he flopped back in his chair. "I could probably stick my arm up in it."

"That never works." Horsey said as she hunched forward. "Trust me."

Bud drooped and kicked his legs back and forth. Then continued to suck the inside of his cheek. *Pop!*

"Mom shot a bear once."

Her mother dropped her hand in her lap. "Laurel! Shush." Horsey sat up straight. Braya leaned forward. Eyes wide. "Woods Road," her mother explained, and Braya nodded.

"I remember that." Una looked to Maxine. "In the dead of winter. It'd been roaming around your house. No one believed you."

Bud leaned in closer. Laurel tilted toward her mother. The rest of the room faded into hospital-beige bricks.

"I don't know why. The tracks were right there. Plain as day for anyone who had a mind to look."

"I shoulda . . . I shoulda looked." Una's face went stern with regret.

Maxine's voice softened. "You did enough."

"I should have checked in on you. Come down to the house. I don't know why I didn't." Her lips all but disappeared into a tight little stitch.

"Maybe you did believe me." Maxine raised a shoulder. "Maybe you were just afraid of bears."

"I am." A dimple formed in Una's chin. "I'm not afraid of much, but I'm afraid of bears."

"Everyone's afraid of bears!"

The dimple deepened, but Una laughed at Braya's wisdom. "I think you're right."

"Hold on." Horsey held up a hand. "You shot that bear? The one . . . The *bearskin?*"

"I did."

"Noooo." Her mouth hung open. She punched the side of her thigh and looked at Laurel. "Your mom killed that bear. Why didn't you say something?"

Laurel nodded with her chin rested on a fist.

"What are you talking about?" Bud looked pissed at being excluded. Next to him, Braya looked from face to face to face, eyes bright, eager to understand something she wasn't ready to know.

The stack of magazines fell over and slid one after another to the floor. The little girl stood back with her hands raised, her fingers opening and closing like she was testing their stickiness. Braya hopped up to help her. She sifted through the magazines, found a *Chickadee* and handed it over. The little girl toddled off with her new magazine filled with colourful animals happy in bright and shiny habitats. Braya restacked the magazines on the table one by one.

"Your dad wanted to keep the bearskin. He tacked that thing to the side of the house and let it dry in the sun. But it was the dead of winter. It froze solid." A hush fell in their corner. Her jacket crackled as she shifted in her seat. "From a distance, it looked like a flayed man strung up all winter long. Laurel wouldn't walk past it. She'd walk all the way around the other side of the house if she wanted to go out back. Remember that? And the snow was always deeper."

Laurel nodded.

When the skin had thawed out in the spring, her dad had taken it down. Laurel had stood back as he spread the bearskin out over the garbage bin. He scraped it with his fleshing knife. A slow steady rhythm that removed dead tissue and revealed the clean skin underneath. He paused, then stuck his finger through the bullet hole. Traced the torn edge.

"Your mother's the toughest lady I know," he told her.

"I thought bears slept all winter." Laurel stepped close to look at the bullet hole.

"This one woke up."

"Mom said it was mad."

"A bear out in the dead of winter? That's a hungry bear. A dead bear. Your mom's a good shot and you're damned lucky. We're all goddamned lucky." He slipped the tip of the knife back under the meat. Shimmied it back and forth to separate hardened flesh from soft hide.

PART FIVE
1997

TWENTY NINE

DECEMBER

Http colon forward slash forward slash www dot yahoo dot com
. . .
. . .

She was as bad as Gran Keane with the remote.
Enter.

Aha! In the search bar she tapped out G e o r g e E l i o t, and spent the next hour clicking through sites and taking notes. Her mother would love this. The web was like the *Encyclopædia Britannica* on steroids; she could only imagine what her mother might try to look up online. It was probably best that she didn't have access.

Bored with her final assignment of the term, Laurel experimented with a few more searches: Most bars per capita in North America. Enter.

Pittsburgh

Most bars per capita in Canada. Enter.

Victoria, Halifax, or *St. John's.* Maybe Stephenville was just a well-kept secret. Laurel looked around the library. She was the only one on the computers, and besides Liz, the librarian, tapping away at the main desk, the place was quiet.

Rick Warren

. . .

Enter.

Nothing. The man. And his death. Didn't exist online.

Winchester .30-30. Enter.

Laurel stared at a picture of her dad's gun. The wooden handle. The lever shaped like her mom's old potato peeler. The long, slender barrel. That gun, the actual *weapon,* was in a police archive somewhere, probably alongside a baggie of her bloody clothes. *Introduced in 1895. The lever-action .30-30 rifle has killed more deer than any other cartridge in North America. While there has been stiff competition in recent years the .30-30 tends to be lighter and easier to shoulder than its longer-range counterparts. It is also on the lower end of recoil for deer rifles, making it a good choice for beginners.*

Her dad had used it for hunting moose, and her mom had taken down a black bear, and Laurel had . . .

You're damned lucky. We're all goddamned lucky.

"Hey."

Laurel jumped as Jimmy came up behind her.

"Ready to go?"

The cursor flew around the computer.

Jimmy held the back of her chair, his face mere inches from hers, and touched the top right corner of the screen. "That X right there."

Laurel closed the page and pushed up from the computer desk. "Thanks for doing this."

"No prob. I was headed home this weekend anyway."

"I just got to check the schedule."

Liz's smile could melt marshmallows. Laurel smiled back, counted to five, then forced her mouth to relax. She'd learned to do that after working a full shift with her earlier that week. Laurel leaned over the main desk and craned her neck to see the schedule tacked to the wall.

"You can come around to this side now." Liz held a pencil like a spear between her two index fingers. She swished it back and forth in a movement that reminded Laurel of Cat Ears' walk.

"Right." Laurel walked past the "Staff Only" sign and made a point not to look at Jimmy, who lingered under the clock by the doors.

"Are you headed home before finals?" Liz smiled. Swished her pencil-spear.

"I *am*." She ran her fingers down the columns under each day of the week.

"Is that your boyfriend?"

"No."

"You're not on till Wednesday. I already checked." *Swish, swish, swish.* "He's a cutie."

"Don't get excited."

Liz giggled. "See you next week."

Jimmy drove with one palm pressed to the steering wheel. The other flat on the console between them. The fan blasted hot air into the cab and the low buzz of OZ FM's top-forty countdown competed with the noise of the heaters. Laurel took off her gloves and relaxed into her seat as the city disappeared behind them and the highway narrowed from four lanes to three to two. A thin strip of snow marked the shoulder of the road, then trees. Dense evergreen monochromatic with frost. Light sliding along branches and needles. The woods alive and breathless.

"There's CDs in here if you want to have a look." Jimmy opened the console and tugged out a heavy book of compact discs. He passed it to Laurel and she flipped through everything from Bob Dylan to Erykah Badu. She closed the book and sat with it in her lap. "Nothing?"

Laurel shook her head, stuffed the book back in the console and closed the lid. She rested her hand in the same spot Jimmy's had been, drummed her fingers on the hard top. A bright December sun beat down on the pavement and melted the frost. Trees just trees as brightness receded up the mountains. Laurel snapped off the radio. Flipped down the visor.

"There should be sunglasses." He ran a hand along a ledge underneath the dash. "Try there." His wrist touched her knee as he pointed at the glovebox.

Laurel popped open the compartment and pulled out a massive pair of aviators. The frames reached halfway up her forehead and to the bottom of her cheekbones. Jimmy's pinky tapped the console soundlessly. The truck quiet save for the steady skim of tires on bare pavement.

"I remember everything. From the gas station." Laurel adjusted the glasses on her face.

"Oh yeah?" Jimmy's cheek twitched.

"I'm not sure how I'd forget. And now I'm . . . now I'm just waiting."

He slid her a sideways glance. "You're that hungry? I know you can't cook for *shit*, but . . ."

Laurel laughed. "I'm pretty much starving."

Jimmy hit the signal light. It *tick-tick-ticked* as the truck slowed. "I got to . . . um . . ." He guided the truck to the side of the road. Tires crunching into snow. "I mean, I want to . . ." Jimmy pushed the truck into park. "I'd like to kiss you." He unfastened his seatbelt, brushed her hair aside and removed the sunglasses. Her hair caught in the hinged elbow.

"Here." Laurel took the glasses and worked the strands free, untangling them from the metal coil one at a time. A semi-trailer rumbled past. The truck shook, buffeted by the drift. She unfastened her own seatbelt, slid the console open and dropped the glasses inside. Her face grazed his as she leaned back, closed her eyes against the rush of her heart. And kissed him.

THIRTY

Kids bundled inside snowsuits climbed on piles of snow between driveways. A little girl sped down on a plastic saucer and brought up solid on the pavement. She rolled across the street, laughed, and threw her arms in the air to show she wasn't even hurt. Jimmy guided the truck into the driveway as Horsey came out through the screen door and waved both hands. She bowed, swinging an arm.

"Welcome back!" she called as Laurel slammed the truck door.

Maxine shouldered out of the apartment with a box hugged to her chest.

"Shit." Jimmy turned back to the truck. "I should back in."

"I didn't know you were coming." Her mother smiled broadly at Laurel.

"I didn't know you were *moving*. Horsey told me."

"I got the best deal on an apartment. It's a duplex. And if my salary goes up my rent stays the same. I thought I'd get everything straightened away and surprise you when you came home for Christmas." Her mother clopped down the steps and gave her a hug.

"You didn't think I'd want to say goodbye to the place?" She hugged her mother back with one arm.

"Do you?"

"Of course I do." Laurel reached for the door. "And you could use the help."

"We haven't touched your room yet." Her mother got out of the way. "It's all yours."

"Well, what were you going to do with it?" She flicked a look skyward and went inside. With the exception of the paint—green in the kitchen and her mother's custom mauve-brown in the hallway, apartment five looked exactly the same as it did when they'd moved in four years before. Boxes leaned together on top of concave bins. Garbage bags stuffed with blankets and pillows sat lopsided on the floor. An apple clock poked out from the top of a bag. Laurel tugged it free of the plastic. She held it up when her mom came in from outside. "Where'd you get this?"

"Arlims. I couldn't help myself. It's the same as the old one."

Laurel turned it over in her hands. The edge on this one was bevelled, and instead of seeds, there were actual numbers. That, and it looked fresh, like a second chance. She tucked it back in the bag. "How's Gran?"

Her mother sighed and tied the bag closed. "A pain in the ass. But I get to use her car to run errands. I have a lot of errands." She laughed. "And as long as she needs twenty-four-hour access to supervised care—me," she pointed at herself. "I need a phone. So she pays the bill. It works. The stuff she says sometimes, though. That woman's dead inside. It really shouldn't be long now."

"Mom!"

Her mother smirked as she hefted the garbage bag into her arms and carried it outdoors.

"Where's Bud and Braya?"

"Playing out here somewhere."

The door snapped closed and Laurel headed upstairs to her room. The latch for the padlock hung open on the doorframe. The actual lock nowhere to be seen. She stood in the middle of her old bedroom and surveyed the contents. Her dresser would be useful if she moved out of residence. And her bed. She'd keep her books, too. It wouldn't be a big deal to lug them back to campus next term, but she could live without everything else. Clothes that she'd collected at yard sales and church basements and never wore. Shoes that no longer fit. Half-empty bottles of gel and hairspray. Horsey came down the hall. She stood in the doorway and clapped a hand to the frame.

"We had some good times in this place. I'm gonna miss it." Horsey folded her arms and raised her eyebrows. "How was the drive with Jimmy?"

Laurel turned to the window. "Fine."

"You're blushing."

"I'm not even looking at you." She chewed the corner of her lip and searched for a four-year-old girl in the crowd of kids running around the street.

"You're practically buzzing. And Jimmy—" Horsey laughed. "Anyway, want some help?"

"Are there any more boxes?"

"I'll grab some garbage bags." Horsey turned to go back downstairs.

"I'd prefer Tupperware!"

"Your Highness!"

Outside, Braya ran from behind a snowbank and fired a snowball at some kid who easily dodged it. She grabbed a handful of snow and squatted down to make a new ball.

Textbooks from school and a few encyclopedia volumes leaned against the wall at the bottom of Laurel's closet. She would let all that go, but the books on the rest of the shelves—the ones from the library she'd loved too much to return, her mom's fantasies and science fictions, and her dad's Louis L'Amours—she'd keep. She pulled *The Daybreakers* off the shelf, one of her dad's favourites, and flipped through thin yellow pages. Held it by the spine and shook. The pages fanned out, but nothing fell to the floor. She tried the other books without any luck. Then checked the encyclopedias and textbooks on the bottom shelf. Something slipped out from the pages of an old math book and flitted across the room. Laurel bent down and ran her hand through the dust underneath the bed.

Horsey dropped a banana box on the floor. "No bins, just this."

Laurel stood, slid the box over to the shelf and began to stack books inside. Downstairs, the door banged back and forth as Jimmy and her mom lugged stuff out to the truck, then she heard Andrew's and Una's voices.

"Mom's here." Horsey bounded back downstairs.

They made short work of the move. Anything could be accomplished in two hours with seven pairs of hands and three vehicles. At least, that's what Andrew said when they loaded the couch aboard the truck and caravanned to the new duplex. Her mother steered Gran's Accord down Main Street, past Esso, Byrne's Shoes and Danny's Bakery. The rear window of the car completely obstructed by boxes and bags. "Don't worry," she said as they turned off Main Street onto Princess Avenue. "We're still royals."

By midnight, bedframes had been bolted back together. Mattresses fitted with sheets. But Baker Dog was missing. Bud said it was fine, but no one would leave the duplex for the night until they tracked down the stuffed toy. What had looked like a tidy move-in turned into the scene of a robbery. Bags were ripped open. Boxes torn apart and left with their insides spilling out. Glassware on the floor. The carpet in the apartment radiated a chemical smell of newness and the light fixtures were marbled glass. Laurel sifted through a bin filled with pots and pans.

Una came in from outside, Baker Dog dangling from her fingers. "He was in the car. Crisis averted!"

Laurel took the dog upstairs to Bud. He and Braya each had their own room. Bunk beds reassembled into a double bed for Bud, and a single for Braya, but Laurel found Braya curled up in bed with Bud anyway. Bud sat up and reached, fingers stretched wide. She tossed him Baker Dog.

"I guess it'll take a while to get used to this place." Laurel pulled the bedsheets up around their shoulders.

"It's too quiet here." Bud tucked the toy under his elbow. "No heavy metal."

Braya pumped her lips and let out a beat. Laurel sat down on the edge of the bed. "That almost sounds like . . . 'Master of Puppets'?"

Braya giggled and nodded her head.

"What about . . . ?" Bud headbanged and nah-nah-nahed.

"'Thunderstruck.' Nice."

"Guess this one—"

"I think it's time to go to sleep."

Everyone had left the duplex by the time Laurel got up again, except Jimmy. He shoved his boots on in the porch and zipped his jacket. He looked up when she came down the stairs. "I guess I'll see ya?"

"Yeah." Laurel couldn't help the smile that pushed through her face as she walked past. "I'll see ya."

He grinned back and waved before disappearing out the door.

She found her mother by herself in the living room, holding an electric kettle. The cord tangled up in the toaster.

"You can sleep with me if you want," her mother said. "Or take Braya's bed."

"I'm good here." Laurel hauled a garbage bag to the couch and tugged out a pillow. Bedsheets and blankets tumbled after it.

Her mother untangled the cord and carried the kettle to the kitchen.

Laurel's cheeks felt oily and a fuzzy feeling clung to her gumline, but she grabbed a fleece blanket and curled up on the couch in the same clothes she'd worn all day. She slipped her arms inside her shirt and unhooked her bra, then shut her eyes, just for a minute.

"Tea?" Her mother stood in the doorway with two steaming mugs.

Laurel cleared her throat and sat up. She hugged the blanket to her chest. "Is there milk?"

"No. There's sugar."

She took the cup and wrapped her hands around it.

"It'd be nice to get some new furniture in here. Maybe a sofa chair." Her mother sat on the couch by her feet and sipped, upper lip barely skimming the hot surface. "The phone'll be hooked up tomorrow." She rolled her eyes to the ceiling. "So Gran can call. Do you know that car has less than a thousand kilometres on it? It just sat in her driveway for years, and there we were . . ." She held her tea in her lap and shook her head. "Anyway." She looked around the room.

A framed picture of Laurel, Bud, and Braya poked out of one of the open boxes on the floor. Laurel and Bud smiling at the camera with Braya, wrapped up in a blanket, squished between them. They were on the front step of the Crown. Laurel couldn't remember it being taken. "It's nice here."

"Not a bad spot to start a new year. And my rent won't go up when I work. I think we can even have pets." Her mother patted Laurel's foot under the blanket. "Bud would love a dog."

"Oh, you have to get Bud a dog." Laurel set her tea on the coffee table. "I have something for you, actually. A few somethings." She kicked the blanket off and went upstairs. It was dark in Bud's room and she felt around until her hand landed on her bookbag. She carried it quietly into the hall, unzipped the front pouch and pulled out *The Daybreakers*. Laurel flipped to the middle of the book then closed it again carefully and returned it to the front pouch. She took out the card she'd gotten from Gran Keane. *MOM* written across the envelope. The two figures on the front of the card. The big red heart. Little squiggly flowers. Laurel slid the card back in the envelope and tucked it in her back pocket. She slung the bookbag over her shoulder and carried it downstairs.

"Here." She dropped the bag on the couch next to Maxine.

"What's that?"

"A bookbag."

Her mother grunted and pulled the bag into her lap. She held it like a dinosaur-egg.

"Open it."

She unzipped it. "Oh Jesus." The bearskin came out in a flourish of rippling fur. Laughing, she gave it a shake, shoved the bag aside and smoothed the bearskin over her lap.

"Andrew used to tie it around his shoulders, like a cape."

Her mother ran her hands through the fur, then threw it over her back and tied the forelegs around her neck. "Like this?" She extended a fist, Superman-style.

"There's more. Front pouch."

Her mother opened the pouch, looked at Laurel, then pulled out the book. "One of your dad's favourites." The book fell open in her hands and she carefully picked out the photograph. "Are you giving this to me? Don't you want to keep it?"

"I want you to frame it and put it up. I can see it when I visit."

"Your dad never . . ." She cleared her throat, then touched a finger to the photograph. Laurel in an oversized snowsuit. Her dad's enthusiastic embrace. "Bud's smile." Her mother put a hand to her mouth. "I'll ah . . ." She nodded, tight and quick. "I'll get a good frame. And is this . . . ?"

"I remember that trip now."

Her mother lifted the flower by a tiny, translucent petal. "Long's Braya."

"Total contraband. I can't believe you let me keep it."

"That was a good day. A very good day. Think I'll get in trouble if I frame this too?" She held the photograph and the flower up next to each other. "They look nice together. And with that?" She gestured at the picture poking up out of the box. "I could start a photo wall. I still have all those brass frames. You know, nothing too bourgeois."

"No. Nothing too bourgeois."

Maxine folded the picture and the flower back into the centre of the book. "I have something for you, too. I've been meaning to do this." She put the book on the table. The bearskin pooled on the couch behind her as she got up.

Laurel leaned back against her pillow, adjusted the bearskin over her feet and sipped her tea.

Her mother ran up to her room. Laurel could hear her rummaging through boxes, then she came back down and rifled through the coats in the porch. When she returned to the living room, she looked empty-handed, but she raised a fist above Laurel and dropped a key in her lap.

"What's that?"

"A key."

Laurel snorted.

"The house. On Woods Road. It's already in your name. I owed some bills and if I left it in *my* name . . . well. It's there. All boarded up, but in one piece."

Laurel picked up the key and turned it over in her fingers. Tarnished brass. Heavy-looking. Almost weightless.

"It's yours."

"What about Bud?"

"You're my oldest. It's yours."

"I own a house?"

"It's practically a cabin, but you can do whatever you want with it. When you're ready. Do it up. Sell it to pay for school. Keep it as a summer . . . place."

"We've been broke for years."

Her mother took a noisy slurp.

"No vehicle. Your phone was cut. Why didn't you sell it?"

"Nobody wants to buy a house out there at the back end of

Woods Road."

"Did you ever try?"

Her mother stared straight ahead, tight-faced.

"Someone would have. Horsey's dad sold land out there for cabins. People want it. Well?"

"Well, what?"

"Did you ever try?" Laurel yanked the bearskin off the couch and threw it at her mom.

She blocked it with an elbow, tea slopped on her hand. "No. I never tried. Okay?" She thunked her mug down on the coffee table. "I think it's time to go to bed. The last thing I want right now is a fight with you."

"Then don't fight! Just tell me why."

"Jesus, give it back if you don't want it." Her mother wiped her leg as she got up. "Good night." The words were serrated as if Laurel had just ruined the most perfect night of all time. Her mother stomped upstairs.

Laurel flung the blanket off. She stomped after her and caught her by the elbow.

Her mother stumbled down a step. "What the hell?" She caught the rail.

"Why didn't you sell the house?"

"I was saving it. For you."

"Why?"

"Because you . . ." Her mother covered her mouth. Eyes wide. Bangs streaked with grey. She blinked at Laurel. "Because you saved my life." She spoke into her fingers. "Is that what you want to hear? You saved my life." Her voice cracked and she squeezed her eyes shut. "And Braya's life. And I'm sorry." She layered both hands over her face and whispered into her palms. "I'm so sorry you had to do that." She bent forward with a hand to the wall. Then leaned against it. Chest heaving, she slid down to the step.

Laurel sat next to her. She laid a hand on her back as she

gasped and sobbed. The carpet underneath them a thick, pale grey, almost white. She ran her fingers over the pile.

"I'm so sorry, Laurel." Her mother shook her head into her shoulder. "If I had done anything different." She drew in a sharp breath. "With Rick. If I had left the woods. If I had left . . . him. Then we wouldn't . . ."

"I know."

"We wouldn't have Braya. And she's . . . she's my world. You all are."

Laurel closed her eyes. "I remember being in the grocery store one day. You had on your leather jacket. With the fringes. Your face . . . there were bruises."

Maxine looked down at her hands.

"I should have walked with you that day. I should have been walking with you in the store, when you saw Aunt Cora."

Her mother looked up and shook her head. "I don't even remember—"

"I should have had your back."

She pulled Laurel as close as she could on the step and held her.

"Braya doesn't know."

"No."

"Did you tell her he died in a hunting accident?"

"No!"

Laurel lifted up. "That's what Horsey said."

"Horsey. Forgodsakes. No. I haven't told her anything." She sighed, deep and shaky. "Maybe we can tell her together."

Laurel rested back on her mother's shoulder.

"All of us. Bud too. Maybe with Tina? She's brought this up before."

Laurel stretched out a knee and rested her foot one step lower. Somewhere in the apartment, a heater ticked to life.

"Mom?" Braya looked down at them in her polka-dot pyjamas.

Her mother looked up the stairs. "What is it?"

"Can I sleep in your bed?" She squeezed a floppy stuffed bunny in her arms. "Bud snores."

"Okay. Go on in my bed. I'll be right there."

Braya shuffled down the hallway and disappeared. Laurel rested against her mother's shoulder for one more moment. Her mother stroked her hair and kissed the top of her head. "I'm giving you the house because it's everything I have to give. I should have done this years ago." She got up and Laurel let her go. "Good night, sweet heart."

Laurel watched her climb the stairs. "Night, Mom."

THIRTY ONE

The Accord accumulated enough mileage running her mother's errands to make up for all the time it had spent stagnant in Gran Keane's garage. Her mother guided the car off Route 460 and slowed over potholes, Woods Road worse now than Laurel remembered it. They passed Una's driveway, twisting into the trees, and continued to the end of the pavement, scraped clean by a recent plough. Her mother parked in front of the Pateys' farmgate and let the car idle. "What do you think? Up for a walk?"

Snowmobile tracks ran a narrow line down their old driveway. Trees tight to the edge. Alder tips spearing up along the sides. The lane didn't look wide enough to accommodate the tiny sedan without scraping paint, even if it wasn't socked in with snow. Maxine turned off the ignition. Laurel cracked the back door open and caught a whiff of manure.

"What *is* that?" Braya climbed out of her booster seat on the other side.

"Goat shit!" Bud had ridden shotgun. He got out, stretched his arms overhead, and inhaled. Braya slapped her mitt over her nose.

The old hay barn was gone, and the old farmhouse, but Jimmy's house was the same. White vinyl siding. Red door. In her memory the house was fancier. A sign on the gate said "Private Property." The sign looked as old and worn as everything else, but Laurel didn't remember it being there. A crusted lip of ploughed snow had built up at the end of their driveway. Her mother stomped into it. She climbed over packed snow and ice chunks and dipped down the other side. Bud held a hand out to Braya. She took it and they started after her. Laurel followed behind.

For the most part, the ski-doo trail held beneath them. Laurel went through once, up to her thigh, and Maxine crashed twice to her knees. Bud moved with his arms airplaned out and practised perfect stealth. Braya skipped along as if weightless. The farm disappeared behind the trees and the house came into view. Grey wood siding. Wide verandah. Windows boarded up with sheets of plywood. Laurel stopped and frowned at her childhood home. She'd expected a flood of memories and a rush of emotion, but it just looked small. Braya blinked at the place like it was haunted. Bud whooped and ran ahead, then crashed through the crust, knee-deep.

The snowmobile track continued past the house and they had to cross a raw stretch of snow to reach the buried front steps. Her mother sank up to her thighs. "Ah . . . !" she laughed. "This might be the end of the line."

"No way!" Bud made a few steps, but even in stealth mode he went down. Maxine tried to haul him out, but together, they just made a pit and sank deeper. Braya stayed on top of the snow, but she headed straight for the pit and crashed into it with them. They laughed hysterically as they tried to roll back out.

Bud managed to haul himself free, but after a few fortunate steps, he crashed through again. He gave up and crawled on his hands and knees, rearing his head from side to side and puffing through flared nostrils like a workhorse. Maxine followed his trail. Laurel plunged forward. Snow pushed up under her pant legs, slipped down the back of her boots and rested against her heels.

She skirted the pit as best she could and followed Bud's path.

"Hold the rail." Laurel gripped it through the snow as she searched for a step with her boot, careful not to rest her full weight on the tread in case the board had rotted through. Braya climbed halfway up, then scooted back down on her butt, packing down a slide. Bud caught on and turned around to do the same. Laurel kept to the side of the steps and climbed up behind her mom.

The front door was streaked with rust. More rust spotted the nail heads in the siding. Laurel hauled off her mitt and dug the key from her pocket. She wedged the key into the lock but it refused to budge in either direction. "You sure this is the right key?"

Her mother pushed in front of her to give it a try. She twisted and jiggled. Grunted. Laurel rubbed her cold fingertips together. The plywood over the kitchen window hung loose in the bottom left corner. She tramped over to it and slipped her fingers underneath the edge. Tugged. Nothing. She braced a foot against the wall and hauled. Wood splintered and cracked. Rusty nails screeched free from the siding. The corner let go and Laurel stumbled back with a broken bit of plywood. The rest of the sheet held fast.

"Not sure if that's the best idea." Her mother looked at the gap in the shutter. "There might be some de-icer in the car. But you're gonna keep at that, are you?"

Laurel gripped another corner and tugged.

"All right." She let loose a heavy stream of breath as she surveyed the chaotic trail they'd made in the snow. "I'll go back and check." Her mother thumped down the steps, legs spread, careful not to ruin the slide.

The board on the window wasn't going anywhere without the help of a hammer or a crowbar, and even if it did, Laurel would need something to pry the window open. She trudged back down the steps, like her mother had, and waded her way around to the back, where she found the shed listing hard to one side, its roof half covered in drift. The door hung open from one hinge and gaped at the top, offering a clear view of the empty interior. A stretch of field that she had once considered her backyard lay fresh and unbroken in front of her. She twisted to look at the house. Cut logs halfway up, then tarpaper. Her old bedroom window with the broken lever. The basement door, buried up to the latch. Somewhere under the snow rested their old picnic table. Laurel turned back to the open field between her and the woods, and forged ahead.

The front of her jeans stuck wet to her thighs and her ankles throbbed with cold. Past the treeline, the snow was impossibly deep. She gave up and sat back on her heels. Laurel watched the trees move. Spruce and fir funnelling up to the sky. A crow cawed, lone and idle. She pulled off her mitts and wiped her face. The crow lifted off and disappeared from view. Its perch, the crooked tip of a spruce, wobbled, then settled back in its rhythmic sway. The tips of the tallest, skinniest trees all bent at sharp angles, pointing east. Bent by the wind that roared down the mountains and across the highway, cutting toward her house.

Do you know your way home from here?

Laurel looked back at the trail she'd left in the snow.

The important thing is to walk in a straight line. Keep the sun in your eyes, or at your back, so you don't walk in circles.

She looked up at a cloudy dimpled sky. A blast of sun.

What do I do when there isn't any sun?

Laurel closed her eyes and fell back in the snow A laugh bubbled up from her chest. When the light failed there was still direction. The trees pointed the way home.

A snowmobile burned across the field and revved outside the tree line.

"Laurel!" Bud called into the woods. "Come on! Mom got the door open!"

The way out was easier than the way in. She half-walked, half-crawled through the trail she'd already made. Jimmy sat on his

Arctic Cat fully decked out in a camo one-piece. His boots tied around his calves. The flaps of his trapper hat over his ears. Braya peeked at her, squished between his elbows and the handlebars. Bud clung to his back. Jimmy gunned the engine. "Hop on."

"Looks pretty full."

Jimmy jerked his head.

Bud shimmied forward and Laurel worked against the soaked denim of her jeans to sit down. Her thighs stung, but she held onto her brother and the snowmobile swung around the other side of the house. It bumped over a drift and Braya giggled wildly. They grumbled to a stop at the bottom of the front steps.

The door hung open.

Laurel climbed off and Bud hopped from the seat to the steps. Each step visible now after their foot traffic. Jimmy lifted Braya from the ski-doo and Laurel helped her off. He killed the engine. "You coming?" she asked him.

The seat creaked as he settled back onto it. "You guys go on."

Laurel squeezed Braya's wet mitts. "Ready?"

She nodded and started up the steps. Her legs moved in arcs to accommodate the puffy snow pants, knees stiff. "You got a nice house."

"Oh yeah? You should see where Horsey grew up."

"She told me. It's a shack." Braya held the rail and Laurel climbed behind her.

"Una always got mad when she said that. But it was a shack."

"Can we go there?"

"To Una's? She doesn't live there anymore. But she'd have put in a good fire and made us tea."

Braya stepped onto the verandah and looked back. Her face flushed with cold. Her eyes bright.

"Here." Laurel picked her up in her wet snowsuit and grunted. She wasn't a baby anymore. "It's dark in there."

"I'm not afraid." Braya slid an arm around her neck.

"No." Laurel kissed her on the cheek. "I'm not either."

Braya gave a very serious nod, back straight, face forward, as Laurel carried her inside.

ACKNOWLEDGEMENTS

To my husband, Marc, for cheering me on every step of the way and being wholly invested in everything I do. To Claire and Jacob, you are my world and my light. My mother, Effie, and my sisters, Stephanie and Alex, for being a constant source of strength and inspiration. Forces of nature, all three of you. My father, Brian, who left us too soon. My mother-in-law, Thelma, who also would have liked to read this. To my father-in-law, David, for helping Marc with the house so I didn't have to. Charmaine Stone, for helping with the kids while I wrote. My editors, Claire Wilkshire and Kate Kennedy, Rhonda Molloy for the layout and cover design, and the rest of the crew at Breakwater Books, thank you for believing in this project. John Vigna, my mentor and friend at UBC, working with you changed my life. Charis Cotter, for reading this book in its infancy and saying, "I think you have something here." Elisabeth de Mariaffi for working with me on another project, pieces of which found its way into this one. Gary Noel, for an early reading that helped me keep going when I was ready to shelve it. Tara and Penny for the "office" drinks. Kristen, for moving to the same places I do. Angela Antle, for throwing me a virtual line when I was lost, and the rest of the Women Writing in Rotting Sheds: Debbie Hynes, Lindsey Bird, Terri Roberts, and Monica Kidd. It's an honour to write with you. A special shout-out to my peers, the OG Crew, and the Thesis Squad at UBC, especially Tena Liang and Emily Cann for those emergency meetings, and to Sabyasachi Nag for remaining calm. Always.

To the Writers' Alliance of Newfoundland and Labrador for their support and mentorship program, the Humber College School for Writers, and the school of creative writing at the University of British Columbia.

And finally, to Newfoundland, this island that is as harsh as it is kind, and the only place I could ever call home.

SHELLY KAWAJA's writing has appeared in several journals and literary magazines, such as the *Humber Literary Review*, the *Dalhousie Review*, *Postcolonial Text*, and *PACE*. Her short story "Shotgun" won the gritLIT 2020 fiction contest. Shelly is a graduate of Memorial University of Newfoundland and the Humber School for Writers and is a current MFA candidate in the creative writing program at the University of British Columbia. She lives in Corner Brook with her family.